Deceive Me Once

Valerie Massey Goree

Parson Place Press
Mobile, Alabama

Deceive Me Once by Valerie Massey Goree

ISBN 10: 0-9842163-0-8
ISBN 13: 978-0-9842163-0-7

Library of Congress Control Number: 2010933671

Dedication

This book is dedicated to my family, especially my husband, Glenn, who supported all my efforts and gave encouragement along the way; to my daughter, Colleen, for being a sounding board; to my son, Kirk, for technical support; to my daughter-in-law, Minerva, for help with the Spanish words and flavor; and to my mother, Gwen Massey, for her quiet help. Above all, I praise God for waiting with open arms to forgive His repentant children.

"If we confess our sins, he is faithful and just to forgive us our sins, and to cleanse us from all unrighteousness." (I John 1:9 KJV)

Acknowledgments

Thanks to writing friends from the Alamo city Chapter of ACFW; special friends Anita and Roberto Garza for providing details about life in Eagle Pass in the 1970s; Chief Deputy Don Berger of the Bandera County Sheriff's Office; Sergeant Moises Peña, Jr. of the Eagle Pass Police Department; and Doctor Sheridan L. Sloan, D.M.V. of the Pine Creek Animal Clinic.

Liberties

Hanson Ridge does not exist, but if you drive from San Antonio to Bandera, you can imagine where it might be. In Eagle Pass, I have taken some liberties with the location of the hotel and the surrounding amenities. Meadow Oaks Rehabilitation Center in Eagle Pass is fictitious.

Deceive Me Once

Valerie Massey Goree

CHAPTER ONE

I scrubbed her blood off my hands and face. My tears mingled with the water escaping down the drain. The abrasion on my forehead still stung from the alcohol cleanse, and my stained clothes lay bundled in a heap on the bathroom floor.

Brutus pushed the door open and sniffed at my clothes. The stench of death clung to him. Without thinking, I grabbed the startled puppy and placed him in the tub. I used my shampoo to bathe the blood and odor away and rubbed his short, brown fur vigorously with an old towel.

After dressing, I plodded to the kitchen and closed the pet door leading outside, then paced the living room on wobbly legs. The sheriff had to drive only fifteen miles from Bandera, the county seat, to Hanson Ridge. What was taking him so long?

A booming car horn shattered the silence. Brutus barked and ran to the kitchen. I attached his leash and secured it to a cabinet handle, and opened the back door.

I traipsed toward the taupe patrol car. The sun glinted off the white caliche stones in the driveway. An officer climbed out of the car and straightened his brown trooper hat. He was probably close to my age, mid-forties, medium height, with solid arms and chest bulging under a khaki shirt, tucked into his brown slacks as if it had been glued down. His purposeful movements and demeanor inspired confidence.

A brief smile creased his bronze cheeks. "Afternoon, ma'am. I'm Chief Deputy Carlos Quintanilla." His deep voice sounded more like he should be in broadcasting and not investigating this sad crime.

I extended my hand, but he removed his mirrored sunglasses, slipped them into his shirt pocket and rested his hands on his thick leather duty belt.

"I believe you found a body, Mrs. McDonough?"

His direct question and accusing gaze made me realize for the first time I might be considered a suspect.

I lowered my hand. "Yes... yes, sir. And a bag filled with money."

His penetrating stare sent ripples swirling in my already queasy stomach.

"Where are they, ma'am?"

I stepped around his patrol car and headed down the driveway. "This way, Deputy."

His long stride brought him beside me. "How'd you get that gash?"

I reached under the hair I'd pulled across my forehead and touched the scraped area. I must not have hidden it as well as I'd thought. "I fell on the driveway. On my way to the house to call your... you."

He grunted.

Our footsteps crunched on the gravel and startled two vultures lingering on the dead branches of a Spanish oak. The skittish birds spiraled in circles above us.

He eyed them for a second, then focused on the brush ahead of us. "How'd you discover the body and the money?"

"Brutus, my puppy—"

"Puppy. Where's he now? Not by the body, I hope?"

"No, no. He's locked up in the house. The dispatcher told me to keep him away."

"Good. Now, tell me what happened."

I stopped and pointed back to the house. "I was weeding that flowerbed and Brutus brought me the corner of a hundred dollar bill. That got my attention, so I followed him. He keeps a stash of treasures on the lawn over there. I saw bits of money littering the area. Dirty, chewed bills. We think he must be part goat, because—"

"Mrs. McDonough, the body, the money?"

I cleared my throat. "Sorry. I talk when I'm nervous. My husband says—"

The deputy pushed back his hat and rubbed his forehead. "What happened next?"

"I followed the paper trail." This time I pointed to the caliche. "See. Pieces of money."

Quintanilla squatted and examined a scrap of paper. "This looks like part of a twenty." He picked it up and stood. "Show me where you went next."

We trekked along the driveway peppered with bits of money and veered off into the brush. This time my feet were protected by boots and my legs covered in jeans. My earlier wardrobe of sandals, T-shirt and skirt had proved no match for the rough terrain.

My husband had cleared a few of our nine acres in the Texas Hill Country northwest of San Antonio. The rest had been left raw. Quintanilla and I trudged through the un-cleared land south of the driveway. We stepped over rocks, clumps of dried grass and scraggy bushes. He reached an embankment before me and stopped.

I indicated the general direction and said, "We have to go up there."

"Lead the way."

I pulled myself up using the rough branches of the mountain cedar trees. Quintanilla followed. Even though I knew what to expect, the unpleasant odor of old boiled cabbage smothered me. I gagged and gasped for air in the stifling August humidity.

We pushed through the thicket of cedars and stepped into the small clearing. In the middle, half hidden by tall, dry grass, the zipper on the charcoal gray canvas glinted in the sunlight. Flies teemed over the bag.

The deputy stopped, surveyed the area and frowned. "Did you disturb anything, Mrs. McDonough?"

"Please call me Chella or Maricella."

"I asked you a question, Mrs. McDonough." He ignored my plea for less formality. His professional tone reminded me again of my precarious situation.

I stepped into the shade and sighed. "Well, just a little. When I got up here my dog dragged out a stack of bills. I picked it up." I could still feel the wet flecks like my face when I'd flipped through the bills, and see the brown speckles on my yellow shirt. I touched my cheek and shuddered. "I also pushed open the bag with a stick. Oh, and I threw up—over there." I pointed to a tree. Sympathetic waves of nausea rose and fell like a barometer. I turned my back on the site.

With his muscled arms folded, he glanced at me. "And what do you know about all this?"

"Nothing. Like I told you already, my dog led me here. We don't come out to this part of our land much."

He bent over the bag and studied the bundles of money visible through the partially opened top. He whistled. "Whew. Quite a haul. Where's the stack you handled?"

I moved closer to the tree where I'd lost my lunch and pushed the grass aside with my boot. "Here." When I'd realized the maroon muck covering the money had been her blood, I'd dropped the bundle like it oozed maggots.

He strode over, glanced at the money and nodded. "Okay, now let's examine the body." He turned and tramped in the direction of the odor.

I followed a dozen steps behind him, reluctance clawing at my feet. Memories of Brutus whining and pawing at an object hidden by the scruffy grass clouded my vision. Goose bumps erupted on my skin as the cabbage odor deteriorated into the suffocating sweet smell of decay. Churning in my gut sent a fresh surge of bile up my throat. I swallowed and clutched a nearby branch.

Quintanilla reached the body and stood with hands on his hips.

I crept behind him. Nothing had changed. I don't know what I'd expected. Someone should have come and straightened her legs, covered her, done something. But there she lay in a contorted heap. Her cobalt blue dress splayed out on the pale rocks like a fan. Shade from the close cedars splattered over the scene. Flies swarmed around; the grass shimmered in the asphyxiating heat.

Her torso was bloated, covered in blood and pock-marked with wounds. Matted long, black hair shielded her face. Her hands clenched across her chest. Her legs buckled at awkward angles, with a long gash on one shin.

The deputy snapped on a latex glove and pulled her hair back, exposing her face.

I gasped and stared. "Oh, she's so young."

"Do you recognize her?"

Stepping closer, I covered my mouth and nose with my hand and shook my head. "I don't think so. It's hard to tell, but no."

"She hasn't been dead long."

A small yellow butterfly drifted over her body then disappeared in the grass. I forced my mind back to the deputy's words. "How... how do you know?"

"State of the body. In this heat and—"

"I get the picture." My vision blurred as I thought of her lying among the rocks while I yanked weeds and pruned rose bushes. "Do you know when, I mean how long she's been here?"

He removed his hand and a few strands of her hair fell across her cheek. "Hard to say. We'll have to wait for forensics and autopsy."

My gaze locked on the girl's legs. One shoe was missing. I tried to dismiss the image of her struggling to walk through the brush barefoot.

Quintanilla glanced up above the trees. "It would be pretty dark here at night, wouldn't it? No street lights?"

"Right. Some properties have an automatic light on their main utility pole, but we don't."

He squatted and examined the area around the body. "Wonder how she maneuvered in the dark? Aha, look here." He lifted the edge of her sleeve with a gloved finger. "A flashlight."

He stood and pulled off the glove. "Any other items around, like clothes, water bottle?"

I swatted a horde of flies away and shrugged. "This is all I've seen. Brutus' stash, the bag of money and the... the body. I haven't looked anywhere else."

Quintanilla took off his hat and ran his fingers through his damp, black hair.

I stared at the girl and wondered if Brutus had caused any of her wounds. When I'd first seen the body, he'd been nuzzling her fist. I clutched my stomach and turned away.

"Well, that's all I can do for now." The deputy put his hat on, pulling the brim low on his forehead. He took my arm and guided me away from the scene. "You can go back inside, and I'll come take your statement as soon as my deputies and the Texas Rangers arrive."

"The Texas Rangers?"

"Yes, ma'am. Since this is considered a death under suspicious circumstances, they have been notified."

Pinpricks like ants with daggers on their feet moved along my spine. *Texas Rangers.* Turning my back on the poor girl, lying exposed to the merciless sun, I stumbled down the embankment and accepted the Deputy's strong arm supporting me.

The return trip to the house was a blur. Next thing I remember, Brutus strained at the leash as I passed through the kitchen.

I staggered into the living room on jellied legs and lay on the couch. My head ached, my stomach churned. A tight band squeezed around my chest. I struggled to breathe.

Death under suspicious circumstances. The deputy must think I was involved. The Texas Rangers were on their way. I thought they only existed in TV shows. Why were they coming here?

Brutus' barking by the kitchen door announced the arrival of more vehicles. I sat up and waited for the merry-go-round room to stop spinning. Then I ventured into the bathroom.

Reaching for the bottle of painkillers prescribed after my recent surgery, I stared at the few remaining tablets. Maybe the medication would remove the hammer in my head and the knots pinching my stomach, but the thought of having to eat something to accompany the strong pills sent a deluge of nausea undulating up my throat. I replaced the bottle in the cabinet and hobbled into the kitchen.

A knock elicited more barking from Brutus. I grabbed his leash and opened the back door. Deputy Quintanilla and another officer filled the doorway.

"Mrs. McDonough, this is Chuck Dayton from the Texas Rangers. We've come to take your statement."

Ranger Dayton tipped his pale Stetson. "Ma'am."

Telephone-pole thin and almost as tall, he stared at me with cold, gray eyes. He wore black jeans, black boots and a blinding white shirt. The Ranger's badge above his shirt pocket gleamed at my eye level. I glanced up at his sandy hair. Would he have to duck to come inside? I stifled a nervous giggle when incessant hammer blows in my head brought me back to serious reality.

No compassion coated Ranger Dayton's words. "Ma'am, may we come in?"

I turned and pulled Brutus behind me. "This way, gentlemen." The effort of holding my head high and striding with fabricated confidence calmed the quivers in my mid-section.

I sat at the round kitchen table with Brutus settling on the tiled floor next to my chair. The men balanced their hats on the nearest ranks to the morning, then sat and produced note pads and pens. Quintanilla pulled a gray bandana from his pocket and wiped his neck and brow.

Ranger Dayton began the questioning. His chiseled features revealed no emotion; his cold voice matched his eyes. His technique ate away at my confidence like a vulture on carrion. My throat constricted, making me swallow every five seconds. I found myself staring out the window or watching Brutus when I replied. Would he misinterpret my actions and conclude I wasn't telling the truth? But I was. I hadn't withheld any information.

Chief Deputy Quintanilla's relaxed and informal style eased the tension. "Mrs. McDonough, Maricella, tell us again, why did you follow your dog?"

"Because of the scraps of money and the blood on his face."

He glanced at the dog. "What blood? He's clean now."

"That's because I just bathed him."

Quintanilla lowered his hand and snapped his fingers. Brutus stood and stepped closer to have his head scratched. "He's a cute little thing. What is he?"

"He's a miniature pinscher, Chihuahua mix—"

"Sheriff?" The ranger's cold voice froze the rest of my reply.

"Right." Quintanilla cleared his throat and deserted the puppy. "You bathed the dog. Did you clean up, too?"

I took a deep breath and looked at my pristine hands. "I had to. Her blood was on my clothes and... and face and hands."

"Where are those clothes, Maricella?"

"In the bathroom, on the floor."

Ranger Dayton pushed back from the table and disappeared down the hall.

"We'll have to take them as evidence." The deputy leaned back in his chair. "But you'll get them back eventually."

I shuddered at the memory of her blood stains. "Please throw them away. I never want to see them again."

"I can appreciate that. Now, back to your discovery of the body. Did you know right away what Brutus had found?"

I steeled my emotions against a rehash of the events. "I've lived in the country long enough to recognize the smell of a dead animal. But when I... when I stepped into the clearing, I knew." A subtle wave of revulsion hit my stomach. "I knew something was different. I can't describe it, but I knew I wouldn't find an animal."

Quintanilla nodded.

The ranger returned with my tan skirt and yellow T-shirt in separate plastic evidence bags, which he threw on the counter. He sat, scooted the chair in and grimaced when his knees hit the table. Pushing back a bit he glared at me as if it was my fault.

Quintanilla closed his note pad and slid it into his pocket. "Thank you for being so cooperative, Maricella." He patted his pocket and smiled. "This will all be over soon."

His tone and smile reassured me. Although they were taking my clothes away, maybe I wasn't considered a suspect after all. I relaxed against the chair in time to see the officers glance at each other, and I'm sure one of them nudged the other under the table.

The calm that had descended over me vanished like mist under a heat lamp. Quintanilla stood, collected his hat and walked to the kitchen door. "I'll be right back, Mrs. McDonough. Have to check on one or two things."

We were back to *Mrs. McDonough* and I was alone with Chisel Face. To keep my wits about me I leaned over to pet Brutus, now lying at my feet. Undeterred, Ranger Dayton continued to fire questions. Where was my husband? Did anyone else live here? What had I been doing the previous evening?

I withdrew under Dayton's intense scrutiny until Deputy Quintanilla opened the back door.

He poked his head inside and said, "Dayton, we're needed out here. The J. P. has arrived."

Bean Pole picked up his note pad and Stetson, and without a backward glance strode through the kitchen and out the door.

My interrogation came to an abrupt halt. I licked dry lips and scooted away from the table. Another knock, more barking.

I shook off the cloak of suspicion Dayton's questioning had thrown over me and called, "Come in."

A female deputy entered and removed her hat. "Mrs. McDonough, the Chief asked if you'd come outside, please."

I stared at her youthful face surrounded by light brown curls. She didn't look much older than the girl among the rocks. "Okay. Do you know why?"

Brutus sniffed her boots and she reached down to pet him. "No, ma'am, but they're getting ready to take the body."

I followed her through the garage. "Deputy, why is the Justice of the Peace here?"

She put her hat back on, adjusted her thick belt and then said over her shoulder, "He'll certify the young lady is dead."

"I could have done that. She was—"

"Yes, ma'am, but this is official. He'll sign the death certificate." Giving me a one-sided smile, she joined another deputy standing by a pickup.

I swallowed the dry rocks in my mouth.

This could not be happening. The body. The deputies. The questions.

My driveway resembled a parking lot. Six vehicles of various sizes and colors jostled for space. Five I knew about, but the sixth? Its long, black shape looked familiar.

A hearse.

My feet rooted to the ground. My insides revolted.

Quintanilla's tap on my shoulder roused me from the numbness encasing my limbs, my heart, my soul.

"Mrs. McDonough, we're almost finished here, and we're getting ready to take the body." He pushed his hat off his forehead. "I know this is not pleasant, but I'd like you to take one last look at her before..."

I nodded and followed him down the driveway, past the row of vehicles. The girl lay on a gurney in an open black body bag, positioned to be slid into the back of the hearse. She was so young, maybe twenty, twenty-five at most. Her features seemed relaxed and peaceful, in sharp contrast to the war raging in my gut. As I stared at her, long-lost images stirred in my memory. Her eyes, the high cheek bones. They reminded me of someone from my past. The deputy scrutinized my face.

Nausea gave me a legitimate reason to turn away and shield my expression from his eagle eyes. Had I concealed my reaction in time?

"Mrs. McDonough, are you all right?" He moved closer. "So, do you recognize her?"

I gulped in air and shook my head. "No. Never seen her before."

Trying to keep upright, I stumbled to Quintanilla's car and leaned against it. Bowed over the vehicle, I watched a man wheel her body into the hearse. Who was she? Where was her mother?

I folded my arms, hugging myself, because I couldn't hug her. "Where will they take the body?"

Quintanilla doffed his hat at the driver of the hearse as it moved away. "The funeral home director will deliver it for autopsy to the Bexar County facility in San Antonio."

"Oh." My maternal instincts couldn't take anymore. "Can I go back inside now? I need to lie down." I rubbed my abdomen and stepped toward the garage.

"Yes, ma'am. Just remember to stay away from the area cordoned off by the crime scene tape, and please keep your dog away from it, too." His intense gaze raked over me. "Are you going to be okay?"

I nodded again. "Yes, thanks. My husband will be home soon. I just need to rest. I had surgery a few weeks ago and my incision is bothering me."

He slapped at a smudge on his pants. "I understand."

The convoy of vehicles, with the exception of Quintanilla's patrol car, left the property. I watched the dust swirls billow and disintegrate. Orange-tinged clouds above the tree line lent a surreal quality to the end of this tumultuous day.

The deputy walked toward his vehicle, but stopped and turned. He leaned against the fender. "I'm sure this has been upsetting for you, but you need to be prepared for more questions, inquiries, et cetera."

I squinted at the sun's last rays and shielded my eyes with a quivering hand. "Why? I've told you everything. The girl, the money. I don't know how they ended up on our property."

"But, ma'am, you've got to admit this is a most unusual case. A young girl, maybe illegal; bag of money, maybe drug related."

Stepping closer to the garage, I murmured, "No, surely not."

"We'll have to explore all angles. And you'll have to come to the Bandera County Sheriff's office tomorrow and have your fingerprints taken."

"Fingerprints. What for?"

"The bag, the money. We need to eliminate your prints." Quintanilla's gaze never left my face.

"But I told you I only touched one stack of bills."

He raised his eyebrows.

I help up my hands in surrender. "Okay, okay. I'll be there in the morning."

"And we'll run a criminal history on you and your husband. So, anything you want to tell me, now's the time."

My mouth hung open. I couldn't digest the words *criminal history* and shook my head. "Nothing. You'll find nothing. Except maybe a speeding ticket." Other unspoken deeds darted through my brain. *You'll discover why I left Eagle Pass. You'll discover I started the fire and I was responsible for...*

I kicked at the caliche stones and concealed my trembling hands in my pockets. Had I successfully addressed the deputy's probing statement and hidden my fear?

Quintanilla rubbed the sprouting whiskers on his chin. "Okay, ma'am. I'll be going now. Here's my card if you need me or remember anything else." He stepped toward me, but held onto the card as I reached for it, forcing me to raise my eyes to his face. "Be sure to call me if—"

I pulled the card from his grasp. "Yes, sir. You can count on me." I backed away from his vehicle before his sincere words could thaw my resolve.

He reversed down the driveway as the sun disappeared behind the trees. Dragging my feet, I stumbled inside and leaned against the kitchen door. Brutus' whining and excited tail wagging brought a touch of warmth to my death-chilled soul. I picked up the puppy, limped into the living room and collapsed on the couch.

Dayton's and Quintanilla's questions unnerved me almost as much as discovering the body had. I'm sure they believed my answers, but they kept digging deeper and deeper into my past. Digging into my past posed a problem. This interview had exposed events buried under layers of years and deceit, and I balked at allowing them to resurface into my present life. There were things from my past my husband didn't even know.

CHAPTER TWO

"Chella, sweetheart, are you okay? Sorry I wasn't available when you called." Tom's familiar voice did much to repair my wounded psyche.

"I'm a little shaken, but, yes, I'm fine now. Tom, she was so young. She—"

I'd called my husband and left him a detailed message after I'd called the sheriff.

"Do you want me to come home? I can reschedule my appointments."

My words rushed out in a torrent. "No, no. I'm fine. Really. Don't change your plans."

"I can see if Cindy can do my route."

"No. That won't be necessary. You don't want to upset the new bosses."

The medical supply company he worked for had recently been bought out, and sales reps were scrambling to keep their territories.

"This is different. They'll understand. After all, it's not every day my wife finds a body on our land."

Visions of the girl's blue dress swam before my eyes. I took a deep breath and blinked. "They didn't understand when Dave rescheduled his Amarillo run."

"Sweetheart, Dave was fired for more than just rescheduling."

"But, Tom, with me not working right now, we need the income."

Tom didn't respond immediately, but when he did his voice softened. "Okay, I'll keep my schedule. I'll be home in two days." He took a deep breath, and I dreaded what he might say next. "Chella, do they, I mean, does the sheriff have any idea who the woman was? Why she was on our land?"

I gulped and squelched the desire to drop the phone.

"No."

"Chella?"

"I said no, they don't. No to both questions."

My hasty response succeeded in hiding the gnawing suspicion the girl looked familiar.

He paused a second, then his voice took on a husky tone. "I'm going to ask once more. Are you going to be okay?"

My answer came out before I had time to consider the question. "Sure. I'm fine."

"Maricella, now don't be hardheaded. You have the Bullock's number, right?" He referred to our nearest neighbors.

"And, of course, I'll keep Brutus close by." I grinned, because other than barking, he'd be no deterrent to trespassers.

After Tom hung up, I fed Brutus, and aware I should eat something, but not sure I could, I opened a can of soup. As I pushed the noodles and vegetables around the bowl, I reflected on my conversation with Tom and spotted Brutus curled up in his bed. If his size ever matched his enthusiasm, he'd be an awesome protector. He did bark when cars entered the property, when deer wandered across the field at the back of the house, when thunder rumbled in the heavens and...

His frequent barking last night in response to neighborhood dogs—had they heard the young girl and her pursuers?

I dropped my spoon. Soup splattered over the tan table cloth. Would the pursuers be back?

I scooted from the kitchen table, and ran to check all the doors. They were locked. Maybe I should have asked Tom to come home early. But I'd still be alone tonight.

After I cleaned the dishes, I showered, put on my old faithful sleeping shirt and climbed into bed. Julia Alvarez's novel, *Saving the World*, stared at me from the bedside table. Maybe I could get lost in her prose, but every little sound in the settling house commanded my full attention. Brutus usually slept in the living room, but tonight I needed his keen sense of hearing to weed out the sinister sounds from the usual.

After being reassured it was all right for him to be on the bed, he curled up at my feet. I opened my book again, but snapped it shut when a thump overhead made me gasp. Cool air circulated over me. Oh, just the air conditioner. Brutus hadn't moved. If he was going to be my barometer, I'd better start paying closer attention to him.

I strained to follow the words of the story, but visions of the young girl floated across the page instead.

Brutus' ears perked up. He raised his head. I dropped the book.

What had he heard?

Donkeys' braying punctuated the silence. Sometimes they sounded like they were in agony. But they weren't. I'd asked the owners, our neighbors.

Brutus snuggled against my leg again. No threat perceived. I opened the book once more and took several deep breaths. Relax.

But no forced technique helped. The events of the day weighed on my mind and heart like a chunk of Everest. Confusion gnawed at me. I didn't know the girl, but something about her face stirred my memory. I tossed the book down.

Finally, I had to admit to myself that although I ached for Tom's return every time he worked out of town, my relief at his absence right now alarmed me. I hadn't been completely truthful with the sheriff or with Tom. I hadn't lied to either, but I could have told them about my suspicions.

Tom knew me too well. If he were home, I wouldn't have had time to build a shield around my responses to this tragedy, and he would have discerned I knew something. He would have pried the information from me. The girl whose body I'd found was connected to my past.

I needed to face this intrusion alone, and find answers before I could allow Tom into the part of my life I'd kept hidden from him.

The hall clock chimed the hour. Midnight. Better take Brutus out before I tried to sleep. I attached his leash, turned on all the outside floodlights and opened the front door. Taking advantage of the retractable leash, Brutus wandered across the lawn, into the flower bed, back to the sidewalk.

After he'd done his business, he scampered as far as the leash would allow and sniffed in the grass, pawing at an object glinting in the light. Curious, I pulled in the leash and bent down to see what he'd found. A gold chain and medallion nestled among the stalks of grass. I picked it up. Where did it come from?

Then I saw the scrap of paper caught in the clasp. A chill seeped up from my toes and I staggered back to the front door. Once inside, I examined the clasp under the bright lamp. The paper was a piece of money. Did Brutus snatch this from the young girl's fist? Had the chain and medallion belonged to her?

My knees buckled and I sank onto the couch. Bits of grass and leaves stuck to the medallion, obscuring its shape. I wiped them away and moaned. Half a heart with a jagged edge. If I hadn't been sitting I would have crumbled in a spineless heap. I knew the medallion—the other half nestled in my jewelry box, buried way at the back.

I rushed into the bedroom and unearthed the broken heart. With shaking hands, I placed the pieces together and read:

Best Friends on one side and *Chella & Eva Forever, 1977* on the other side.

Images of the dead girl's face swam before my eyes. A tug at my hand reminded me I still had Brutus on the leash. I unhooked the dog and sat on the bed, trying to hold the heart pieces together, but my hands shook as if I held a jackhammer.

"Eva, my friend, why did she have your necklace? Is she your daughter?" I turned the pieces over and shook my head. "But that's not possible. I know I witnessed your death in 1977."

CHAPTER THREE

Monsters usually disintegrate in the light of day, but vestiges of mine lurked around every corner. I ignored the sunshine pouring in through the bedroom's east window and stumbled to the door to switch on the overhead light.

Rumpled sheets indicated someone had slept in my bed, but it couldn't have been me. After finding Eva's necklace, I knew I'd crawled into bed and blubbered for hours. How could I have fallen asleep?

I stared at the scattered pillows and pulled at the neckline of the sleep shirt threatening to choke me. Brutus' ears perked up and a low growl bubbled in his throat. Goose bumps spread over my skin like leprosy. His shrill bark at the chiming door bell sent me at least three inches off the floor.

When I landed, I flattened myself against the wall and grabbed at my chest to keep my heart from bursting through.

After oxygen supplied my brain with a degree of sanity, I convinced myself the murderer wouldn't ring the front door bell. I crept to the door to peek through the peephole.

My sanity flew up the chimney. It was Quintanilla. I gulped. Did he already have my criminal history report? Was Ranger Dayton with him?

Through Brutus' constant barking I heard the chimes again. I'd have to let the deputy in. Get dressed? No time. Robe? Yes.

I headed for the bedroom, but turned and yelled, "Just a minute." And ran back to the bed.

My robe lay on the floor, half buried under the spread discarded during my wild night. I grabbed it, then remembered the necklaces. Maybe Quintanilla didn't know about the dead girl's necklace, and he sure wasn't going to find out about mine. Where were they? I had to find them before I let him in.

I tossed the pillows aside, scoured the wrinkled sheets, then saw them tangled on the floor next to my slippers. I scooped them up.

The door bell chimed again and the sheriff bellowed, "Mrs. McDonough. I just need to tell you something. Will you be long?"

Just tell me something. Not arrest me?

"I'm coming."

I threw on my robe and tied the belt, but on the way out of the bedroom I dropped one of the necklaces. Brutus snatched it up and pranced into the living room. I called, but he refused to come, choosing instead to dash under the dining table.

Propped next to a chair leg rested a red rubber bone, his favorite chew toy. One squeak and he rushed out to chase it when I threw it down the hall. I retrieved the necklace and shoved both into my pocket. No time to hide them. Quintanilla knocked just as I opened the door.

"'Morning, Deputy. Sorry it took so long. I was. . ." The sharp points of the heart pieces dug into my hand.

"No problem. Good morning, Mrs. McDonough. First, I won't come in. Just wanted to let you know we're back at the crime scene and we'll be talking to the neighbors. Please keep your dog on the leash again."

"Oh, yes, sure." I looked over his shoulder. No Dayton.

Brutus came to the door with the red bone in his mouth, and I let him stand there. If I picked him up I'd have to let go of the necklaces, and I was sure if I did they'd burn a hole in my pocket, and slither down my leg and land at Quintanilla's feet.

"Mrs. McDonough, are you all right? Did you have a good night?"

Although the rest of my body felt like a block of granite, I slid my foot out to prevent Brutus' exit from the house, with my long robe aiding in the maneuver. While my appendage seemed to act independently, replies to the deputy's questions warred in my brain. Sure, everything's just peachy, Sheriff. I had a great night. I'm used to finding bodies and bags of money 100 yards from my house. Or I could tell him I'd jumped at every noise and cried myself to sleep.

But I stooped, took Brutus' toy bone, threw it down the hall again, then peered into Quintanilla's dark eyes. "Not good."

He mumbled "Sorry Ma'am question."

We stared at each other. He backed away from the door and tipped his hat.

"Don't know how long we'll be here. I'll let you know when we release the crime scene, so you can let your dog loose."

"Thank you." I'd almost closed the door when I remembered a task I had lined up. "Oh, Sheriff."

He stopped and looked over his shoulder. "Yes, ma'am."

"You said you'd be talking to the neighbors. The Baileys, two properties over, at number 207, they're on vacation. I've been feeding their cats and watering the indoor plants. As soon as I'm dressed, I'll be going over there."

Quintanilla returned to the small front porch. "Wait a minute, ma'am. You say they're on vacation. How long have they been gone?"

"They left last Friday and will return tomorrow. That'll be a week."

He pushed his hat back and scratched his forehead. "You can't go by yourself. I'll have to send a deputy with you."

"Why?" Before the word left my lips I knew the answer. "Oh, right. The girl could have been there. The killer could have been there, or could still—"

"Don't worry." The sheriff straightened his hat and gave me a reassuring smile. "With all the law enforcement activity in the area, I'm sure the suspect is long gone. I just want to make sure no evidence is compromised."

"I understand."

He headed down the sidewalk. "Let me know when you're ready and I'll send a deputy with you. And don't forget to have your fingerprints taken."

When Quintanilla disappeared around the house, I closed the door and dashed into the bedroom. The sharp heart pieces were embedded in my palm. I pulled them out and placed them together, ensuring I hadn't damaged the edges. They still fit perfectly. I wrapped them in a tissue and secreted them away in the back compartment of my jewelry box. The indentations in my palm hadn't broken the skin. They would recover.

One gawk in the bathroom mirror explained why Quintanilla had asked after my health. My shoulder-length black hair, which usually had a decent wave, stuck out in all directions, like I'd been practicing back-combing for a '60s bouffant hair style. Coffee brown eyes glared back at me through puffy lids, and a dark scab graced the middle of my forehead like a new-age tattoo.

Disgusted, I retreated to the kitchen, fed Brutus and forced myself to eat a slice of whole wheat toast. An hour later, with hair reasonably under control and the ravages of my agitated night disguised with makeup, I collected my purse and the Bailey's house keys and opened the garage.

Two Bandera Sheriff's patrol cars and an unmarked pickup lined the driveway, preventing me from backing out. I took off in search of Quintanilla. Voices from the vicinity of the crime scene directed my steps, but before I reached the embankment the men tromped around from the left. Two deputies and a Texas Ranger. Not Dayton. Whew.

"Mrs. McDonough, I see you're ready." Quintanilla rubbed his chin. "Um, I think I'll send Deputy Weaver with you."

The middle man, a young black deputy, stepped forward and inclined his head. "Ma'am."

"Call if you see anything suspicious, Weaver."

"Yes, sir." He headed toward the driveway.

"Which vehicle are we taking?" I hurried to catch up with him.

"Vehicle?"

"Yes. The house is about a mile away. All these properties are pretty big. The Bailey's driveway is almost half a mile long."

"I guess we'll take mine. This way, ma'am."

I followed him and climbed in the front seat. *Rather the front than the back,* I thought, and clung to my purse. He swung the patrol car around and drove out the gate which had been propped open. I directed him to turn left at the road, then right at the second driveway.

"Is the gate locked?"

"No. It's a bump gate like ours."

Weaver slowed and bumped the rubber-sleeved arm, then drove through. I've used these gates thousands of times, but by force of habit I checked the side mirror to make sure it closed automatically behind us.

It didn't.

"Hey, that's odd."

"What?" Weaver asked.

"The gate didn't close."

The deputy stopped the car and peered out the back window. "Has that happened before?"

"Not since I've been coming to feed the cats."

"I'll check it on the way out."

When we reached the house, he cautioned me to stay in the car while he examined the perimeter. Minutes later, a thumbs-up sign allowed me to leave the car and unlock the front door. Weaver entered first and I followed him down the hall, but when he stopped in the archway to the living room, his right hand clasped his holstered gun and his left arm barricaded my entrance.

"Stay back."

Glancing over his shoulder, I could see evidence of a major struggle. Pictures hung askew. Knickknacks were knocked off display shelves. Sofa cushions lay scattered on the floor, and a lamp teetered on the edge of a table.

Weaver gestured for me to be quiet and remain in the hall while he investigated the rest of the house.

I watched him crouch-walk through the living room and disappear into the kitchen beyond. A deathly quiet enveloped the house. Where were the cats? The Baileys had three old felines who usually slept inside all day and would greet me as soon as I opened the door.

Fronds in a large Boston fern on a pedestal by the window quivered. I stopped breathing. Where was Weaver?

Rustling and twitching.

I exhaled and stepped into the room. More twitching in the fern. I moved closer. Gray feathers intertwined with green leaves. A bird.

To keep cat hairs off the dark furniture while they were gone, Barbara Bailey had placed old towels on the armchairs and sofa. I grabbed the nearest towel and threw it over the top of the plant. The startled bird flapped about, but couldn't escape. I secured the towel around the frightened creature and headed for the front door.

When released, the uninjured bird flew to a low hedge, and after squawking and twittering its opinion, took off into the clouded sky.

Stomping footsteps from the house alerted me to Weaver's approach.

"Ma'am, what do you think you're doing? I told you—"

"It was a bird, Deputy. I've just released it." I showed him the pale yellow towel where tiny gray feathers fluttered in the breeze.

"What do you mean?"

"Come."

We returned to the living room and I indicated where I'd found the bird. We examined the area and noticed little feathers dotted about on the floor and sofa.

"One of the cats must have brought the bird in through the pet door sometime yesterday, and the three of them have been having a field day in here."

"It *is* the only room that's messed up."

"Those scoundrels. Wonder where they are? I'll put out their food and water, then check outside."

"We'll do that together, ma'am."

How could I forget? "Of course. And before we go out, I want to tidy up the living room."

Weaver nodded and picked up cushions and straightened pictures, while I took care of the cats' dishes. When satisfied with our handiwork in the living room, we headed to the barn, Weaver in front, me traipsing behind. The heavy door stood ajar.

"Is this how it was yesterday?"

I moved closer to him and shrugged. "Don't know. I haven't been out here all week."

"Wait outside, ma'am."

Again Weaver drew his weapon and entered the barn with caution. My heart beat in my throat until he called, "All clear."

The door creaked as I pushed it wider. Hot, musty air swirled around me. There were stacks of hay bales in the corner and various yard tools strewn about. Loose straw and dry leaves crunched under foot. The three cats blinked at us from their snug resting place curled up next to a duffle bag on a hay bale.

Weaver kicked at the debris. "Do the Baileys have livestock?"

"Sometimes they raise half a dozen calves or so. But they didn't this year. The hay must be left over."

The orange tom cat, Hodges, stood, stretched, and ambled over to rub against Weaver's legs. The deputy reached down to pet the feline, then straightened and backed away.

"Whoa. That's blood." He pointed to spots on the ground leading up to the bag.

◆◆◆

Brutus strained at the retractable leash as Chief Deputy Quintanilla approached the back porch. I sat on the steps to give the puppy a taste of freedom, since he wasn't used to this confinement.

Quintanilla pulled off his hat and perched on the top step. "Weaver said you had your fingerprints taken."

I raised one hand and nodded. "While you were over at the Baileys."

He pulled out his bandana and wiped his forehead. "Good."

Hummingbirds hovered at the feeders on the eaves of the porch roof above us.

I petted Brutus whose little curlicue tail wagged at high speed. "That's a fancy machine you have."

"What?"

"I expected to get my fingers dirty on messy ink pads."

"No. We've had the Identex touch print machine for a while." He cleared his throat. "Mrs. McDonough, I have more questions." His tone terminated casual conversation and brought me back to the morning's discovery.

"What are the ages of the Bailey's children?"

"They have two boys, eight and eleven."

"Boys. So, no young girls on the property?"

Despite the humid air swirling around us on the porch, tiny bumps of goose flesh popped on my arms.

"Why? What was in the bag? Did it belong to her?"

The deputy gazed out across the open field, over the hills in the distance and sighed. "Can't say at this point, but since the Bailey children are boys, I'm pretty sure the items don't belong to them." Then he turned and stared directly at me. "We did find this close to your fence."

He pulled a small plastic evidence bag from his shirt pocket. It contained a yellow velvet jeweler's bag, the draw string tangled in oad knots.

"Is it yours?" He held it up for my inspection.

I stared at it and shook my head. "It's very dirty."

Quintanilla returned the bag to his pocket and in one fluid motion stood and vaulted down the four steps.

Facing me eye to eye, his hard, flat voice cut deep. "In my expert opinion, Mrs. McDonough, that's not dirt. It's blood."

CHAPTER FOUR

Daniel Ward, the preacher of the Community Church we attended, raised his bushy gray eyebrows. "Any more news from the sheriff?"

I shook my head as Tom placed his arm around my shoulders. His closeness churned the guilt like a tornado in my soul.

I relied on years of practiced deceit to reply in an unaffected voice. "No. They still don't know the name of the girl, or how she ended up on our property."

"We're supposed to meet with the Chief Deputy tomorrow. Maybe we'll know more then." Tom squeezed my shoulder.

"Well, we'll keep you and the young girl's family in our prayers. See y'all next Sunday." Daniel turned to greet the couple behind us, and we walked to our car.

Tom and I returned home after having lunch at a Mexican restaurant in Bandera. He preferred my *carne asada*, but I hadn't prepared many full meals since my illness. He understood and even took over the kitchen when home for more than a day. We settled in our side-by-side recliners to read our favorite sections of the newspaper.

I read the same paragraph in the Metro section for the third time. Words swam before my eyes, and I placed the paper on my lap. Tom devoured the section he held. Although we'd been together many years, my heart still filled with love and admiration for this mountain of a man, the solid foundation of our family. Our two sons took after him physically. Tall, muscular, and good-looking, but they were also developing his spiritual qualities of service and devotion to the Lord. Although twenty-year-old Joey had a rebellious streak, his heart was attuned to God.

Guilt threatened to choke me and I groaned. Tom dropped the paper, turned and peered at me above his reading glasses. "You all right, sweetheart?"

I nodded and placed a hand over my abdomen. "Just a twinge." Which wasn't exactly a lie, but at this point, I couldn't distinguish between post-operative pain and the consequences of years of deceit.

Tom took off his glasses, and his blue eyes searched my face. "Sure? Kidnapped, it seems to me this business with the money and the girl has really taken its toll on you."

"It has been traumatic, but I'm fine. Really." I picked up the paper again.

"I could cancel my next trip. Leave on Thursday instead of tomorrow."

"No. No, don't cancel." To detract from my hasty reply, I added with a smile, "Don't cancel tomorrow's trip. I'm relying on you to be back in time to accompany me when I go to Dr. Fordyce for my final checkup on Friday."

Tom replaced his glasses and grabbed another section of paper. "Okay, Chella. Just take it easy. You've been through so much these last few months."

I gave him my best reassuring smile, and he returned to the NFL fall schedule which captured his full attention.

No article kept my interest for long. I discarded the paper and reached for my book on the side table. But Tom had placed his Bible there when we'd come in, and I ran my fingers back and forth over the worn cover. I picked it up and enveloped it in my arms, hoping the words of comfort would seep through the pages and minister to my tormented spirit.

It didn't help.

I rested against the chair and stared at my husband's legs, elevated next to mine. The crease in his navy slacks, the matching socks, and polished shoes brought a fleeting smile to my lips. Tom and his clothes. Socks always matched, or, at least, coordinated with pants, which had to have a defined crease. He even sent his blue jeans to the cleaners so they'd have a crease. I didn't mind doing load after load of laundry, but I refused to iron blue jeans. My easy-going Tom had this one quirk, which I often teased him about.

The lump in my throat grew bigger and threatened to suffocate me. When he found out the truth about my past, would I still be doing his laundry? Would I wish I'd ironed those blue jeans?

I couldn't sit next to him any longer. I eased the footrest down, pushed up from the chair and tiptoed past my now dozing husband. Once out on the back porch the oven-like air engulfed me, but instead of grimacing as I usually did, today I relished the warmth. I sat down and the puppy joined me, providing another reminder of the girl who'd entered our lives in such a brutal way.

The waterfall splashing into the nearby fish pond lulled me into false contentment. I picked up Brutus and stroked his curled up body. The repetitive motion eased the tension holding my shoulder muscles captive. Haze over the distant hills flowed down the valley and entered my soul, filling the cavities with a modicum of solace. I slumped in the chair.

The afternoon dragged by, like a herd of turtles pulled it uphill. Avoiding Tom's concerned glances, avoiding the guilt a closed Bible evoked, avoiding the hidden heart necklace and its connection to the dead girl, all intensified the tangles in my nerves, and drained the energy from my body.

Our neighbors, Emma and Larry Bullock, owners of the donkeys, invited us over for the evening. I couldn't decline without Tom becoming suspicious. Being in such a small, close-knit community, they knew about the money and the body, and naturally we discussed the situation. I managed to maintain my best guest manners and disguised how this repetition acted like acid eating at my gut.

♦♦♦

We arrived on time for our ten o'clock appointment with Chief Deputy Quintanilla. He ushered us into his office. Would he attribute my clammy hand shake to nervousness? Utter dread weighed me down like a cement block.

"I have a bit of information for you folks and also a couple of questions. First, we located the young lady's fingerprints in AFIS. Her prints were taken when she applied for citizenship. Her name is Angelica Valdez, aged twenty, from Eagle Pass."

The deputy's voice drifted in and out of my roaring eardrums. Angelica. Eagle Pass. I wiped away the sweat spots on my upper lip. The struggling window air conditioner unit did little to combat the heat and humidity.

Quintanilla's shrewd eyes fixed on my face. "Mrs. McDonough, are you all right? Is there something you want to ask or tell me?"

"You know I've been sick, had surgery, and now this. It's been a rough couple of days."

Tom leaned forward. "Deputy, I'm not sure I like your tone."

I placed my hand on his arm and forced a smile. "It's okay, honey. I'm just feeling a little hot and uncomfortable."

The deputy angled the small desk fan in my direction, and reclined in his creaky leather chair. "Eagle Pass, Mrs. McDonough. You're from there, aren't you?"

I nodded. Words caught in nervous tangles stuck in my throat.

Tom stepped in. "So are a lot of people. Doesn't mean Maricella knows... knew the girl."

Deputy Quintanilla pursed his lips as he twisted a pen between his fingers. "You're right, but I had to ask. And another item of interest. All the money in the bag is old, dated in the 1970s. About $75,000."

The pen twisting ceased, the creaking chair stopped rocking, and the deputy leaned across the desk. "You left Eagle Pass in the '70s, didn't you, Mrs. McDonough?"

I glanced from Quintanilla to Tom. Was the anguish gushing through my body evident on my face?

Words croaked out. "That's right. I came to San Antonio in 1977. But I still don't know why you're asking. I've never seen that bag of money or the girl before. I'm certain." At least my conversation contained a scrap of truth.

Tom placed his hand on my leg. Its nervous shaking ceased. I gulped down air, closed my eyes and fabricated a calm façade.

Quintanilla's next words, however, shattered the fragile hold I had on normality.

"She was stabbed. Three times."

My eyes widened. "Oh, no."

The deputy nodded and kept his gaze on me. "Yes. Stabbed. But not where you found her. And not in the Bailey's barn either. Haven't determined where yet. The autopsy should tell us approximate time of death and how long she lived after the stabbing." He paused. His eyes bored into my soul. "Other than mine, there were only two sets of footprints where you discovered the body, yours and hers. Human, that is. We also found deer, jack rabbit, and coyote prints. And she bled profusely."

He paused for a millisecond, just long enough for me to grab Tom's hand.

"We followed the blood trail across the Bailey's field to their barn, across the road to your property. And the scrape on her shin was from the bump gate post. She must have stumbled into it and damaged the automatic release. We tested the mechanism and it works some of the time." He nodded slowly, rocking with the motion. "By the way, it *was* her blood on the money and in the bag."

The room spun; my oxygen-deprived lungs burned; tears filled my eyes. The picture of her body in the clearing fogged my vision. "Her... her blood. Tom."

I turned to him and he enveloped me in his strong arms, while my body heaved.

"Deputy, I think that's enough. Unless you have any more questions for my wife, we're leaving." Tom took a tissue from a box on the desk.

I sat hunched over in my chair and wiped my eyes.

Quintanilla leaned back again. "I'm sorry, but there were just too many coincidences." He laced his fingers and placed his muscled arms behind his head like sunbathing on a beach. "There is one more thing." He rocked slowly back and forth, my agitation growing with each movement. "Mrs. McDonough, I'm giving you another chance. Hindering an investigation, like tampering with evidence or withholding information, is a third degree felony, punishable by a hefty fine, possible jail time." The rocking stopped and his serious, dark eyes focused on mine. "Now, do you have anything to add?"

I shook my head, using the tissue to camouflage the fear I knew covered my face. "The body, the bag of money, I didn't tamper with them." The truth.

"Sweetheart, calm down. I'm sure Deputy Quintanilla is just covering all bases. Surely, he doesn't think you're involved." Tom looked at the officer. "Do you, sir?"

The deputy stood. "It's my duty to inform you. That's all. You have my card, ma'am, if you need to contact me." He extended his hand.

We rose and shook hands.

"I understand." Emotions held in check by decades-old chains, I stared him in the eyes. "I'll be sure to tell you if anything new turns up."

I hadn't lied. If I found anything new, I'd tell the deputy, but I kept knowledge of the necklace locked away in my private vault.

Turning to Tom, I placed my arm through his. "Let's go, honey."

"One more thing." Quintanilla sat on the corner of his desk, arms folded across his broad chest. "The clothes in the duffle bag were Angelica's. One T-shirt even had ANGEL embroidered on it." He pushed off the desk and raised his eyebrows a fraction. "The blood on the jeweler's bag was hers. Wonder what was in it?"

I gave him my best *nothing you say can get to me* glare, and pulled Tom to the door.

We left the cramped office and headed home, rehashing the events of the morning. Tom showered concern over me with his glances, his words, and his touch. My outward composure cloaked the turmoil and shame of guilt boiling inside. I struggled to keep my past in the shadows, as I had done for so many years, reassuring him I was fine in a practiced, self-controlled tone.

He packed for his next out of town trip while I heated leftover chicken *fajitas* for lunch. Savory smells from the meat, onions and peppers almost overpowered me.

Tom and I sat at the kitchen table and ate in silence. I picked at my food.

"You're unusually quiet." Tom took the last bite of chicken.

I studied the food on my plate to keep him from scrutinizing my face. "I've been thinking about the girl."

"Wish I didn't have to leave for Kerrville this afternoon." Tom took his plate to the sink. "Why don't you call Joey? See if he can spend a few days with you." José, our youngest son, lived in student housing at the University of Texas in San Antonio.

"No. I'll be fine. Joey can't come because he's got a group project for one of his classes, and besides he's working nights this week." He worked at a grocery store warehouse during the summers.

"If you say so, sweetheart. Well, I'm ready to go, but let's have a prayer before I leave."

I clung to Tom as his sincere words of praise and petition surrounded me and almost broke through the wall I'd place around my past. My guilt chomped away at the barricade, but it held fast. I suppressed a groan and forced a mumbled amen through trembling lips. When Tom's arms slackened their hold, I kept my head bowed and walked back to the living room. I returned a minute later with a stiff smile in place and worry lines deliberately smoothed off my forehead.

"Here's your Bible." I placed it in his briefcase.

"Thanks, sweetheart. See you Thursday."

We kissed, and he held me in a tight embrace, and then drove off in the company van to his afternoon appointment at the hospital in Kerrville. From there he'd spend two days in the Midland and Odessa area, providing training to the hospitals' ICU staff on the use of the new cardiac catheter equipment.

After cleaning the kitchen, I ambled back to the bedroom. My jewelry box on the dresser beckoned. I reached into the back compartment and pulled out the tissue wrapped heart necklaces. I held the two pieces together. The words *Chella & Eva, Forever* blurred as tears stormed and spewed down my cheeks.

Quintanilla's warning of withholding evidence loomed like a monster in my soul's closet. But what would giving him the necklace accomplish? He already knew the name of the girl. Did he have to know the necklace could have been in the jeweler's bag, and that I had the other half? Would that knowledge help him find the murderer or answer questions about the money? Rationalizations soothed my guilty conscience.

Besides, I wasn't ready to let others into the dark recesses of my previous life. What if I was wrong? What if the young girl wasn't the daughter of my childhood friend? But her name—Angelica. My friend, my childhood friend, the one who owned the half-heart necklace, her name was Eva Angelica Cuellar.

Her name tore open a memory. The photograph. Glancing around to verify no one could see me—absurd I know, but logical thinking had flown out the window—I closed the blinds and even shut the door. I pulled the stool from my dresser into the closet and located the old, dust-covered shoe box. I carried it to the bed and examined the contents. A variety of photographs, letters and memorabilia. Buried at the bottom, I found the envelope I sought. Two photographs inside, both yellowed with age, had not been handled for most of my married life. One of my parents; the other of Eva and me.

My parents sat in a café on their honeymoon in Monterrey, Mexico, holding hands and smiling. My mother's dark curls were surrounded by a ridiculously large hat, and my father's wide tie covered half his chest. I remembered her giving me the picture and describing how happy they'd been.

The other picture showed Eva and me standing arm in arm, dressed for church and grinning big-cheese smiles. Long, black hair pulled back by white ribbons, our Sunday best dresses, white socks and black shoes. I turned it over and my mother's handwriting could still be seen: *Eva Angelica Cuellar and Maricella Maria Farias, age fourteen, Eagle Pass, Texas.* It had been taken a year before the fire, the guns, my running away.

I turned the photo over again and studied Eva's face. Tears fell in an open torrent. I clutched the fragile piece of paper to my chest, my intense sobs chasing Brutus off the bed. Now I knew for sure—the dead girl was Eva's daughter. The necklace, her name and the face. Although I'd seen her for only a heart-stopping moment before the funeral home director had zipped up the body bag, I now stared at the same face in the photo.

"Eva, my dear friend, why did your daughter come to me?"

As certain as I was Angelica was Eva's daughter, I was just as certain she'd been on her way to see me.

Now I had to find out why—on my own. I knew deep in my being the answers would be connected to the night we gave each other the heart piece necklaces. The night I celebrated my coming-of-age party, my *quinceañera*. The night my parents were killed and my childhood ended.

CHAPTER FIVE

"How are you, Mama?" My oldest son's voice vibrated with concern.

"Doing fine, Mike. Did Daddy ask you to check up on me?"

Silence on the phone confirmed my suspicion that Tom had asked Mike to call.

"You know him so well. But are you okay?"

"Yes, I'm fine, and he'll be home tomorrow."

"I have another reason for calling, Mama. The training I told you about, well it's been scheduled for next week, and I was wondering if Teresa could spend a couple of days with you."

Mike and Teresa had been married six months. She wouldn't start her final year at the university for several weeks, and I knew time lay heavy on her hands. Being from New Mexico, she missed her family and still felt like a stranger in San Antonio. Her parents had been hesitant about the marriage at first. They would have preferred she marry a full-blooded Hispanic, but after meeting Mike, they were more accepting when they recognized his Christian qualities.

"Sure. That'll be great. In fact..." My mind raced through disjointed plans to visit Eagle Pass. "She can stay for the whole week, and maybe we'll go on a little trip. I'll give her a call."

Mike shared more details about the training course he had to attend in Dallas for the computer company he worked for. They'd hired him the previous year, right after graduation.

After he hung up, I continued answering my e-mail. When I had completed the task, I straightened up the desk and picked up Mike's wedding picture. He looked so much like his dad. Light brown hair with a hint of red—a gift from Tom's

Scottish ancestors—sparkling blue eyes, and a smile to melt your heart. Teresa's radiant face, surrounded by dark curls and white lace completed the picture. She looked more like my daughter than my daughter-in-law. Mike and Tom were the only ones with light hair, eyes, and skin. José, Teresa and I were three peas in a pod with black hair, chocolate eyes, and olive skin.

I reminisced about how we'd named our boys, and wondered if fate had had a hand in the process. When they were born, all we could see were healthy little babies, but now as adults, their names matched their physical characteristics and personalities. Tom and I agreed when I was pregnant with our first child that he'd provide the name for a boy, and I would for a girl. Michael Thomas had been born first. Then when our second child had also been a boy, we decided I'd have my turn. I'd chosen José for my father and Manuel for my grandfather.

But I'd never told Tom why I'd chosen those names.

I'd given him as little information as possible about my family. Now I'd have to revisit the past to find out why Angelica had come to Hanson Ridge.

◆◆◆

With Tom out of town, I'd been busy at the library and on the Internet. I kept my emotions locked away behind a barbed wire fence, and read with dry eyes and a cold heart. I'd found the *News Guide*, the Eagle Pass newspaper on microfiche, and searched for June 1977. My parents had been murdered the night of my *quinceañera,* June 25, 1977. I'd fled Eagle Pass the next morning.

The brief article relayed the events in antiseptic clarity. The restaurant had burned to the ground; seven bodies were found; some had died from gunshot wounds and others from smoke inhalation and burns. The names of the deceased were not mentioned.

When I checked the obituaries, I found my parents listed. I read their names with detachment. José and Maria Farias. Just another couple. Somebody's parents, somebody's family.

Eva's parents were listed with other names I recognized, but no Eva. Speculating she may have died days after being wounded, I checked the files for several weeks, but her name never appeared. I checked other databases and could not locate her obituary anywhere.

Although the ceiling fan in the office circulated the cool air, sweat popped on my forehead. Eva could still be alive. She could have survived the gunshot, the fire. I fanned my face with a sheet of scrap paper and leaned back in the chair. These past twenty-nine years she could have been a few hundred miles away and I'd never tried to find her, never used this type of research before. But, I had to remind myself, I'd seen her shot, I'd seen the pool of blood. And at fifteen, what resources did I have?

I'd run away and tried to forget those awful events from my past. I'd even tried to run away from my Hispanic heritage. But now I had to face these truths that modern technology had presented me.

Eva could be alive. But her daughter was dead.

Armed with the new details, I formulated plans for a trip to Eagle Pass. I knew I'd told Mike that Teresa could stay with me when he traveled to Dallas, and at first, having her accompany me seemed like a good idea. But now I realized I'd have to air a lot of dirty laundry and wasn't sure I should do that to my new daughter-in-law.

And Tom. What about Tom? I'd have to plan this venture during his next out of town trip. Because as much as I loved and trusted him, I had to do this on my own. My past was mine and mine alone. This venture could damage or even end my marriage, but I had to go. Intrigue and subterfuge suffocated my brain cells. My head ached.

I turned off the Internet and glanced at a bundle of three by five inch index cards Tom kept on the desk. In his Bible study time he'd write down scriptures he wanted to remember. I flipped through a stack and quickly dropped them before I deciphered the words and they seared my soul.

Oh, how much more guilt could I bear? I'd caused the argument that led to the shooting, the fire, the deaths of my parents. I'd misrepresented myself, and the ultimate deception. I'd attended church services with Tom in body but never in spirit. Tom was such a fine Christian man, always had been, and I was a hypocrite. After our marriage, I'd attended church with him, and as the years sailed by, just kept up the pretense. I believed in God and the Bible, but I had no relationship with the Lord.

My whole married life had been one deception after another. And yet, I still could not bring myself to tell Tom any of this face to face. Not until I had more answers than questions.

The accusing cards lay scattered all over the desk. I ran out of the office to the kitchen and clung to the counter. Enough. I needed to get out of the house which held too many reminders of my perfidy.

Quintanilla had released the crime scene several days ago, so I no longer had to keep Brutus on the leash. With his freedom restored, the puppy seldom spent time indoors. I grabbed my purse and climbed into the car, Brutus nowhere in sight. The drive to Bandera would take about fifteen minutes along the narrow, winding two-lane highway. Hanson Ridge sported a gas station, feed store, post office and small café. When I needed to shop, I had two choices—congested San Antonio, or convenient, but smaller Bandera. Bandera won. Most of the time.

Entering the grocery store, I grabbed a cart and strolled up and down the aisles, selecting items at random. In the produce department, I stood examining the tomatoes when a man bumped into me.

"So sorry, ma'am. Wasn't watching."

I glanced up. "That's all right. No harm done."

He kept staring. "Excuse me, but don't I know you?" He had a strong Spanish accent.

Giving him my full attention, I focused on the short, stocky man, several years my senior, with a bulbous nose, and weather wrinkled cheeks, in sharp contrast to his smooth, bald head. The smile on his thin lips scarcely affected his piercing eyes.

"Wasn't your picture in the paper last week? Something about a body?" He took a wrapped cigar out of his shirt pocket, which explained the strong odor of tobacco on his breath.

My mind raced back to *The Bandera Bulletin*, our county's weekly newspaper, and recalled the vague details the report of the incident had contained. How could this stranger have identified me armed with information from the publication?

"What are you talking about?"

He fingered the cigar. "Didn't you find a body on your property?"

I stepped back, finding his closeness oppressive.

He pulled off the clear wrapper with a red and gold band and scrunched it into his pocket, and then placed the fat cigar in the corner of his mouth.

With my cart angled between us, I said, "I did, but why do you want to know?"

"Did she have—" A commotion at the front of the store caught his attention.

Peering around him at the direction of the noise, I saw a red-faced woman and young boy pick up cans knocked off a display. Then two police officers entered the store and headed toward the produce department.

I returned my focus to the man in front of me and the terror in his eyes shocked me. Even his swarthy skin couldn't disguise his bloodless face. His hawk-like eyes darted back and forth between me and the door. Intrigue replaced my initial repulsion at his presence. Sensing his desire to escape, I discarded my grocery cart as soon as he ran to the door, and followed him out.

When he saw the police car in the front row of the parking lot, he slowed. He eased along several rows of cars. I snuck behind an elderly couple pushing a loaded cart until I reached the row of cars on the other side. When the cigar man stopped by a vehicle, I stepped behind a van so he couldn't see me. I heard a door slam and peeked out to see what car he'd entered. A tan sedan, same make and model as Mike used to drive in college, a Chevy Cavalier.

The man revved the engine and pulled out of his space. I strained to read the muddied Texas license plate, but could only decipher an *A* and a *T*.

The vehicle did, however, have identifiable characteristics. The trunk and left rear fender were both a dark, rusty brown, like replacement parts.

As I watched him drive out of the parking lot onto the main road, the Sahara took over my mouth and the knot in my stomach twisted until I doubled over in pain. I'd seen that car before. Yesterday, when I'd taken Brutus for a walk on our road, the car had been parked several hundred yards from our driveway. It hadn't concerned me then, because the rancher who lived down there often hired workers who'd leave their vehicles by his gate.

I staggered back to my car, ignoring the groceries I'd abandoned, slid inside and fastened my seat belt. Before I started the engine, I glanced in the rearview mirror. My hair was a mess, dark smudges underscored my eyes. Another knot of pain pinched my gut. The man said he'd recognized me from my picture in the paper. Impossible. My picture had not accompanied the article about the body.

How did he know me? Did he have a connection to the body? To Angelica?

CHAPTER SIX

After checking the doors one last time, I climbed into bed. While Tom was home, Brutus had been relegated to sleeping on his bean bag in the living room again. But tonight I wanted the dog close. If that cigar man with the two-tone car came anywhere near the house, I wanted Brutus to sound the alarm. Maybe it was time we invested in an electric gate. And a twelve foot fence.

Sleep delayed its coming. I know I glanced at the clock every ten minutes until at least midnight.

When I finally succumbed to slumber, it was not peaceful. I awoke, panting for air and drenched in sweat. I sat up and pulled the sheet around my body. Visions from my nightmare danced in the dark. After drawing in sufficient oxygen, breath by forced breath, I relaxed against the pillows.

All the visits to my past had born fruit in my sub-conscience. My nightmare had been laced with events I'd buried years ago, but were now as fresh as if they'd happened yesterday. I'd tried not to rehearse those memories, but alone in bed I couldn't locate the brakes to my run-away reels of tape. My black and white past resurfaced in vivid, persistent Picasso colors.

Eva and I had been friends since second grade. We'd lived in the same neighborhood, and over the years, our parents had become good friends, too. Our mothers shared a unique and tragic trait—they'd both suffered several miscarriages before giving birth to their daughters. Based on the closeness of our families, our fathers agreed to go into business together, to open a restaurant. The plans were in the making for a year or more. Many evenings, I remember hearing Eva's dad, Juan

Cuellar and my dad, José Farias, discuss and argue late into the night.

The name of the restaurant caused one of the loudest arguments.

"*Resaurante Cuellar.*"

"*No. Casa Farias.*"

Louder and louder each repeated his choice till my mother's soft voice interjected, "*Casita Bonita.*"

Pretty Little House. That name had satisfied both parties.

A week after the restaurant opened, I sprinted to Eva's house, but when no one responded to my knock, I dashed around to the back. I could see into the kitchen through the open screened-in porch door. Mr. Cuellar bent over the kitchen table.

He counted objects and placed them into a large plastic bag. "*. . . tres, cuatro, cinco...*"

He stopped when he dropped something, and as he stooped to pick it up, I saw bundles of money on the table. I retreated and ran back home. Telling anyone what I'd seen never crossed my mind. My mother always said if we kept our noses out of other people's business, we'd keep out of trouble.

The restaurant had been open for a month when we celebrated our *quinceañeras*. Eva and I had birthdays two weeks apart. Our parents pooled their resources and planned the biggest celebration for our fifteenth birthday party our neighborhood had seen in years.

After mass, our families, friends, and the shared court of fourteen girls and fourteen boys gathered at the restaurant. Tables had been pushed against the walls and *luminarias* cast flickering gold light over the guests. We'd already received our tiaras, and our flat shoes had been exchanged for heels when there was a lull in the ceremonies.

I clasped Eva's hand and took her to the kitchen. There we gave each other the heart necklaces we were so proud of. We'd saved our tips from helping serve the summer guests since the restaurant's opening, and had enough money to have our names and the date engraved on the back of each necklace.

Eva heard her mother call and returned to the party. I stayed in the kitchen and latched my necklace in place. That's when I overheard our fathers in the storeroom arguing again.

Their Spanish flew back and forth, and I almost dismissed it as another verbal battle in their relationship, when I heard my father's question. "Where's the money, Juan? The bills are coming and the business account is empty. What happened to the money?"

The loud festive music drowned out Mr. Cuellar's mumbled reply.

My father's voice grew angry. "The money, Juan. We need the money. Have you been gambling again?"

A loud thump, like a fist hitting the table, echoed in the small room. "No, I have not. I'll give it to you tomorrow."

I stayed to listen, because I'd seen Mr. Cuellar with bundles of money. Was it the money he owed my papa? When a third voice entered the script, I crept closer to the storeroom door.

The unknown man spewed a long diatribe of threats. "Your loan is overdue. Pay up or I may have to take one of your pretty little daughters and—"

I gasped and my father looked up. "Maricella, what are you doing here?"

Side-stepping into the doorway, I leaned against the frame. "*Papi*, don't worry. He has the money. I saw it."

Three faces looked my way; two in shock, one in anger. The visiting man pulled a gun from his belt and aimed it at Mr. Cuellar. I stumbled backward, not yet used to the high-heeled shoes and knocked over a metal container. The distraction enabled Mr. Cuellar to reach for a gun he had in his coat pocket.

My father glanced from gun to gun and yelled. "Run, Chella! Run!"

I'm not sure what happened in the storeroom, but in my haste to find my mother, I think I knocked over one of the *luminarias*. The numerous paper decorations caught fire, and smoke swirled about the room.

Voices raised in alarm had guests running for the door. My father entered the dining area, grabbed my mother and searched the chaos for me. I could see them through the throng of people rushing by, and then I heard the shots.

As if in slow motion I turned toward the sound and saw Mr. Cuellar stagger in. He grabbed his wife, holding Eva's hand, and stumbled to the floor. Guests swarmed. The stranger came in and fired. I ducked down next to a table and heard several more shots accompanied by shouts and screams.

The smoke made it almost impossible to see, but I recognized the shirt and pants of the stranger as he ran past me to the door. When I crawled out, I saw Eva on the floor, surrounded by her parents. Oozing blood stains grew around the still bodies.

Creeping farther to the other side of the room, I grabbed a napkin from the floor to hold over my nose and mouth. I found my parents. Papa lay still, his unfocused gaze fixed on the ceiling, but Mama's rasping breath gave me a shred of hope.

"Chella, *mija*... take the box. Go. Go to *Tia*. Run!"

Her head flopped to the side and her eyes closed. I knew without touching her that she was dead. A cold spray from the ceiling showered us like giant tears. The need for fresh air forced me outside. I could hear the sirens; my throat and eyes burned; my heart ached. I ran down the street, oblivious to the calls from people running to the scene.

All I could hear were my mother's dying words. "Go. Go to *Tia*. Run!"

She'd always been prepared for the worst. I can remember as a young girl she'd sit me on the kitchen counter and take a small metal box from the top shelf of the cabinet. She'd show me the contents as she added a bill or two. Five, ten, twenty dollar bills stacked neatly under a beautiful lace scarf and the envelope of important papers.

"Es para emergencias."

She'd say the same words every time. And now, here was my emergency. I ran to the back door, pulled the key from the flower pot and crept inside without turning on the lights. I took the special box down and made my way to the bedroom. I threw the box and a change of clothes into my backpack and sat on the bed, wet and exhausted.

Sirens wailed in the distance. My heart pumped so hard I placed my hands over my chest to keep it contained. I squinted at my damp dress. Light from the street revealed rips and soot stains on the intricate white lace. My spirit was as broken as the heels of my new shoes, and like my tiara, my innocence had vanished.

I kicked off the shoes. One landed on the bed. Uh-oh, no shoes allowed on the bed. What would *Mami* say? I picked up the scarred shoe, but my mother's prone form swirled in front of my eyes. Tears stung. Grief pinched my throat. I threw the shoe back on the bed and tore at my dress.

As I left my bedroom, clothed now in jeans, T-shirt and sneakers, I glanced back at the discarded pile of smoke infused lace. My *quinceañera* was supposed to signal my passage from childhood to womanhood. Instead, it catapulted me from the safe, secure home I'd known all my life into the insanity of an unknown world.

A knock at the front door sent my heart racing, and I shivered as fingers of fear tickled my neck. Who was it? Could it be the man with the gun? I grabbed my backpack and tiptoed to the back door. Certain I'd never see this house again, I dashed outside. Cutting through the neighbors' yards I avoided whoever had been knocking, and reached Main Street where I hid behind a Dumpster until dawn.

I don't know how I survived the night. I just remember a numb coldness filling my mind, soul and body, until sleep gave me a scrap of relief. Finding my way to San Antonio to *Tia* Gloria was easy compared to the evening I'd just endured.

Memories of the early morning bus ride were surfacing in my consciousness when the phone rang. Ice water thrown in my face could not have made me any colder than I felt at that moment.

Three o'clock in the morning. Who was in trouble now?

"Hello."

"Mama, it's José."

"Joey? What's wrong?"

"Can you come get me? I'm... I'm at the police station."

Halfway to San Antonio, the seriousness of the situation hit me. Joey, my son in jail. Words of dread for any parent. What could he have done? Already drained by guilt and sadness the memories of my *quinceañera* night had invoked, I now compounded the gnawing in my gut by adding frantic worry to the mix.

When I arrived at the police station I had to wait fifteen minutes for an officer to see me. The acid in my stomach almost erupted before he came to get me.

"'Morning, ma'am. I'm Officer John Kelsey. Follow me, please." He led me back to an interview room where my son waited.

José's bowed head and slumped shoulders conveyed his despondence. I sat next to him, but he refused to look me in the eyes when I placed my arm around him.

Officer Kelsey stood against the wall. "Mrs. McDonough, José is not under arrest. After completing these forms he'll be free to go."

I glanced from him to Joey. "Then why is he here?"

"Mama, I didn't know. I promise."

"What didn't you know?"

"The guy I told you about, the one with the fancy new truck. I think he's involved."

Without mentioning names, Officer Kelsey explained several young men in the student housing complex where Joey lived had been selling drugs from their apartments. That night, when Joey had arrived home from work, the campus police were raiding the apartments. Joey had parked in his assigned spot, which was below one of the apartments being raided. When the occupants were aware the police were coming, they had thrown bags of drugs over the balcony. Joey had seen these bags next to his car when he'd stepped out and picked them up. A campus officer had caught him holding two bags and arrested him with the other students.

"Of course, we verified his alibi after we brought him in. And his apartment also checked out." Officer Kelsey sat and shuffled the papers on the table. "So, he's in the clear."

Joey turned and looked at me then. "But, Mama, because of the arrest, I can't go back to student housing till the fall semester begins, and my car is still—"

"We will need to keep it a while longer." Kelsey picked up a pen.

I nodded and tried to digest all I'd heard. "So, can I take him home now?"

"Yes, ma'am. José, just complete these two forms and sign each one." The officer handed him the papers and a pen.

Joey completed the required information and we left the station half an hour later. He sat in silence for most of the forty-mile trip.

But when we turned off the highway and pink tinged the eastern sky, he mumbled, "Please don't tell Daddy."

"But Joey, your father and I don't have any secrets. And besides he'll be home later today."

"Yeah, right."

Unnerved by a surly tone I'd not heard from him in years, I stared at him. "What was that?"

"You and Dad don't have any secrets? I happen to know you do."

My knuckles turned white from the gorilla grip I had on the steering wheel. What had he discovered?

"What... what do you mean?"

"Remember last semester in sociology I had that family-tree project? Well, I found out a few things."

I fought to keep my voice calm. "What are you talking about? What things?"

Joey slumped down in the seat. "You always told us your parents were dead."

"Well, they are."

"But you had us believe they died in a car wreck. I found out how they really died." He glared at me. "They were shot. You lied and you've been lying to Daddy, and Mike and me all this time."

My throat constricted. I struggled for breath. I almost ran the car off the road, but veered back before the wheels left the pavement. What should I do? Tom couldn't find out about my parents yet.

As I slowed at the bump gate, I turned to Joey. "I won't tell Daddy about your arrest if you don't tell him about my parents."

He stared at me as if I had stepped off the moon.

"Please, Joey. I promise I'll give you, Mike, and Daddy the whole story soon. There's something I have to do first, then I'll tell you all the truth. Please."

Before I came to a complete stop in the garage, he climbed out of the car and fumbled for his back door key.

When he opened it, he turned accusing brown eyes to me. "And you call yourself a Christian."

I stepped out of the car. My knees buckled under the weight of guilt and I dropped to the ground. With eyes scrunched up tight, I held back the tears. Brutus came out of the pet door and nudged my legs.

The first heart wrenching prayer I'd uttered for many years escaped from my lips. "Dear God. Please don't abandon me as I have abandoned you."

The sun peeked over the trees and light flooded the garage. I opened my eyes and patted the dog, finally giving him the attention he craved. He bounded around, eager to show off his newest treasure. He ran to the lawn and came back with a stubby brown object in clear paper with a red sticker. Dropping the prize at my knees, he sat with ears straight up, eyes wide, and tongue lolling out of the corner of his mouth. I picked up his offering and twisted it round and round. I'd seen that red sticker before, but where?

"No!" I dropped the piece of cigar before the contamination could travel from my fingers to my soul. "The man in the grocery store."

CHAPTER SEVEN

The only outright lie I'd told Tom and our boys was how my parents had died. But there were so many other things I hadn't told them. The details of my early life; the role I'd played in the fire and the other deaths that night. Those lies of omission ate at my soul. During our courtship and twenty-four years of marriage, I'd tried to convince myself Tom knew all he needed to about me. He didn't need to know all the guilt-encrusted details.

And now I had to tell him another lie. He was due home late afternoon, and Joey's presence would have to be explained. Joey and I had spoken all of ten words to each other since we'd returned from the police station. After sleeping for several hours, he'd taken Tom's car to his apartment to collect clothes and other personal items, then drove on to work. His shift ended after midnight. Therefore it would be up to me to tell Tom.

I'd rehearsed several stories, but each one acted like a dagger piercing my heart. Finally, I decided to use Joey's forced presence to my advantage. I'd called Teresa and reiterated my willingness to have her stay while Mike traveled out of town, but also asked if she'd like to join me on a little trip. She agreed, eager to see more of Texas. I didn't have the heart to tell her the scenery between San Antonio and Eagle Pass would not be anything she hadn't seen before. She would think she was back in New Mexico.

Since we'd be gone four or five days, and Tom's schedule usually had him out of town a day or two each week, I'd need someone to take care of Brutus. Now I had a real reason for having Joey in the house, and it would not be a lie. Having him stay would help me out, since I'd be gone for several days.

I still had not resolved the duplicity of involving Teresa in this pilgrimage into my past, when I resisted sharing the intimate experience with my husband. My reasoning contained gigantic holes, but I latched on to it, nonetheless. Teresa and I still had a lot to learn about each other, and I knew the deceit wouldn't last long. I would tell her the truth at some point in our travels. And we shared two other traits: our cultural heritage, and we were women.

With Tom, the years of silence, lies and half-truths were so deep I wasn't sure I could extricate myself and come out a whole person and keep our marriage together.

As I pushed the hamper to the laundry room, I passed an oblong wooden plaque in the living room that Tom's best man had given us as a wedding present. It read: *As for me and my house, we will serve the Lord. Joshua 24:15.* I'd ignored it many times over the years, and even tried not to display it when we'd moved to this house three years ago. But Tom had unearthed it and placed it in a prominent spot in the living room. The gold lettering seemed to jump out and attack me this time. I did not serve the Lord in telling my husband half-truths, in conspiring with my son to deceive his father, in concocting excuses to travel to Eagle Pass. I averted my eyes and pushed the wheeled hamper faster.

The lump in my throat wouldn't budge. I swallowed and swallowed, and threw towels and sheets into the washer. After adding detergent and bleach, I closed the lid and punched the appropriate buttons. As the tub whirled and the water trickled in, mixing the smell of chlorine with the floral bouquet of soap, I leaned over the machine. The sorrow, guilt and fear choking my spirit bubbled out in wracking sobs. Why couldn't I find a spiritual bleach to cleanse my soul?

The telephone ring jarred me from my pity party. I wiped my face and dashed to the office. I talked with Linda Mueller, the director of the orthopedic clinic where I worked—or at least used to work before my recent health problems. She asked about the status of the next article for the *Texas Physical and Occupational Therapy Journal.* I reported it needed a final revision and promised she'd have it by the end of the day.

Not to add another lie to my resume, I plugged in the flash drive and opened the appropriate file. I added a concluding paragraph, completed the final revision, and e-mailed it to Linda. I also reminded her I had my follow-up appointment the next day, when I hoped the doctor would tell me the date I could return to work as a physical therapist. The intense abdominal pain prior to, and the complications resulting from, my gall bladder cancer surgery had required I take a three-month leave of absence. But in order to keep in good standing with the organization, I had agreed to write the monthly article the clinic was obligated to provide the *Texas P. & O. T. Journal.*

Last month's issue lay on top of the file cabinet. I thumbed through it and stopped at my article where my photograph graced the upper right hand corner. Running my finger over the picture, the face of the man in the grocery store flashed in my mind. A shiver through my body sent the journal fluttering from my fingers. I picked it up, and winced at a twinge in my abdomen. I stared at the cover. Could the man have seen my photo in the *Texas P. & O. T. Journal?* But why would he read such a publication? I threw the journal back onto the file cabinet.

Answers to my questions proved elusive, but a burning in my soul convinced me he had a connection to Angelica, to Eagle Pass, and maybe to Eva. This morning when Joey and I had come home, I'd picked up the cigar piece and wrapper Brutus had so proudly presented me, and placed them in a plastic baggy. Even now, thinking about that man and how he must have been on our property, sent the hair on the back of my neck signals to stand at attention. I decided I couldn't keep calling him *that man*, and since he had a preference for cigars I would call him Cigar Breath.

I should tell Deputy Quintanilla about Cigar Breath, but then I'd have to explain my suspicions and my connection to Angelica's mother. Would this be construed as concealing evidence? My desire to find answers to troubling questions far out-weighed my fear of Cigar Breath or the deputy's threats. I had to resolve these issues on my own. I wouldn't involve Tom or Quintanilla in this pursuit. I was adamant. No Tom or Quintanilla. I just knew I had to have all the answers when I did tell Tom.

After I placed the clothes in the dryer, I took out the plastic baggy containing the cigar stub. Brutus always scoured our property for interesting treasures. In the past, he'd collected bits of trash that blew in from neighboring properties or from the road. This cigar didn't necessarily come from Cigar Breath. It could have belonged to Norm Harrison, a neighbor at the end of the road who smoked cigars. He often walked his dogs past our place. Maybe he'd dropped his cigar.

Believing Norm had dropped the cigar, eased my fears, allowing me to look forward to Tom's return.

Due to an accident and congestion on Interstate 10, he arrived home much later than expected. He'd called so I would go ahead with dinner. Little did he know that it'd been a week since I'd been able to face a plate of food with anything resembling anticipation.

Later in the evening, I told him Joey would be staying a week or two. Tom accepted my explanation without question, adding another sack to the burden of deceit I had lashed to my soul. And then when he asked where Teresa and I were going, I nearly suffocated on my words and had to get a drink in the kitchen.

When I returned, I had an answer. Not a lie, but also not the complete truth. "We're going antique hunting. I think we'll stop in Comfort and Kerrville, then maybe head down to Uvalde."

"Uvalde. That's not known for antiques, is it?"

"I heard they have a new flea-market that draws dealers from all over. Anyway, it'll be something different." I ravaged through the pages of a catalog to hide from any further inquiry.

"Different is right. Well, even if Teresa doesn't find much of interest, you two will have a great opportunity to visit."

Another half-truth told. Another wedge between us. Another brick added to the wall separating me from God.

◆◆◆

"Mr. and Mrs. McDonough, good news," Doctor Fordyce said. "All the tests are normal and the incision is healing well. As I said before, you were very fortunate we caught the cancer so early."

We both sighed, and Tom patted my hand resting in the crook of his arm.

"Great news, doctor. But what about the twinges I feel occasionally?"

He leaned back in his chair and removed his glasses. "The internal stitches. Some have dissolved sooner than others. Nothing to worry about, but no heavy lifting for a few more weeks."

"That was going to be my next question. When can I return to work?"

"Any time, but as I said, no lifting. Can you guarantee you won't strain your abdominal muscles? You know we did more than remove your gall bladder. The exploratory surgery we did in your abdomen is the holdup at this point. So, maybe give it at least two more weeks."

I rubbed my hand over my stomach and nodded. "Sounds good. I'll be happy to get back to the clinic."

"But you mustn't overdo it. Two more weeks. We can handle that." Tom shifted in his chair, ready to stand.

Doctor Fordyce motioned for him to stay seated. "There is one more thing."

Tom and I glanced at each other. I clung to him. "What's that?"

The doctor smiled. "Nothing too serious. Sorry if I alarmed you. It's just your blood pressure, Maricella. It's a little high. Not high enough for medication, but you must take it easy. Watch your diet and stress levels."

My breath whooshed out in relief. I knew what caused the rise in my blood pressure and it had nothing to do with food.

"Sure. I'll take it easy. In fact," I turned to Tom and gave him my sweetest smile, "my daughter-in-law and I will be taking a little vacation next week."

"That'll do the trick. Hope you have a great time." Doctor Fordyce stood and extended his hand. "Unless you have any problems, I won't need to see you for two months."

We shook hands and left his office. Since it was close to lunch time, we ate before returning home. A sidewalk bistro close to the medical center offered a variety of salads, sandwiches, and homemade soups.

After enjoying a leisurely meal, we ambled to the car and Tom's phone rang. He groaned when he recognized his boss' name on the caller I.D. Tom had been looking forward to having five days at home, but the boss calling on Friday afternoon did not bode well.

I sat in the car while Tom completed his conversation. When he joined me, I could tell his plans had changed.

"That was Kurt. I have to attend another training session in New York next week."

"You weren't scheduled for your refresher course until September."

"I thought so, too, but Cindy has a big contract to finalize in Dallas, so I have to take her slot."

When Tom had initially received training on the use of the new Intra Aortic Balloon Pump, we knew he'd have to attend a follow-up session in New York City. Given the tenuous situation in the company, Tom couldn't refuse the New York trip.

He thumped the steering wheel, then started the car and glanced at me. "Is this all right with you? I'll be leaving Sunday and not returning till the following Saturday."

"Sure. Don't forget José will be home and I have the trip with Teresa." I stared out of the window at the rolling hills, avoiding Tom's scrutiny.

Inwardly, I jumped up and down. Tom's week out of town would suit my plans perfectly. I could spend several uninterrupted days in Eagle Pass, and he wouldn't have to know exactly where I was. I would need to convince Teresa not to tell Mike. Another deception, another story.

Tom bumped the gate open and turned into our driveway where we saw Brutus lying on the grassy edge. He appeared to be sleeping, but as we approached and he remained motionless, my heart raced and fear nibbled at the corners of my mind. All I could think was Cigar Breath had been here.

"Tom, stop. Brutus. Something's wrong."

I jumped out of the car and ran to the brown heap in the grass. Tom was close behind. The dog's little body moved up and down a fraction with each breath.

"He's alive." Tom turned the little bundle over. "No sign of open wounds. Maybe he was bitten."

Or poisoned.

"Take him, Chella. Let's get him to the vet."

I took the unconscious puppy and ran back to the car. Tom raced to the veterinarian clinic, five miles away. We had Brutus in an examination room within minutes.

The vet confirmed no physical injuries, but did find puncture wounds on the dog's right hind leg. Dr. Slaven shaved the area around the bite, and by the spread of the punctures, assumed Brutus had been bitten by a rattlesnake. She immediately gave anti-venom, took blood, and inserted an intravenous catheter. The assistant carried away our little brown puppy, assuring us he would be well taken care of for the next few days.

Driving home, I kept on the lookout for a tan sedan with a dark trunk. Although Dr. Slaven's diagnosis of a snake bite as the cause for Brutus' condition, I couldn't help thinking Cigar Breath was trying to send me a message. Tears tracked down my cheeks. I sniffed.

Tom placed a comforting hand over mine. "He'll be all right, sweetheart."

The tears turned into a deluge. Oh, Tom. How I love you, but my tears aren't just for Brutus. They're for Angelica and Eva and... you and me.

CHAPTER EIGHT

"I'll call you every day. And every night. I love you."

Tom kissed me and I clung to him. "I love you." I held onto his comforting form. "Please remember, no matter what happens, I love you."

He pulled away and his blue eyes searched my face, but I averted my gaze before he could discover the pain I endeavored to hide.

"What was that?"

I clung to him again. "Nothing. Just that I love you, too."

He picked up his brief case and smiled, a dimple creasing his cheek. My heart constricted as it had done the first time I'd seen him in freshman social studies class. He waved and mouthed, "I love you," and meandered through the line at the security check point.

I waved and blew him a kiss. "Oh, use my cell number when you call—"

He turned and the crowd swallowed him.

Driving out of the airport parking lot, I sighed with relief. With Tom on his way to New York, my plan to discover what had happened to Eva was well under way. During our marriage, Tom had worked for three different medical supply companies, and always had a combination of South, Central, or West Texas as his territory. In his absences, I'd been the one who had to handle two young boys, make on-the-spot decisions, and deal with family celebrations and crises alone. When Tom returned home, he barged in and took over. Sometimes I resented how he assumed control so matter-of-factly. But if this was my major complaint about him, I suppose I could consider myself fortunate.

As I drove on the interstate out of San Antonio toward the Hanson Ridge exit, I tried not to be overjoyed at his departure. Had fate intervened and given me a clear path to travel?

Used to making decisions on my own, I vowed to see this one through to a successful conclusion. I sighed and set the cruise control.

When I arrived home, Joey met me in the kitchen, brown-bag meal in hand, ready to go to work. His late shift required him to sleep during the day, which resulted in him spending little time with Tom. I admit I'd avoided Joey because I didn't want to be reminded of our deal with each other. But since I would be leaving the next day, I needed to give him last minute instructions about Brutus.

We'd been called by the veterinarian's office late Saturday afternoon. Brutus was alert, seemed to be suffering no adverse side affects from the bite, and could go home. He had to be given antibiotic medication twice a day, and the wound site observed for signs of infection. I showed Joey the medication in the refrigerator, and gave him a list of important phone numbers.

Joey did not look at me the whole time I spoke, but on his way to the back door, he turned and his lips twitched in a brief smile. "Hope your trip's successful, Mama. And thanks for not telling Dad."

I ignored his bowed head and hugged him. "And thank you for keeping my secret. You'll soon have the truth. I promise." I patted his shoulders. "Drive safely, and remember I love you."

He had his own car back. I walked him to the driveway, waved and watched the red taillights disappear into the darkness.

After giving Brutus his evening medication, I began packing. When I had all the necessities for a week, I carried my dresser stool to the closet again and pulled the box off the shelf. The photograph of Eva and me lay on top of my keepsakes. I took it out and replaced the box. I returned the stool to my dresser, extracted the necklaces from my jewelry box and placed them in an envelope with the photo and held it to my heart.

"Eva, I'll know soon."

I opened the small zippered section of my suitcase and secured the envelope inside.

Surprised at how fatigue weighed me down, I slipped into bed early, but awoke several hours later when Brutus barked. I climbed out of bed with heart quivering, palms clammy, and opened the bedroom door in time to see Joey slinking to his room.

"Sorry, Mama. Guess Brutus is not used to me being here yet. Good night."

Relieved that Joey had caused the commotion and not someone sinister, I returned to bed, but not to sleep. My mind tossed and turned as much as my body did.

I know the impending trip played hide-and-go-seek with my memories, and before long I sat on the bus that had taken me from the chaos of my fifteenth birthday party to *Tia* Gloria in San Antonio.

Tia—actually my great aunt—had been expecting me. She said the police in Eagle Pass had called her as next of kin and to report my disappearance. She enveloped me in her arms and in her heart.

Those last years of high school were only bearable because of her. All but one of my friends in Eagle Pass had been Hispanic. There had only been two or three Anglo kids in the whole school, but now the harsh reality of racial and cultural differences cut into my young, impressionable spirit.

Tia would comfort me. "*Mija*, ignore them. You're smart. You're talented. You'll rise above this."

The summer I turned sixteen, an event I refused to celebrate, I started working at a local clinic on the Westside.

The school counselor had recommended me for the position, and I'm sure it pointed me to a career in the health care industry. I know it spurred me on to getting the best education I could.

Right before graduation, I'd received a college scholarship based on my good grades, and had just enrolled in UTSA when *Tia* died. With her death, the last tie to family shattered. We were the only family each other had. Her two daughters had died in infancy, and her son, who served in the army during World War II, had succumbed to his wounds right after his discharge.

As a college student living and working in the northern area of San Antonio, I began to disassociate myself from my past—family, friends and heritage. Looking back, I'm not sure if I tried to break those ties because of shame, or because I wanted to forget the hurt and guilt associated with that part of my life.

Papi, forgive me for dishonoring you in this way.

After Tom and I began dating, I gave him just the barest details about my life prior to enrolling in college. Even after he'd proposed in our sophomore year, I refused him access to that part of my life. His parents accepted me, maybe because I didn't flaunt my Hispanic culture and because I readily attended church with Tom, but they objected to our wanting to marry so young. We ignored their protests and married anyway.

I've often referred back to the decision and wondered if I'd chosen marriage to keep me out of financial crises, or because I truly loved Tom. Over the years, I've realized it was because of love, a love which has developed and changed and grown. During those early years together, I continued to ignore my past, and even though we lived in San Antonio, I shied away from cultural reminders.

When I return from Eagle Pass, I know I'll have to confront the ghosts of the past, and ask my family for forgiveness.

I glanced at the clock. Three-thirty. Four more hours, then I'd pick up Teresa and we'd be on our way. I rested back in the pillows, cradling Tom's in my arms. The faint scent he'd left behind calmed my troubled heart. Would he forgive me? Would his God forgive me? A lone tear bubbled up and spilled down my check. His God. Even after all these years, I'd never come to think of Him as my God.

When we were dating, I'd go to church with Tom, never having graced the doors of any church since leaving Eagle Pass. Even *Tia* did not leave home to go to church. She'd say her daily prayers, had crucifixes and holy pictures throughout the house, but always said her age and infirmities kept her home. I remember how she struggled to walk, with every movement eliciting a moan or gasp. God would understand, she'd say.

Tom's sincere belief in his God wasn't even enough to convince me to openly accept the Lord. Why would God want me? I was so unworthy. I had caused the deaths of my parents, my friends. I could lie anytime—had done so most of my life. I could hardly keep truth and lies separate anymore. Tom's God wouldn't want me.

I threw Tom's pillow to his side of the bed, and since I couldn't sleep, climbed out of bed to work on the next article for the *Texas P. & O. T. Journal*. Before I opened the file, I logged onto the Eagle Pass newspaper Web site. They had publications listed for the past month. I scanned the stories, searching for anything. Nothing.

Maybe I'd find Eva Valdez's name somewhere. I assumed since Angelica Valdez was her daughter's name Eva's last name would be Valdez. Nothing. No Eva Valdez. I kept searching, going back day by day. Even after twenty-nine years, some names stirred the cobwebs, but nothing helped me in my quest.

A wedding. A summer family reunion. A new store opening. A drug bust. A car wreck.

I stopped. The name of the injured woman was listed as Eva Alonzo. Words in her story jumped at me. Severely injured. Aged forty-four, same as me. A daughter named Angelica.

Could this be my Eva?

CHAPTER NINE

Teresa already knew about the body. I'd told her and the boys the day after I'd found the young girl, but had kept my connection to Angelica to myself. I'd given my daughter-in-law a fact-based reason for making the trip to Eagle Pass. I told her I'd recently discovered a childhood friend I'd presumed dead was alive and possibly living there. That part of my story contained a nugget of truth.

Knowing eventually I'd have to tell Tom and my sons the real reason for moving to San Antonio so long ago, I rehearsed my revelation by giving Teresa a preview.

We'd left San Antonio early in the morning and traveled west to Uvalde where we stopped for a breakfast of pancakes and fruit. Maybe because we shared a common heritage, or because Teresa was a captive audience, she accepted the details of my life prior to marrying Tom without question. She'd listened with wide-eyed amazement, horror and sometimes disbelief, but if she had comments, she kept them to herself.

After breakfast, we visited the large flea market. Now the sharp points of my conscience could turn without hurting quite so much, because I could tell Tom truthfully we did stop in Uvalde. Before leaving home, I'd pulled out a Texas map to plot our journey. A quick scan and I realized if we included visits to Comfort and Kerrville, we'd travel northeast, the opposite direction to Eagle Pass. But when Tom found out I'd lied about the whole trip, it wouldn't really matter if we didn't make it to the antique stores in those two towns.

After breakfast, Teresa took over the driving as we headed south. We had another hour's drive ahead of us, and the closer we got, the quieter I became.

She gave up trying to keep the conversation alive and poked my arm. "Is something wrong? You haven't said a word in miles."

"I'm thinking about my friend, Eva. Wondering if I'll find her. If she's okay."

Teresa nodded and concentrated on the long, shimmering ribbon of tarmac ahead, while I closed my eyes and rested my head against the seat.

What would I find in Eagle Pass? Who would I find? As these questions paraded through my muddled mind, I wondered if I'd also find closure, forgiveness, peace. Last night, when I'd read the *News Guide* newspaper article about Eva Alonzo's car wreck, I'd hoped it might be my friend, but later I'd dismissed it as too coincidental.

But now, as the flat country around us seemed to invade the car and remind me I'd left behind my safe haven, people and places and events from my past came marching into my present. The knots in my stomach took turns unraveling and twisting into tighter bundles. I almost had to ask Teresa to stop the car, but after shifting in my seat and taking a sip of water, the roller coaster motions settled down to a mild churn.

Names and faces of people from my childhood popped into my memory. I took out the notebook I'd brought along to help keep track of vital information and jotted down the names. As I wrote, I tried to remember any Valdez boys who could have been Angelica's father—Eva's husband, but none came to mind. Thinking about the Eva from the car wreck, I tried to recall Alonzos from my childhood, and vague memories of a man by that name floated in and out of the fog. But he would have been too young to have a son Eva married and too old himself. No. Eva Alonzo, injured in the car wreck, could not be my Eva.

"Eagle Pass, five miles. Almost there."

Teresa's words brought the curtain down on the past. "Good. The hotel won't be hard to find since it's east of town, just off Main Street, and I know where that is." I'd booked the rooms online and had printed out the accompanying map.

The growth of the city amazed me. New building construction to the left and to the right. Signs advertising a new medical center. Would I still be able to locate the old neighborhood?

We checked into our rooms, then had a pasta salad lunch in the hotel dining room before venturing out. I'd asked Teresa to drive again. I couldn't trust my quivering muscles to safely maneuver the car.

The ride down Main Street brought memories flooding over me. I recognized many buildings and yet so much had changed. Gone were the department stores, the drug store, the grocery store. They'd been replaced by vendors catering to tourists. Colorful embroidered dresses and piñatas hung at eye-level fluttered in the breeze. Black sombreros stacked on boxes threatened to spill onto the sidewalk. Traffic slowed our progress. I soaked in the atmosphere, not sure if it was a balm or a penance.

Down a side street, I saw a row of Dumpsters. Teresa kept driving, but I stared at the trash-filled receptacles, sure I could see a young girl huddled by the wall, cradling a backpack and wearing a heart shaped necklace.

My childhood home, four blocks off Main Street, took an eternity to reach. The band around my chest grew tighter and tighter, forcing me to gulp in air.

Teresa placed her hand on mine. "I know this has got to be hard."

I gulped again, swallowed and attempted a smile. "You're right, but I have to go."

She followed my directions and slowed when we arrived at the house. My house. One of the many long, narrow, siding-covered look-alikes. I'd been taken there as a ten-day-old infant, and had never known another home until *Tia* Gloria had given me sanctuary. Somehow in my dreams it appeared bigger, prettier, cleaner.

This shabby place needed a coat of paint. The big tree from the front yard had been uprooted and lay decaying on the brown grass. I wanted to get out and knock on the door and tell them I used to live here, but I couldn't do it. My hands were glued to the seat; my feet were chunks of concrete. The churning in my gut and the pain in my heart forced my eyes to close.

"Drive on. Please, drive on."

Teresa drove and stopped around the corner. "Do you want to go back to the hotel?"

I opened my eyes and shook my head. "No, no. I must see Eva's old house too. I'm okay now. It was just such a shock."

Eva's house, one block over and one street down, always seemed so far away on foot. As we drove along I retraced the often traveled path I'd taken to her house.

I could still hear my mother say before I'd set out, "Don't walk on the grass, Maricella. Stay out of the neighbors' yards. Remember to show respect."

For the most part, I had followed my mother's instructions, but there were times when the urgent need to visit Eva forced me to take a short cut. I knew just which fence was down, or which hedge had a gap.

"Over there." I pointed and Teresa stopped the car.

Eva's house looked attractive compared to ours. It appeared to have been newly painted pale green, and the garden showed signs of care, although the lawn could have done with mowing.

Next door, I noticed an elderly woman in a rickety rocking chair on the porch. Teresa and I climbed out of the car and approached her. She motioned for us to come closer and we greeted her in Spanish. She invited us to join her, indicating we sit on a bench along the railing. I explained I'd been a friend of the girl who'd lived next door twenty-nine years ago.

At first the woman stared at me and then at Eva's house, as if my words had no meaning. Her wispy gray hair fluttered in the breeze and flopped over her eyes. When she raised her arm to push the strand off her face, the short sleeve of her navy blue floral dress fell back to reveal a birthmark on her upper arm. I gawked. She noticed and dropped her arm.

"Mrs. Hernandez, the mark on your arm. I apologize for my rudeness, but I've seen it before."

She shook her head and stared off into the distance, ignoring us. Embarrassment clouded her face. But I could remember when she'd shown the opposite emotion.

Sometimes when I had visited Eva, her mother would send us next door to deliver a stack of hot tortillas, or fresh tomatoes from the garden. I'd been fascinated by the stories the neighbor woman would tell of her youth in the mountains near Mexico City. At the time of those visits, she must have been about fifty years old, much older than my parents. The first time I'd seen the birthmark, which when viewed from a certain angle, resembled a fire-breathing dragon, she had told us a magnificent tale about how she'd acquired it. Gullible and innocent, we'd believed every word. She'd probably forgotten the elaborate yarn she'd spun.

"Mr. and Mrs. Cuellar were your neighbors, and I used to come and play with their daughter, Eva. Remember, Mrs. Hernandez? The fire, the shooting?" I waited as I could see her eyes widen and the expression on her face soften.

"Yes. Yes, I remember. You girls were always together. Like sisters. Until—" She lowered her gaze and shook her head. "It was so sad." Mrs. Hernandez glanced at me and smiled "But she's back."

I touched the woman's hand. "*Señora*, what do you mean?"

Teresa, who had ambled over to examine scarlet flowers in a hanging basket came and stood behind the woman. She shrugged and mouthed, "I don't think she knows what she's saying."

I patted the wrinkled hand. "Eva's not here anymore."

But Mrs. Hernandez pulled her hand away and pointed to the house next door. "She came back with a new husband. A few months ago, I think, or maybe a few weeks ago. But she's not there now."

She rocked back and forth. The wooden porch planks creaked with each movement. A glazing engulfed her eyes.

Teresa returned to the bench. I wanted to believe the old woman's words. I wanted to reach into her head and pull out more. Panic and hope vied for supremacy in my throat, leaving me speechless.

Teresa placed a hand on Mrs. Hernandez's shoulder. "Do you know where Eva is now?"

The old eyes focused on Teresa, then the woman turned and encompassed me with her gaze. A tender smile eased the corners of her mouth. "When you see her in the hospital, give her a kiss from me." She puckered her lips and touched them as if blowing a kiss.

Hospital. The car wreck. It must be Eva. My hand shook as I tapped the old woman's knee.

"*Señora*, what... what is her last name now?"

The rocking stopped. With great effort, she pushed herself up and grabbed onto the porch railing next to the bench where we sat. After gaining her balance, she shuffled to the front door. Had she heard my question? Before I could ask again, she stopped and turned, her eyes alert and focused.

"She married that no-good Hector. The one who's a big shot at the casino. Never liked him."

"Hector? Hector who?" Panic rushed up my spine sending spasms through my body. Afraid we'd hear no more from her, I slumped against the bench.

The stooped frame reached the door and she pulled open the screen. As she stepped inside, she stumbled on the threshold. Teresa rushed to help and prevented the old woman from falling.

"*Gracias. Gracias, mija.*" Mrs. Hernandez held onto Teresa's arm. "I'm fine, thank you. Go, now. I need to rest."

Still supporting the old woman's elbow, Teresa asked, "What is Hector's last name? Please, we have to know."

"Alonzo. Hector Alonzo."

◆◆◆

I don't remember leaving the porch nor getting in the car.

Out of the fog, a voice repeated over and over, "Where's the hospital, Maricella? Where's the hospital?"

Teresa's touch on my arm jerked me back to the present.

"Not sure." My voice spluttered out. I couldn't remember ever visiting the hospital when I lived here. "We'll have to ask for directions."

Teresa stopped the car. "I'll check at this restaurant."

While waiting for her, my connection to reality gradually returned. I gazed around and familiar sights popped into my consciousness. That house, those buildings. Coldness crept up my body, and when it touched my heart, I shivered, although the stifling summer heat seared my skin and created a desert in my throat.

This had been the location of my parents' restaurant.

Memories of the fire swamped me. *Mami y Papi.*

Acrid fumes assaulted my nose. Smoke stung my eyes. People scurried. Shots. Blood.

The ringing of my phone brought me back to earth with a violent jolt. I stared at my purse. My heart thumped like a kettle drum. I blinked. The phone rang and rang. I pulled it out of my purse. *Caller Unknown* flashed on the screen. Who was it? I had to know.

After three deliberate deep gulps of air I answered it. When I heard Deputy Quintanilla's voice, my hand shook and I scanned the street. Where was he? How did he know I was in Eagle Pass?

Reason resumed control. He'd called my cell number and I could have been at home or in Timbuktu—if I had service that far away. I answered with forced nonchalance, and fanned my face with my notebook, waiting for him to dispense with the greeting. Why had he called?

He got straight down to business. "Just wanted to keep you up to speed. We have the autopsy results for Angelica Valdez." The deputy paused, and when I didn't respond, couldn't respond because my heart beat in my throat, he continued. "She basically bled to death."

I'm sure I must have said something, but the booming in my ears drowned out my thoughts, not to mention my words. Quintanilla needed to take sensitivity lessons—unless he aimed to shock me into revealing more, into slipping up.

"Mrs. McDonough, do you want to hear the rest?"

"No, I mean, yes, Deputy. Please tell me what else you've discovered."

"We found a bus ticket stub in Angelica's pocket and were able to retrace her journey. Working with officials from the area, we determined she'd taken the regular bus from Eagle Pass to Uvalde. There she'd purchased a ticket on a small private bus to Bandera. We're not sure how she traveled the fifteen miles to Hanson Ridge."

administration hub nurses' station. These spokes then dead-ended into a ring of additional halls.

I placed my hand through Teresa's arm as we followed the signs down one spoke to Eva's wing. Lingering fumes of disinfectant mixed with lavender air freshener.

Wrinkling my nose, I squeezed her arm. "This isn't good."

"Why?"

"It means Eva must be... must be seriously injured, because she's not coming in for therapy—she's been admitted." We turned into the next hall.

Teresa stopped and nodded. "Here's the room. Let's find out."

The door stood ajar. I peered into the room. Muted light entered through the blinds and played across the sleeping figure in the bed. We tiptoed in. A small bandage on Eva's forehead identified the only visible sign of trauma. I'd expected her to be hooked up to a swarm of machines, but she didn't even have an I.V. Teresa stood behind me, a palatable source of strength, while I gazed at my friend. After nearly thirty years, I recognized her. The dark, wavy hair, the high cheek bones, a little scar on her chin. She lay on her back with her face turned to the side, her hair spread on the pillow.

I wanted to hold her in my arms and melt away the years, erase the mistakes, but my feet were glued in place. Teresa tapped my shoulder and pointed to a chair next to me. The breath I'd been holding escaped in little puffs, and I sat down on the edge of the beige vinyl chair. Teresa gestured and stepped into the hallway, closing the door behind her.

Eva stirred. My heart skipped. She opened her eyes, but didn't see me. The covers moved and she pulled her hand out to brush the hair from her eyes. I couldn't control myself any longer.

I leaned forward and whispered, "Eva. It's Maricella."

I placed both hands on the rail and stared. Her unfocused eyes moved back and forth until they lingered on my face, and a gentle smile graced her lips.

"Chella, my friend, have you seen Angel? She's so beautiful. Have you seen her?"

I shook my head. How could I tell her about Angel? Surely, this lie would be excused. "No, I haven't seen her."

"No, no. It's happening again." Eva moaned, pulling the covers over her head.

The unexpected reaction caught me by surprise. Standing, I tried to remove the pale pink sheet from her grasp. "Eva, please. What's wrong?"

Inch by inch, she pulled the covers down, her dark eyes peering at me over the edge.

"Maricella, is it really you?"

"Yes." I straightened the sheet around her. "Who did you think it was?"

Eva plucked at the sheet as she sighed. "I've had the strangest dreams. You and Angel and Hector—"

Her voice trailed off into the distance. Had she drifted back to sleep?

Then she grabbed my hand. "You're here. Really here." She fumbled with the control panel and raised the head of the bed. "Oh, my friend, after all these years, it's so good to see you. How did you find me?"

Eva tugged at the neck of her hospital issue green print gown. "These things are such a pain."

I adjusted the ties of her gown, and she rested against the pillows. "I spoke with Mrs. Hernandez, your neighbor."

"Oh, yes. But—"

A knock interrupted us and a nurse bustled in, followed by Teresa.

"Good afternoon, Mrs. Alonzo. I see you have company. Good, but we still need to take you to therapy. Right now." The nurse lowered the bed's railing and glared at us. "*Señoras*, you can't accompany her, but you can wait here if you like."

I stepped back to join Teresa while the nurse moved to the other side of the room and brought over a wheelchair I'd not noticed before. Wheelchair. That's okay. Eva was probably still weak. But when the nurse lowered the bed and held up a transfer board, I realized Eva's injuries were more extensive than my cursory observation had revealed.

My hand over my mouth, I watched as she struggled, with the nurse's encouragement, to transfer herself from the bed to the wheelchair. Eva was paralyzed—I surmised from the waist down.

Once situated in the wheelchair, sweat drops speckled over her forehead, Eva grimaced and waved. "Will you be here when I get back?"

I nodded. Words stuck in my throat. The nurse instructed Eva to propel the chair with her hands on the big wheels and opened the door. Once they disappeared around the corner, I sank onto the bed, bawling like a lost kid.

Teresa produced a tissue and sat next to me. "I tried to find out what happened, but the staff wouldn't tell me anything."

After I wiped my eyes and blew my nose, I walked to the window. "Not family. They're just following procedure." My health care knowledge kicked in and chased away the shock. I shrugged off the tears and stuck my hands on my hips. "We need to see if we can find Eva's husband, or ask her to sign a consent form so we can talk to her doctors and read her records."

While waiting for Eva's return, I asked the desk nurse for the necessary paperwork. Anxious to find out the extent of her injuries and her prognosis, I completed as much of the form as I could. I also needed to know if she'd been told about Angel. In all this mess, I'd been thinking about myself until now, but what had Eva endured? The wreck, pain, paralysis, and the loss of a daughter.

I paced by the window, but stopped when a bird landed on a nearby tree branch. The tiny feathered creature fluttered among the leaves, then hopped onto the window ledge and focused its glassy eyes on me.

I had to pull myself together, get my emotions under control, and use my professional skills to help my friend cope with and understand her situation. The bird flew away and calmness settled over me. A sensation I hadn't experienced for a long time.

Teresa joined me at the window and placed her arm around my shoulders.

Taller than me by several inches, I glanced up at her. "I'm so glad you're with me, Teresa. Thanks for your support."

"That's okay. I'm thankful you chose me to share this special time with you." She squeezed my shoulder. "How about... how about we have a prayer?"

I nodded. No way could I have voiced a prayer with my heart so full of guilt and shame.

Teresa's soft words surrounded me with strength, just in time to greet Eva with a sincere smile when the nurse wheeled her back into the room.

"That was hard work. I'm tired." Eva propelled her wheelchair to the bed.

We watched the nurse supervise her transfer back into bed. Teresa pushed the wheelchair into the corner and I stood by Eva's side.

"We won't stay much longer." I brushed the hair from her face.

"Don't leave. Please don't leave." Eva reached out to me and I sank into the chair near her bed.

"Eva, my friend, I'm here, and I'll stay as long as you need me."

She smiled and looked at Teresa, frown furrows between her eyes.

I motioned for Teresa to step closer. "This is Teresa, my daughter-in-law."

Eva's face contorted. "Daughter-in-law. That means you have a son. Oh, Chella, we have so much to talk about. I have a child too..." her voice trailed to a whisper and she turned her head away. "I had a child, a beautiful daughter. Angel. She was my Angel."

"What happened—?" But before Teresa completed her question, I put my finger to my lips and motioned for her to say no more.

Eva began to cry, the soft sound tearing at my heart. What could I say? How could I comfort her?

I attempted to change the subject. "Where's Hector? Has he been to see you today?"

She shook her head, and turned toward us. Tear tracks stained her face. "No, and I don't want him to."

Teresa pulled her chair closer. "Why not?"

Eva raised the bed, her eyes dark and forlorn. "He's changed. He's not the man I married six months ago. I don't ... trust him anymore."

I smoothed the sheet over her legs. "So maybe he's not the person I should talk to about your recovery."

"No. Don't have anything to do with him. Ever. He's evil. If you want to know about my legs, talk to my doctor."

Handing Eva the consent form, I explained why she needed to sign it and fill in the places I'd left blank. I hesitated to ask for more details about Hector. Her expression seemed to indicate that was a closed subject. For now.

There were so many questions I needed to ask her, but I didn't know where to begin. Before I could utter the words, Eva introduced the one foremost in my mind.

"I sent her to you, Maricella, but she didn't make it. My Angel was killed before she found you."

"Eva, what do you mean you sent her to me? How did you know where I lived?"

"Open that drawer." She pointed to the bedside table. "Somewhere in there you'll find a magazine."

Moving aside a hospital gown, I located the magazine and pulled it out. Last month's issue of the *Texas P. & O. T. Journal* stared at me. Now I knew. It contained my article, accompanied by my photograph and a brief biography.

"I saw your picture and found out where you lived." Eva's weak smile slid from her face before it reached her eyes.

"But why did you have this journal?"

"They gave it to me when I first came here. Dr. Contreras wanted me to read about my condition." She looked down at the still appendages. "My legs..."

For a few seconds, the only sound in the room came from the wall clock.

Then Teresa took the journal and thumbed through it. "How did you receive your injuries?"

"Car wreck. Three weeks ago." Eva tapped the site of the bandage. "Banged my head. It's healing now, but the spinal injury is the problem."

Although I'd read the brief newspaper article, I wanted details from Eva. "How did the wreck happen?"

She sighed and squinted, as if recalling the event made her head ache. "I was going to get Angel from work and a... an old green pickup ran a stop sign, and next thing I knew, two days had passed, and my legs were paralyzed."

"Was the other driver ever located?" I asked.

Eva raised her head, glancing from Teresa to me. "I haven't told anybody this. Didn't know who I could trust. Hector has friends everywhere. Come closer."

Teresa and I moved our chairs and Eva whispered, "I think I recognized the driver. I think it was Hector."

CHAPTER ELEVEN

A nurse with sergeant-major posture entered the room, stifling our responses to Eva's revelation. She stabbed at her watch and scowled at the wall clock. "*Señoras*, visiting hours were over a long time ago."

Her tight lips and frown halted my request to stay longer.

I stood and hugged Eva, forcing my eyes to stay dry. "We'll be back tomorrow, *mi amiga*."

"I'm so thankful you found me. We'll tell each other everything. *Mañana*."

The relief on her face and gratitude in her voice ripped my heart in pieces. I wanted to take her with me, but knew I couldn't.

"*Adios*." I squeezed her hand.

Teresa pulled me to the door, stepping around the rotund nurse standing at the foot of the bed.

We passed the nurses' station and I slowed. "It's still early. Do you mind if we read Eva's records before going to eat?"

Teresa shrugged. "Of course, not. Let's see what they can tell us."

I handed over the signed consent and waited while the nurse located Eva's file. Teresa and I took the folder to the waiting room and studied the contents.

The blow to Eva's head had caused minor bleeding into the brain, but the second CAT scan done the day after the wreck showed the bleeding had stopped. Once she'd regained consciousness other tests revealed normal brain activity and reflex responses, except in the legs. Her spine had been injured at the L4 vertebra, in the lumbar region, resulting in paralysis from the waist down, as I had surmised. The rehab staff was helping her build her upper body strength, so she could get herself in and out of bed, the wheelchair, and the bathroom, and to be as independent as possible, until such time as she regained lower body muscle use.

Who would help take care of her once she was discharged? There was no Angelica now and her records indicated no other children, and Hector appeared to be a lost cause.

"She'll have to come home with me when she's discharged. That's all there is to it." We returned to the station and I handed the file back to the nurse. "Maybe when we come tomorrow we can talk to Dr. Contreras."

"Dr. Contreras is here now," said the nurse. "I'm sure he would want to talk to you. We've been very concerned about Mrs. Alonzo."

After a few minutes back in the waiting room, the doctor joined us. Middle-aged, with kind, sincere eyes, his confident demeanor put me at ease.

He took us to his office and asked about my connection to Eva.

"I'm a childhood friend visiting from San Antonio."

"That's good because we have a couple of major issues. I know she doesn't wish to see her husband, but even so, we have not been able to contact him. Her daughter accompanied her when she transferred here, but Eva's had no other visitors. Do you, um, know about her daughter?"

We both nodded.

"I see. Well Mrs. Alonzo will likely be discharged next week, but I can't send her to an empty house. Do you know of any other family members or friends we can contact? She has not shared any names with us."

"She can come home with me. I'll talk to her about it tomorrow. I'm sure she'll agree."

"Good, but it won't be easy. She will have to—"

"I am aware, Doctor." I poked a finger at my chest. "I'm a physical therapist. Our house is all one level and I have access to any equipment she may need."

Dr. Contreras raised his eyebrows. "Wait a minute. I knew your name sounded familiar. You're *that* Maricella McDonough. I just read your article. In fact, I gave it to Mrs. Alonzo to read."

I smiled. "That's me."

"Excellent news." The doctor closed the file and scratched his head. "There is something else you should know." He leaned back in his chair and rocked back and forth a few times. "Mrs. Alonzo's spinal injury is, well, minor, and I don't understand why she's not responding to therapy nor showing signs of regaining muscle use."

Teresa glanced from the doctor to me. "What do you mean?"

"The swelling caused by the initial trauma has dissipated and her last MRI indicated no permanent damage. I'm leaning more toward it being—forgive me for saying this— psychosomatic."

Having had some experience with patients exhibiting psychosomatic ailments, I nodded in agreement.

"The trauma of the wreck, which was three weeks ago, her adamant stance on not seeing her husband, and, of course, the news of her daughter's death. All pretty heavy burdens. I wouldn't doubt if her depression is negatively affecting her recovery." Dr. Contreras stood and stepped around his desk. "Mrs. Alonzo going home with you—that might just be the medicine she needs. Got to do my rounds now. Good evening, ladies."

We left his office, signed-out and walked in silence to the parking lot. Teresa took the car keys from me and pushed the remote to unlock the doors.

Once behind the wheel she said, "I'm bushed. Hotel or supper first?"

"Let's eat first then we can relax. And I have something I need to discuss with you."

Grateful she read my mood and kept conversation at bay, I rested against the seat and wondered how Tom would respond to me wanting Eva to come stay a while. Staring out the window, all visions of my husband vanished and anxiety nibbled at my gut when I caught a glimpse of a tan sedan with a dark trunk in the parking lot. I turned and stared out the back window.

"Anything wrong?"

"No." I suppressed the alarm bubbling in my throat. "Just thought I recognized someone. Never mind, my mistake. How about steak for supper? There's a steakhouse in the Mall."

Cigar Breath's car in Eagle Pass? Surely not.

In my present state of mind, I must have imagined the car with the dual paint colors.

◆◆◆

When Teresa knocked on our connecting door later in the evening, I knew exactly what I needed to tell her. She deserved to know the truth, the whole truth. I could only hope for her forgiveness, for misleading her from the beginning.

Tom had already called from New York City, and I'd told him we'd traveled to Eagle Pass and had met Eva. So now he knew the truth, or at least part of it. I still hadn't told him about Angel, the necklace, or how my parents really died. I knew if I'd told him all, he'd be on the next plane down here, and I couldn't deal with him face to face right now.

His disappointment in me, although not expressed in words, but manifested in tone, stabbed at my soul. But I'd eventually convinced him Teresa and I were fine. I told him we were visiting the old neighborhood and old friends. I did not tell him I wanted Eva to come home with me. That revelation needed to wait until his next phone call.

My dichotomous soul split in two. On the one hand, I was proud of myself for preparing to tell Teresa everything, but on the other hand, I persisted in deceiving my husband. The saving grace I awarded myself was that I did intend to tell Tom—just not yet.

Teresa came in, already showered and ready for bed, her dark hair piled on top of her head, her face free of makeup. Not that she wore much, or needed to. She sat in the armchair and tucked her long legs under her robe. My son had married a strong Christian woman; one who, unbeknown to her, had put my spirituality to shame on more than one occasion since we'd left San Antonio.

I held the notebook I'd used to document everything I'd discovered so far and stood by the window. Peeking through the curtains, I glanced at the city lights twinkling in the darkness, and willed my hesitant spirit into calm action. I had to tell her now. I moved to the desk and pulled out the chair. I sat and placed the notebook on my lap.

My sentences fell over each other to fill in all the missing details. When I reached the part about the necklace, I picked up the envelope from the desk and showed Teresa the two pieces.

"Tomorrow I'm going to tell Eva about finding Angel's body, and give her back the necklace. And I have to ask about the money." I held open the notebook. "See. Here's my list of questions and all the information I have."

Teresa hadn't shown much expression during my confession, but she had asked clarifying questions along the way.

Now I stared straight into her eyes. "I'll understand if you want out of this mess. I'm sorry for deceiving you and making this trip under false pretenses. I hope you can forgive me."

She smiled, untangled her legs and stood. "I don't completely agree with what you've done, but I think I understand. At least, some of it anyway." She stepped over and placed her hand on my shoulder. "But don't worry. I'm not leaving. I want to see this through to the end."

"Thanks, Teresa." I stood and we hugged. "It means a great deal to me. I couldn't have gone this far without your strength."

"It's not my strength you need right now." She pointed heavenward. "It's His."

"I can't ask Him for anything. Would you?" As I bowed my head, I realized I'd never before asked someone to pray for me. It was a humbling experience.

Teresa prayed for guidance, for strength, for wisdom, and thanked God for keeping us safe.

After saying amen, I dabbed at my eyes.

"I'll pray for you, with you, any time, Maricella. Just let me know when. I'm going to bed now. Feeling really tired. See you in the morning." Teresa closed the connecting door behind her.

I plopped onto the bed. It had been embarrassing to explain past mistakes to my daughter-in-law. But she hadn't walked out. She hadn't scolded or abandoned me. The experience gave me courage to store away for the time I'd confront Tom and our sons. And my God.

My cell phone rang. Joey, reporting on Brutus. The dog was fine and there were no signs of infection in the wound.

Although my topsy-turvy emotions calmed after Joey's call, adrenaline on a high speed chase through my body kept sleep away. I paced back and forth, pulled out the Bible from the drawer and tried to read it. I even turned on the TV, but nothing brought me a semblance of peace or calm. Opening my notebook, I perused the notes I'd taken. I read Eva's brief account of her car wreck, and the possibility she'd recognized the driver as her husband. I checked my watch. Only ten o'clock. On the spur of the moment, before I could talk myself out of it, I decided to do a little investigating.

I grabbed my purse, turned off the light and closed the door with the faintest click. The well-lit parking lot increased my confidence and I marched to my car. The drive down Main Street to the old neighborhood took less than ten minutes. No one appeared to be in my former home. The corner street light illuminated the peeling paint and sagging porch, dimming my enthusiasm for a moment. Swallowing the lump in my throat, I drove to Eva's house. As I slowed to a crawl, I made a mental note to ask her why she'd moved back here.

Several lights shone from her house: the front bedroom, the living room. For a second, I contemplated introducing myself to Hector, but sanity returned and I remained in the car. What if he was responsible for Eva's accident? He wouldn't be pleased to see me.

A glow coming from the side of the house caught my attention. Curiosity won and I inched the car forward, peering around the house at a detached garage at the end of the driveway. The owners must have built it sometime after Eva's parents had been killed. In my enthusiasm to gain information from Mrs. Hernandez, who lived on the other side, I'd not noticed it the day before.

Light spilled out from the partially opened doors—not the roll up type, but those hinged at each side. I could see a man working under the hood of a vehicle.

I stopped my car and opened the window. He banged on a part of the engine, making a horrendous noise. As I watched, he moved over, exposing the vehicle. It was green. Before I could draw in a breath, he closed the hood and switched off the garage light. Thankful I hadn't turned off the engine, I drove away, and kept going until I stopped in the hotel parking lot.

I rested against the seat, chest heaving like I'd run a marathon. Hector and a green vehicle. Could it be? No. Surely, I'd been mistaken, Eva had been mistaken.

Needing a tissue to wipe the sweat gathering at my hairline, I opened the glove compartment and located a travel pack right next to my flashlight. After crumpling up the used tissue, I fingered the flashlight and turned it on and off. Maybe I could check out the garage. No, what a ridiculous idea. I couldn't, *shouldn't*.

But I did.

Driving back to Eva's home, I parked one house down from her driveway, and turned off the engine. No lights were on in the front rooms of her home this time. Climbing out of the car, I pushed the door closed without a sound. I hid by the neighbor's hedge, listening for Hector or whoever had been working on the green vehicle.

Other than night insects and the occasional car horn, all I heard was the blood thundering in my ears. I licked my parched lips and made my way down the driveway, keeping to the grass to avoid crunching gravel.

When I reached the garage, I shone my flashlight on the latch. No lock. I flipped the metal strip and eased open one door. A mouse-like squeak, another pull and I slipped inside, closing the door behind me. The flashlight's yellow beam turned the vehicle a sickly green, but it was green. A beat-up old green pickup, with rust patches dotting the hood and sides.

Quite pleased with what I'd discovered so far, I shone the light on the front bumper. Severe damage on the passenger side exposed shiny metal with no rust. That could only mean one thing. The damage was recent.

A noise outside. My scalp tingled. My heart fell to my feet and giant butterflies cavorted in my stomach. I turned off the flashlight. Feeling my way along the vehicle, I crept to the back of the garage where I crouched behind the truck.

The garage doors opened. The overhead light illuminated the scene. My breath stuck in my lungs. The person, Hector, I assumed, opened the driver's door and fumbled around inside the truck. He cursed and slammed the door, then turned off the light. Tomb black. I blinked.

My knees ached and the churning in my gut threatened to erupt. He hadn't closed the garage doors, but I did hear the porch screen door bang closed. I stood and leaned against the truck. My hand shook so much as I wiped my face, I almost gave myself a black eye.

When the blood circulation had returned to my legs, I stepped around the truck, and headed for the sliver of light coming through the door. I peered out. The coast was clear.

Slipping through the opening, my Capri pants caught on a nail. While trying to unhook the fabric I heard movement from the back porch. Should I go back behind the truck, or get out and hide by the side of the garage? With an extra pull the nail loosened its grip and I dashed around the garage, willing my last intake of air to sustain me until he'd gone.

The man came back to the garage, closed the doors and fumbled with the latch. I heard metal on metal then a key turn. He'd placed a lock on the doors. I gasped. Did he hear me? No. His steps crunched on the driveway back to the house.

I would have been locked in if I'd stayed in the garage

Not being a good judge of time passing without a watch to consult, I don't know how long I stood beside the garage. It seemed like hours, but when an insect crawled up my leg, fear of discovery lost out to abhorrence of creepy crawlies on my person.

I needed to escape. The neighbor's hedge blocked my exit to the side. The only way out was down the driveway. Peeking around the garage I saw no one, heard nothing.

I took small, slow steps on the grassy verge, but the hairs on the back of my neck prickled and galvanized my legs into a panicked run. The same sensation I'd had as a child leaving a dark room with unknown monsters chasing me.

The remote door opener pressed, I jumped in the car as if an army of Hectors pursued me. It wasn't until I'd parked outside the hotel again that I realized I'd left my flashlight in Hector's garage.

CHAPTER TWELVE

"Wish you'd told me." Tom's words cut new gashes in my conscience. "Since this is your first visit back to Eagle Pass, it would have been great to be with you, to meet your friends, see your old home."

My guilty heart weighed me down like an armful of wet clay. I should have told him from the start I had planned this trip to Eagle Pass. He wouldn't have minded. I could have told him that much without revealing what I knew about Angel and the necklace and my parents' deaths. His voice still conveyed drops of disappointment, but I had to convince myself I had a good reason for the deception.

To change the subject, I told Tom about Eva needing a place to convalesce. His response to my suggestion of taking care of her typified his caring, Christ-like spirit.

"Do what you think is best, sweetheart. Sounds like she really needs you right now. I'll support your decision. Just remember, don't strain yourself physically."

Relieved he hadn't asked about my evening, which had strained more than my body, I hung up and knocked on Teresa's door. In response to the unrelenting heat in the Valley, Teresa wore a white sundress with yellow sunflowers appliquéd along the hem. My summer uniform consisted of Capris and T-shirts, both in fuchsia today, a cheerful color for my next meeting with Eva.

We followed another guest to the lobby for the continental breakfast. Teresa had a glass of juice and a toasted bagel. My traumatic night had given me a ferocious appetite. But I ate sensibly, limiting my meal to a vegetable omelet, not wanting to gain the pounds I'd lost during my illness.

When the crowd had dissipated, guaranteeing privacy, I told Teresa about my venture to Eva's home. Her eyes popped when I recounted hiding behind the truck and almost being locked in.

"Maricella, you're crazy. You could have been caught, or worse." She pushed the half eaten bagel aside and took a sip of juice. "Why didn't you wake me?"

"Because you would have talked me out of it."

Teresa raised her eyebrows and cocked her head. "Exactly."

"But I did discover the green truck with fresh dents and scrapes."

"What are you going to do about it?"

"Since visiting hours at the rehab center don't start for," I consulted my watch, "another two hours, I think we should go straight to the police station and file a report or something."

"File a report on your trespassing?"

I gulped on a mouthful of coffee. "I hadn't thought of that. No, wait. Eva is my friend. I was at her house."

"Snooping in the garage?"

I gathered the disposable cups and plates. "Maybe the officer will be very understanding."

Teresa smiled and pushed back her chair. "Maybe."

As we headed down the hall to our rooms, I put my arm around her. "You didn't eat much. Feeling okay?"

"Not very hungry, but I'm fine. Let's go find a friendly cop."

The daylight ride down Main Street was easier this time. We stopped at a traffic light, giving me time to examine the stores. An electronics outlet on the next block advertised a stock reduction sale.

I parked across the street. "I've been thinking I'd like to record Eva's story. I'm going to buy a tape recorder before I forget. Want to come?"

Teresa opened her window. "No, thanks. I'll wait here."

The size of the newfangled recorders surprised me. Some didn't even use tapes anymore. The clerk explained with gusto how the tiny cell phone-sized digital voice recorder worked. It could record up to one-hundred-forty-four hours, more than enough for my needs.

I hurried back to the car with my purchase. Teresa helped me open the package and insert the batteries.

"Perfect. Can't believe how small it is." I placed the recorder on the armrest console. "I think I'd like to find people who knew my parents and record their recollections of my family, too."

Teresa stuffed the packaging materials into the plastic bag. "Great idea. It would be wonderful to share those recordings with Tom and Mike and José."

I inserted the key in the ignition and nodded. Teresa's innocent statement pierced my soul. I should have done this a long time ago. Tom should be here to share these discoveries with me. Why hadn't I trusted him?

Vehicles occupied all the parking in front of the police station. I found a space across the street. When we entered the police station, Teresa chose a seat in the foyer while I explained to the receptionist what I needed to report.

She made a phone call, then buzzed me through the security door. A young officer met me and directed me to a long hallway lined with chairs. He told me to wait there for the officer who would address my concerns.

Men and women in uniform scurried about, phones rang, voices overlapped. I sat transfixed by the commotion, until a man's laugh in an office across the hall caught my attention. I stood and peeked through the open door in time to see him place the phone receiver down on the cradle, his dimpled smile still splitting his cheeks. The twinkling brown eyes, military-cut black hair and broad shoulders had probably sent many hearts fluttering. Mine was no exception.

The smile remained as he stared at me. He stood, pointed in my direction and stepped around his desk. "You look familiar. Have we met before?"

His question confirmed the initial opinion I had of him—a ladies' man. Disappointed, I shook my head. "I don't think so."

But as the words left my mouth, I pulled open a memory drawer, and that smile, those dimples, the eyes, all came together. Yes, we had met. In fact, we had been in the same class in junior high.

"Ray?" He came closer. "Raymond Reyes?"

"And you are Maricella Farias." He extended his hand, but when I reached for it, he enveloped me in a hug. His solid body in a well-fitting dark blue uniform towered over me. I told him my married name, but the warmth of his greeting lingered.

"So, *Mrs.* McDonough, what are you doing in our police department?"

I cleared my throat. "I... I have some information about a car accident. The other vehicle involved left the scene."

Ray's smile evaporated and he rubbed his chin. "Sounds serious. Come to my desk and I'll take down the particulars."

I sat across from him and told him of Eva's suspicions and all I could remember about the green pickup truck.

Ray took notes on a legal pad, then turned to his computer and punched a dozen keys. His eyes scanned the screen. "Eva's accident is still an open case. I'll enter the information you've just given me, but her statement to you that Hector may have been the driver can't be taken as evidence. I'll send an officer to take her official statement, and get a search warrant for the garage." He punched a few more keys and pushed away from his desk.

"This may be enough to issue a warrant for her husband's arrest." He stood and picked up his hat. "I need to leave now. Come, walk out with me."

When we entered the waiting area I introduced Teresa to Ray.

Ray placed his hand over his heart. "I meet two beautiful women the same day and they're both married. Just my luck."

Teresa and I giggled.

"Is there anything else I can do for you before I leave?" His genuine smile, displaying a toothpaste advertisement's white teeth, encompassed us both.

"Yes, there is. Sometime while I'm here, I'd like to find out about my... the fire, my parents'..." I couldn't complete the sentence.

He patted my shoulder. "Sure. I'll check it out for you." He reached into his shirt pocket. "Here's my card with my cell number on the back. Give me a call later today."

Teresa watched him leave and turned to me. "Wow. What a hunk. Are you sure he's a cop?"

Laughing, I nodded. "I remember in ninth grade all the girls were crazy about him. He formed part of our *quinceañera* court. He filled in when—what was his name? Oh, right. Jesse. Jesse Rodriguez. Ray filled in when Jesse fell and broke his leg."

We crossed the street and stopped at my car. "He's still charming. But he is going to investigate Hector and the green pickup. Good-looking or not, we've got a cop on our side."

"What did he say about you snooping in the garage?"

I pulled sunglasses from my purse and shrugged. "Nothing. Seems Hector Alonzo has been a person of interest for other reasons. Ray was anxious to hear my evidence. He's working on an arrest warrant."

On the way to visit Eva, I stopped at a florist to purchase a balloon bouquet for her, and at a convenience store for gasoline. José called as we entered the rehab center parking lot. He'd opted to work a double shift and wanted to report on Brutus before clocking in. The puncture wounds were healing with no sign of infection, and Brutus appeared to be almost back to his usual rambunctious puppy-self.

Visiting hours began at ten o'clock. We arrived soon after the facility opened to find Eva in a wheelchair by the window of her room.

She grinned and extended her hands to us. "Chella, Teresa. Good to see you. Oh, I love the balloons. *Muchas gracias.*"

I tied the balloons to the bed rail "Going to therapy?"

"No. Just got back. Something new. They had me on my stomach and raised my legs up and down, and moved my ankles round and round."

"Range of motion. It's to keep your joints limber and your muscles active." I pulled a chair closer and sat.

Eva described other exercises she'd done and indicated satisfaction with her performance. Overall, she exhibited a more positive demeanor, which even elicited a comment from the nurse who came to check her blood pressure.

Reminding me I'd forgotten the tape recorder, Teresa returned to the car for it. While waiting for her, I told Eva about our encounter with Ray. She remembered him and was thrilled about the possible arrest warrant for Hector.

I asked Eva if she'd allow me to record her story. We all laughed at how strange our voices sounded when I played back the trial conversation of the three of us practicing exaggerated pronunciations.

After the nurse left, I placed my hand on Eva's shoulder. "Eva, where will you go when you're discharged?"

Her expression darkened. "Not sure. I don't want anything more to do with Hector. Maybe I can go back to Mexico. I still have family there."

"How would you like to come home with me while you recuperate?"

Eva almost fell out of her chair. Excited squeals alternated by tears answered my question.

Teresa scooted her chair close to the window where she propped her feet on the sill. "Has Dr. Contreras told you when you can leave?"

"Not yet, but he hasn't been in today." Eva's exuberant mood dissolved. Her head sank. "What about Angel? I can't leave Eagle Pass. They haven't sent her body, and I need to bury her before I can consider leaving."

"Eva, I have so much to tell you. In fact, I may be able to find out about Angel." I took my cell phone from my purse. "You can come home with me, and we can return to bury Angel. I'm going to make a call. I'll be right back." I stepped into the hall.

Under any other circumstances, I would never have called Deputy Quintanilla, but the situation required action. He was surprised to hear from me and more surprised at my question.

"Angelica Valdez's body? Why do you want to know?"

More lies or the truth? "After you told me her name, I found out I knew her mother, Eva Alonzo. I'm in Eagle Pass with Eva now." I couldn't believe I told him. "And we want to make funeral arrangements."

Quintanilla's grilling questions burned my ears. I explained I'd only confirmed Eva was Angelica's mother yesterday.

"Do you know why she was coming to see you, because it's now obvious she had a reason for being on your property? And what about the money?"

"No." The truth. "I don't know." I described Eva's circumstances and asked Quintanilla to contact Officer Raymond Reyes with the Eagle Pass Police Department for additional information about the car accident.

"Mrs. McDonough, I warned you—"

"But I've told you everything this time. Office Reyes can give you details. And whatever Eva shares with me, I'll report to him." I sat down on the bench and hesitated a moment. "Am I still in trouble?"

Quintanilla chuckled. "Yes, ma'am. But at least you're in touch with the EPPD. That will give you a few extra points in your favor. But seriously, I'm not sure about the body. Will check on the status and then contact Officer Reyes."

I returned to Eva's room, relieved I hadn't been raked over the coals and threatened with arrest.

"Eva, *mi querida amiga*, before I tell you what I just found out about Angel, I have something else to share." I grabbed her hands and related the events which began with Brutus finding the bag of money and her precious daughter, and ended with me discovering the damaged green pickup truck.

My voice cracked several times, and I was surprised Eva and I made it through without tears.

That is until I gave her the half heart-necklace. She held it to her chest, head bowed, shoulders shuddering from the force of the grief.

Teresa knelt by the wheelchair, her hand on Eva's shoulder. "Can I pray with you?"

Eva sniffed and nodded. I envied the ease with which Teresa talked to God. Would I ever be able to pray like I was having a conversation with... my father?

At the conclusion of the prayer, silence permeated the room.

Dr. Contreras pushed open the door. "*Buenos dias, señora.* Oh, your visitors are back. Good." When he noticed Eva's red, swollen eyes, he stopped by her chair. "What's wrong?"

She shook her head. "Nothing you can fix. I just heard more about how my Angel died." She propelled the wheelchair to the window, forcing Teresa to stand, and turned her back on us.

Dr. Contreras stepped behind her, hands in the pockets of his white coat, folder tucked under his arm. "What was that?" He pointed to Eva's feet clad in hospital-issue gray socks.

Teresa and I rushed to Eva.

"What?" Our words erupted in unison.

Dr. Contreras turned Eva around and crouched down, the folder slipping to the floor as he cradled one foot, then the other.

"I thought I saw her toes twitch." He pulled off one sock and ran his fingers from her heel, across her arch, and up over her toes to her ankle. "Eva, can you feel this?"

The toes wiggled.

"*Excelente*. Now let's try the left foot." He followed the same procedure, but this time the toes remained still.

He picked up the folder and stood. "Well, sensation in one foot is a start. This is wonderful." With the folder open, he scribbled away.

Eva stared at her feet, right toes wiggling up a storm. We giggled like we were watching a baby take her first step. Which, when I thought about it, we were.

"Thank you, Lord." Teresa's words of praise reminded me we weren't alone in this struggle.

I hugged the beaming Eva, who had pushed aside the recent devastating news for the moment, and then touched the doctor on the arm. "We have a question for you, sir."

"Yes, Doctor," Eva peered up at him. "When can I leave?"

"Leave. You want to leave us?" He tapped his pen on the folder. "Hmm. That depends."

Raised eyebrows in my direction were answered by my nod. "Yes, sir. She can come home with me."

"Then I see no reason to keep you, Eva. I knew you'd gain muscle use sooner or later. I'll write up a care plan and you can leave," he consulted her folder, "how does day after tomorrow sound?"

CHAPTER THIRTEEN

I turned on the recorder. "Okay, Eva, I'm ready."

After lunch, she had indicated she was tired of sitting in her wheelchair, and we watched as the nurse supervised her transfer to the bed. I noticed a marked improvement in Eva's ability to maneuver her lower body, and attributed it to repetition, good news of wiggling toes, a discharge date, and a place to go.

Teresa and I had purchased lunch in the rehab center's small cafeteria. We would not make that mistake again. Limited choices, greasy entrees and wilted salad convinced us to try a nearby restaurant next time. I ate as little as Teresa did. How did that girl survive? Eva had also picked at her food.

Instead of asking hundreds of questions, I opted to let Eva tell her story in her own time. I just wanted to know what had happened to her over the past twenty-nine years, and why Angel had come to me with a bag of money.

"I have to start at that awful night, our *quinceañera* night …" Her voice trailed off.

"Take your time. Teresa and I have all day."

Eva took a deep breath and picked up the recorder. She began, stuttering and floundering, but gained momentum as the words flowed like lava.

The morning after our tragic birthday party, when she had regained consciousness in the hospital and the bullet had been removed from her abdomen, the doctor gave her the news her parents were dead.

"I couldn't find out anything about you, Chella. They told me your parents were dead too, and later they told me your body hadn't been found in the restaurant. It wasn't until I read your article in the physical therapy journal a week ago that I knew for sure you'd survived."

Teresa leaned closer to the recorder. "What did you do? Did you stay in Eagle Pass?"

"I had no other relatives in Texas, and my godparents died in the restaurant fire. When released from the hospital, I traveled to a cousin in Mexico. So far away from Eagle Pass, I had no way of inquiring about you, Chella, or other friends in Texas. I concentrated on the immediate job of graduating from high school."

She'd met Angel's father, Miguel Valdez, when he'd visited relatives in the area. They dated for several years, but waited until Eva turned twenty-one to marry.

"That's one year after Tom and I married."

Teresa stretched out her legs and asked, "Did Miguel live in Mexico or Texas?"

"He was born in California, but traveled with his job all over Mexico. We moved frequently, and when Angel turned ten, we settled in San Diego."

Eva talked of their life in California and how different it was from Mexico and even Eagle Pass. Angel celebrated her *quinceañera* in San Diego.

Try as I might, I couldn't resist asking questions. "Was that difficult for you? I don't know how I would have handled organizing a celebration when ours had been so disastrous."

Eva closed her eyes for a moment. "I tried to put all those bad memories behind me, and when the time came, Angel's excitement carried me beyond my pain." She opened her eyes and stared at the ceiling. "Miguel's love for us, and faith in God did much to help me focus on the future and not the past. Angel had a wonderful *quinceañera*, but our happiness didn't last."

Miguel's work sent him to Eagle Pass the next year, but his health deteriorated. Their finances were stretched to the breaking point by medical bills, and Miguel succumbed to complications from diabetes and hypertension. He died a month before Angel graduated from high school.

"I had to get a job, because Miguel had limited retirement funds and we wanted Angel to attend college." Eva rested against the pillows, with the sadness the memories evoked etched on her face. "Those were rough times, but Angel and I managed."

I took the recorder from her weakened grasp and held it close to her. "When did you meet Hector?"

Eva sighed and lay in silence for a moment, then gazed out the window. Her face devoid of emotion, she began Hector's story.

Eighteen months after Miguel's death, Hector had visited the insurance office where she worked. Although more than fifteen years her senior, his charisma caught her attention. They married after a six-month courtship.

At first, she saw him as a positive influence in their lives. He provided financial security and his charm enchanted them.

The problems surfaced when Hector refused to tell Eva what type of work he did. Weeks after they married he took her to visit an office where he indicated he worked, but when she returned several weeks later, the staff told her they'd never heard of him. When questioned, Hector admitted he'd lied and now worked at the Lucky Eagle Casino.

"That's when I knew I'd made a mistake in marrying him. He became very possessive. Tried to control my life. He wouldn't let me have friends over. He..." Eva raised the head of the bed and stared at her legs.

I paused the recorder.

Teresa opened her purse and removed her billfold. "Anyone else thirsty? I'm going to the soda machine."

We gave her our orders and I turned the recorder back on. "Did he mistreat you?"

"No, not until I found the money, but I'm jumping ahead." Eva frowned and settled back on the pillows. "There's more."

At first, they lived in an apartment. After a few months, Hector rented a house without consulting Eva. When they drove up in the moving van, she recognized it as her childhood home.

"When I saw my old house again, part of my heart died. All the pain and grief of losing my parents resurfaced to crush the air out of me. But my anger at Hector took hold and jolted me back to reality."

Teresa returned with two cans of Coke, and one Sprite.

Eva took one of the Cokes and opened the can. "After Hector found out about the house, he at least had the decency to admit he should have taken me to see it before signing the lease, and agreed we didn't have to stay after the lease expired."

I took a sip of my Coke and placed the can on the table. "I can't imagine living in my old house. I couldn't even get out of the car when we drove by. How did you manage?"

"I've learned to... manage a lot of things. It was hard at first, but after unpacking and decorating, I found peace in creating a home full of love and joy, like my mother had done."

Eva raised her arms and placed her hands behind her head. "I worked at forgiving Hector, and told him I wanted to stay in the house. He even came to church with me."

I squirmed in my chair, sure accusing fingers pointed at my soul, but Eva and Teresa hadn't moved. The pointing fingers had escaped from my conscience. Hadn't I been *going to church* with Tom all these years?

Unaware of my discomfort, Eva's narration took us deeper into her world.

After they had been in the house a month or so, Eva began preparing a vegetable garden in the back yard. She'd remembered her mother had always grown a variety of produce each season.

At first, the soil turned over easily, but when her shovel hit a hard object, she thought she'd reached a layer of rock.

"I scraped away more dirt to expose the rock—shiny, black rock. But when I touched it, I knew it was no rock. It was plastic. I carefully dug around until I could pull it out." Eva moved her arms and gestured the bag's size. "A large, black garbage bag."

Teresa and I sat on the edge of our chairs.

"I'd punctured a small hole in the plastic with my shovel. I could see money inside and squatted down next to the bag. I looked around, and satisfied no one could see me, heaved the dusty bag onto the back porch."

Dumping the money onto the old table, Eva found all denominations, some loose, some in bundles, bound by paper tape or disintegrating rubber bands. Hundreds, twenties, tens. She didn't count it, but estimated thousands of dollars. She peeked in the bag and saw a piece of paper in clear plastic at the bottom.

"You're not going to believe this, Chella. It was a note. From my father."

Teresa and I gasped. My mind raced back to the money I'd seen him count, the money he'd told my father—

"What did he write?" Teresa asked.

"I read it over and over. I'll never forget the words. He wrote the money belonged to the restaurant, to your dad, Maricella. He'd been gambling—I thought he'd overcome that addiction—and lost his share of the bank loan. He had to borrow from a loan shark to replace the money for the restaurant, and now the loan shark was hounding him, threatening him. He said he'd been lucky on some of his bets, and there was more than enough money for the restaurant."

Her voice faded and I handed her the can of soda. After a sip she rested against the pillows, weariness creasing her face.

Her distress ate at my soul. I stood and touched her cheek. "Do you need to stop?"

Eva shook her head. "No, now that I've started, I have to finish the story." She swallowed and handed the can to me. "Papa said he hid the money and would take it to the bank after our *quinceañera*. He also said he left a note in his desk drawer about the money. I guess I'll never know what happened to it."

Tears clouded her eyes. "He must have suspected trouble because he ended the note asking whoever found the money to give it to your dad, and to tell Mama and me he loved us."

Rivulets channeled down her cheeks.

I handed her a tissue and leaned closer. "The loan shark. He must have been the man I saw in the storeroom that night with our fathers."

Eva mumbled through the tissue. "What are you talking about?"

I described what I had witnessed the night of our *quinceañera*, pinpricks of fear still piercing my spine with each word.

"He killed them, didn't he?" She crumpled the tissue and threw it on the bed.

Remembered gunshots echoed in my head as I nodded. "More than likely. I've asked Ray to check on their murders. Check their files." I cleared my throat. "I've never tried to find out before, have you?"

Eva rubbed her temples and sighed. "My cousins in Mexico told me to forget about it. At age fifteen, in their debt, I couldn't do anything anyway. All I did was visit the cemetery when we moved back here." She clutched my hand. "Your parents are close to mine. Have you visited their graves?"

A groan generated from the depths of my past, escaped my trembling lips. I slumped over the bed rail. Eva rubbed my shoulder; Teresa came over and crouched next to me.

The ache in my heart deepened. "Oh, *Mami, Papi.*"

So successful had my rejection of the past been, I'd never questioned the burial of my parents.

Teresa turned off the recorder. "I believe we all need a break."

The silence in the room engulfed me. I couldn't think clearly. But when Teresa stood with our purses in hand, a semblance of rationality returned.

"Yes, a break. Eva, you look tired. How about we let you nap and we'll come back." I looked at Teresa for confirmation. "After a couple of hours?"

Teresa handed me my purse. "Good idea. I'm in need of a nap, too."

We waved and pulled the door closed behind us, neither speaking until we reached the car.

"I was serious, Maricella. I want to go back to the hotel for a nap. Don't know what's gotten into me. Do you mind?"

"Not at all. In fact, that will give me a chance to transcribe Eva's story from the—oops. I left the recorder in her room. I'll just go back for it."

Teresa took the car keys. "I'll meet you at the entrance."

As I meandered through the parking lot, I noticed a smaller parking area to the side of the building. A handful of vehicles were parked there, but one caught my attention. A tan Chevy Cavalier. Could it be? Curiosity won. I hurried toward it, scanning the area for a bald man.

As I rounded the corner, the sight of a dark brown rear fender and trunk took my breath away. He was here. Cigar Breath was here.

"Eva." If he was connected to Angel, then he could be connected to Eva, too. I ran inside, traversing the halls as fast as I could. Why did her wing have to be at the far end of the facility?

Wing C. I squeezed past a group of patients in wheelchairs and apologized. Wing D. I rounded the corner and saw a man leave a room. He glanced my way and turned in the opposite direction, disappearing through a door at the end of the hall. Short, stocky, and bald. It had to be Cigar Breath.

I kept my eye on the room he'd left—it was Eva's. Pushing the door open, I rushed to her side. Before I touched her or could call her name, she opened her eyes.

"You forgot this." She pulled her hand from under the covers and handed me the recorder.

Trying not to alarm her, I took it and asked, "Has someone, a man, come into your room?"

Eva frowned. "No. Just you. Why?"

Smiling, I tried to be reassuring. "No reason. Thought I saw someone leave, that's all." I leaned over and kissed her forehead. "Rest, Eva. See you soon."

She closed her eyes again.

My nose twitched. My husband always teased me about my heightened sense of smell. I put it to use now.

Tobacco. I smelled cigar tobacco. Nothing smells like cigars.

Cigar Breath had been in Eva's room.

CHAPTER FOURTEEN

I dashed down the hall to the door I'd seen the man enter. It had a glass panel down the middle, revealing stacked chairs, a broken bedside table, and numerous boxes. A storeroom, lit by a high window.

Before I turned the handle, I glanced about. The hall was empty. The door opened into a pantry-sized room. No place for a man to hide. He must have slipped out when I'd been with Eva. The tobacco odor hung in the confined space.

I ran back to the nurses' station. "Has Eva Alonzo had another visitor?"

The nurse dialed the front reception desk and asked, then shrugged and hung up. "She said no one else has signed in for Mrs. Alonzo. Why? What's going on?"

I related what I'd seen and she assured me they would check on Eva more frequently, and the security guard would be alerted.

When I climbed in the car, I told Teresa what had kept me so long. She knew about Cigar Breath and my suspicions he'd been involved in Angel's death.

"We should tell Ray."

"You'd better believe I will. But first, do me a favor. Drive to the other side of the building." I indicated the way.

"Why?"

"I saw a car parked there, just like the one I told you Cigar Breath drove in Bandera."

The space was empty.

"It must have been him. I'm going to call Ray later to ask what he's discovered about my parents' murder. I'll tell him about Cigar Breath's car then."

Teresa drove to the hotel. Once in her room, she closed the connecting door behind her. Fatigue had taken the spring from her step and the luster from her eyes. I hoped she'd be able to nap. I paced the room, sleep the furthest thing from my mind.

But the pacing back and forth solved no problems. Ray had not responded to my message yet and he wasn't at the police station. I stopped at the window and pulled aside the sheer curtain. Cars, people, shimmering heat rising from the street, all blurred into a colorful fog. Tears slithered down my face as if my heart melted.

Now what? I sat on the bed and grabbed a tissue. Tears for me? For Eva? Her words about seeing my parents' graves kept pulsing in my brain. The tears were for a lost youth, a lost family.

I pulled the hotel stationery from the drawer and wrote to Teresa, telling her I'd be back in an hour. After slipping the note under her door, I ran to the car.

When I arrived at the cemetery, a funeral procession had just entered. I located the caretaker and he gave me directions to my parents' final resting place.

The plain white headstone, shaded by a lone mesquite tree, had a profusion of thick, ugly weeds growing at its base. I stepped closer, crouched down and began pulling them out.

I pulled and pulled, anger swelling with each yank. The rough, prickly stems tore at my palms. I groaned and grunted. Why were the flowers so colorful? They were weeds. They had no business growing here. Kneeling on the gravel, I threw the last offensive plant aside.

Chest heaving from the exertion and emotion, I clenched my teeth. "*Mami, Papi.* I'm sorry I haven't come before. Please forgive me."

I bowed my head, but a bird's call drew my attention to the swaying branches above. Blue sky peeked through the lacy leaves. I squinted in the mid-day light. My hands tingled. I raised them toward the branches, the sky, the heavens.

Words burst from my mouth. "Oh, God, forgive me. Forgive me."

Silence. No birds. No traffic. No people.

Then the funeral party's hymn floated on the hot air and entered my soul, soothing the raging waves of guilt and anger. I knelt in silence, trying to remember my parents' faces, ignoring the last images I had of them.

"Tom, you were right. You should be here with me now."

How I longed for the warmth of his arms, the reassurance from his lips, the strength of his spirit. He'd know what to say. He always did.

I stood and brushed dirt, dried leaves and gravel off my pants. I stared at my hands, then looked up at the tree. Did God hear me? I couldn't describe what had happened, the warmth radiating through me, but something was different.

I shook my head and touched the headstone. "I'll come again, *Mami y Papi*. I'll bring my Tom, and your grandsons."

Another hymn escorted me out of the cemetery.

Teresa called as I climbed into the car.

"I read your note. Where are you?"

"I've been at the cemetery. Visiting my parents' graves. I'll be back in five minutes and will tell you all about my... experience."

At my first knock, she opened her room door.

Discussing my visit to the cemetery with her brought a sense of something I couldn't quite define. Not peace as much as fulfillment. Facing the demons from my past and dealing with them head-on, completed a part of me that had been empty for twenty-nine years.

My soul ached with its new inhabitant, and for the first time I heard words of praise leave my lips. "Thank you, Father."

Teresa stared at me. "Maricella."

She'd been sitting on her bed, but now she came to me in the armchair. I stood and hugged her.

"I've been praying for healing. For your healing. Praise God! It's begun."

I searched her face for comprehension. Then I knew, as if I'd been struck by a heaven full of lightning bolts.

Plopping back into the chair, I grinned. "It was the weeds. Look what they did to my hands." I held them out and stared at the scrapes and cuts. "Those obnoxious things made me so angry. How could they grow there? Yanking them out made me aware of how pent up anger at my loss had stifled my spirit." I clasped my hands in a symbol of prayer. "I'll never look at weeds the same way again."

"Pray with me, Maricella."

Teresa's words flowed from her heart. Mine staggered out, but she assured me God heard them.

We sat in silence for a moment, then I glanced at my watch and jumped up. "It's time to go back to Eva's. Are you going to come?"

Teresa picked up her purse and headed to the door. "Wouldn't miss it. Don't forget the recorder. I think you need to attach that thing to your wrist."

I dashed into my room, grabbed the recorder and shoved it into my pocket. After washing my hands and dabbing on lotion, I floated to the car.

◆◆◆

The sight of Eva's empty bed sent panic waves surging around my stomach. But when I noticed no wheelchair, I surmised she'd gone to therapy. Teresa checked at the nurses' station and reported Eva would be back in ten minutes.

While waiting for her, I prepared the recorder. I never did transcribe what I'd already recorded. There'd be hours of work when I finally got around to it. Maybe Eva and I could do it together when she came to stay.

Eva's and the nurse's voices echoed as they came down the hall. I glanced at Teresa. "I'm not going to mention my suspicions about Cigar Breath to Eva. It could all be my imagination—a man with a penchant for cigars in Bandera and now in Eagle Pass." I fiddled with the recorder and shrugged. "I don't want to alarm her unnecessarily."

Teresa raised her eyebrows, but nodded and sat by the bed.

Once settled close to the window, toes wiggling inside the gray sock, Eva smiled. "They worked me hard this afternoon, but I feel stronger. I can almost transfer out of bed by myself."

With hands raised, Teresa said, "Thank You, God."

"Yes, praise be to the Father. And thank you to friends." Eva reached for my hand, her eyes awash with tears. "I feel renewed since your arrival. You don't know how I prayed I'd see you."

Joy and humility filled my heart. Why had it taken a tragedy to reunite us? I dabbed at moisture gathering in my eyes.

Eva pointed to the recorder. "Is that thing set? Let's continue before this dissolves into a crying fest."

She took the recorder from me and held it to her mouth. "Earlier I told you about finding the money. Since I never knew when to expect Hector home, I buried the bag again. I smoothed over the area, trampling down the dirt and even threw small rocks about. After sweeping the back porch, I put away the garden tools. But while washing my hands in the bathroom, I heard Hector drive up to the garage and enter the back porch. He didn't come inside." Her eyes widened at the memory.

"I panicked. I'd tried to clean up the dirt and couldn't imagine what had delayed him. As I dried my hands, I remembered the note. I'd put it on the chair when I refilled the bag with the money. But I'd forgotten to pick it up."

"Oh, no. Did he find it?" Teresa asked.

Eva heaved a giant sigh and nodded. "I'd dropped to my knees in fear and prayed, closing the bathroom door so he wouldn't see me. But he came crashing through the kitchen, down the hall, yelling my name, and I knew I'd have to face him.

"I opened the door and he pushed me back into the bathroom. Waving the note around like a wild paper fan, he asked where I'd put the money. I tried to tell him I didn't know about any money, but I'm not a good liar." Eva bowed her head.

Swallowing the boulder-sized lump of guilt, I glanced away.

Hector continued to harass Eva, but she refused to divulge the money's whereabouts.

Surprised she escaped harm, I clasped her hand. "You're a strong woman, Eva. Did you stay with him?"

She hiked a shoulder and chewed on her lip a moment. "Angel and I had no place to go, and Hector had calmed down by the time I had to leave to get Angel from work. On the way home, I told her about the note and the money, and where I'd buried it. I knew she'd never tell Hector. We agreed if things got worse, we'd take the bag and run away."

A petite nurse wearing neon pink scrubs bustled in and pointed to the wall clock.

I took the recorder from Eva and punched the pause button, then looked at the nurse and pleaded. "I know, but please, please can we stay a few more minutes?"

"Fine. But only thirty minutes."

We all smiled our appreciation. I punched pause again and positioned the recorder closer to Eva.

She described how Hector rummaged through drawers, boxes and closets when she wasn't home. Two days after she'd found the money, he confronted her. His threats grew more and more violent, but Eva kept the secret.

Going to pick up Angel from work the next afternoon, Eva decided she'd had enough. She would tell Angel and they'd leave as soon as possible.

"I never made it. That's the day of my car wreck. I'd just turned down the side street and had the right of way through the next intersection. The green pickup came flying down the cross street and hit my side of the car. I remember seeing the truck out of the corner of my eye."

Eva moved her wheelchair to face the window. "The shock of the impact spun my car and I stared at the merry-go-round houses and trees through the shattered window. When the car stopped, it hurt to breathe and I tried to move. But it was like I was frozen. I couldn't move my arms or legs. Blood from my head wound dripped into my eye. I couldn't focus. But I know what I saw. Hector, or someone who looked a lot like him, pulled open the passenger door, I thought to help me, but he just checked on the floor and peered over the seat to the back. I'm also sure he opened the trunk."

I turned her chair around and searched her face. "Did he ever check on you?"

Eva shook her head and propelled the wheelchair until she reached the bed. "I don't think so. Next thing I remember, I awoke in the ER."

Teresa stood and opened the blinds which allowed in a little more light. While looking through the slats, she said, "That's terrible. Was he the driver of the truck?"

Eva motioned for me to give her the recorder. I handed it to her and she placed it on her lap.

"I've relived those few moments over and over, and each time more details emerge. Now I'm sure Hector drove the truck. And he was looking for the money."

"More information to give Ray when I talk to him later." I glanced at the clock. Our time was running out. I cleared my throat and asked, "Why did Angel have the money?"

Facing the window, Eva's eyes glazed over and her lips quivered. "I thought I was saving her life, but... I..." She held up her hand. "Just give me a minute."

We waited while she regained her composure.

When she continued, her thick voice wavered. "Angel accompanied me when I transferred here from the hospital. We read your article together, the one in the therapy journal. When I discovered where you lived, I knew we had an escape. I told Angel we'd leave as soon as I could walk."

Eva reached for her water glass and drained it. Exhaustion played on her face, but I knew she wanted to complete her story.

Hector visited her the day after she'd transferred to the rehab center. He yelled at her, threatening to harm Angel if she didn't tell him where she'd hidden the money. The commotion he caused alerted the staff, who escorted him out.

"I was petrified for Angel. I called her and begged her to come see me immediately, and to avoid being alone with Hector. She already knew I thought Hector had caused my accident." Eva's fingers twisted into a tangled knot.

"When she arrived, I told her the time to escape had come. She needed to wait till night—it was Sunday and Hector would be busy at the casino—to dig up the money and take the heart necklace. I knew you'd recognize it and take her in."

Clutching the necklace which she now wore, Eva's chest heaved with anguish and pain. "I told her to save herself. That I'd be okay here with the staff knowing I didn't want Hector to visit anymore."

With her hands covering her face, we strained to hear the words. "That was the last time I saw her."

Teresa and I both knelt at her wheelchair, enveloping her in our arms. What could I say to console her? What words would heal the hole in her heart? My nascent trust in God was too unfamiliar to aid me.

Even Teresa remained silent. The only sounds in the room came from the depths of Eva's grief as she groaned over and over. We remained close to her, till she dropped her hands and sucked in air.

I will never forget her expression of despair. Words of comfort formed in my mind, but before I could utter them, Teresa's soft prayer broke the silence.

"Father God, send comfort down like spring rain. Cloak Eva in your grace and love. Hold her soul in your caring hands and heal her body."

She didn't say amen, but seemed to be waiting for someone else to speak.

I'd never prayed aloud in front of people before. Not since I was a little girl. But the words that had been floating in my mind wanted release. I remembered how I'd compared Teresa's praying to talking to her father, so now I talked to my father, my Heavenly Father.

"Please Father, bring peace to my friend. I don't understand why these things happened. Help us to serve and follow you even when we don't understand."

When I said amen, my dry mouth attested to my nervousness, but my heart wanted to sing.

Eva looked at us, her eyes tired, but calm. "Thank you."

I pushed myself up and Teresa's arms encircled me.

The nurse who opened the door glared at us, tapping at her watch. "*Señoras*. I said thirty minutes."

I wiped a hand across my face. How had I made it through without crying? "I know, I know. We're leaving now."

As Eva transferred to the bed, I turned off the recorder, placed it in my purse and winked at Teresa.

She gave me a thumb up sign. "Good for you."

Once Eva settled among her pillows, I hugged her. "We'll be back tomorrow. Sleep well."

On our way past the nurses' station, I latched my half-heart necklace in place. I hadn't worn it since my *quinceañera* night.

Dr. Contreras, standing behind the counter, motioned for us to join him. "Just the ladies I need to talk to. I have the care plan written for Eva and the name of a specialist in San Antonio I'd like her to visit."

I took the card he offered. "I know Dr. Flores. She's great. I'll schedule an appointment as soon as we get home."

"There are a few more exercises I want Eva to work on tomorrow, then I'll discharge her the following day." Dr. Contreras placed his hand on a stack of folders.

"Oh, Doctor, one more thing. Could the staff check on her in a while. She's been talking about her daughter and I'm concerned about her emotional state."

"Sure, I'll go down there now." He picked up the folders, nodded in our direction and strode away.

When we reached the parking lot, I scanned the area for a tan Chevy Cavalier. No two-tone Chevy anywhere in sight. I sighed with relief.

The restaurant we'd chosen for supper had a large patio where we found a table in the corner. Teresa ordered blackened snapper with mango salsa, and I chose dill encrusted salmon. After we'd eaten, Mike called Teresa. Most of the patrons had left, allowing her some privacy.

I ambled over to admire the fountain in the middle of the patio and glanced at my daughter-in-law from time to time. It was a blessed day when she came into our lives. Mike had become a fine husband. Wonder who his example could be? And Teresa complemented him.

She glanced up and smiled as she held the phone to me. "Maricella, your son wants to talk to you."

We chatted for a short time. He had two days remaining in his training session and naturally missed his wife. I told him we'd be home on Thursday, with Eva.

Teresa and I ordered caramel cheesecake for dessert. She ate more at this meal than I'd seen her eat all week. I kept checking my phone, but Ray still hadn't returned my call. The gathering dusk reminded us of the time and we returned to the hotel. It had been a relaxing, refreshing meal, a balm to our spirits after the harrowing story we'd heard from Eva.

Arm in arm, we walked down the hall to our rooms, giggling like teenagers at an anecdote Teresa told about her childhood.

But our laughter ceased when we saw my room door ajar.

CHAPTER FIFTEEN

We backed away from the door, clutching each other. "What should we do?" Teresa whispered, as we kept moving.

"Go to the front desk and tell them. I'm going to stay here at the corner and watch the room. See if anyone comes out."

I concealed myself behind a large, plastic ficus and peered down the hall at our doors, then down the hall Teresa had taken. I placed my hand in my pocket and touched Ray's card. I pulled it out. Why not give him another try? With my eyes on the door, I dialed his cell number.

Please answer this time, Ray. Please. He picked up on the sixth ring. In choppy phrases, I described our plight. He had just completed his shift and was driving home down Main Street. He'd be right over. But my vigil behind the plastic plant seemed to last for eons.

Teresa returned, shaking her head. "There's only one person on duty right now. She said she'd send someone as soon as she could."

"Don't worry. I just called Ray. He's on his way." I glanced behind her. "There he is now."

The sight of a big cop in uniform, striding toward us, chin squared, business frown in place, calmed our frantic nerves.

"Maricella, Teresa, where're your rooms?"

We pointed down the hall. I'd already given him the room numbers on the phone.

"Stay here, ladies."

Ray drew his weapon and walked toward our doors. He pushed open the door to my room, gun raised and stepped in.

Nibbling my bottom lip, twisting my purse strap, I waited with Teresa. Minutes crawled by.

After tension morphed seconds into decades, Ray poked his head out Teresa's door. "All clear. There's no one here. You can come in now." He stood by the door and motioned for us to join him.

We slipped into Teresa's room and looked around.

She checked her belongings on the desk, clothes hanging on the rack and opened her suit case. "I don't see anything out of place. How about your room, Maricella?"

I passed through the connecting door and scanned the area. Everything seemed to be in order. Even my toiletries were as I'd left them in the bathroom.

"Nothing's missing." I turned to Ray standing in the doorway.

"Good. Maybe the maid just didn't close the door properly. The automatic piston closure mechanism seems to be broken." He swung the door back and forth to demonstrate.

Teresa came into my room. "Whew. All that worry for nothing."

I held my hand out to Ray. "Thanks for coming so quickly. We appreciate the help."

"I was just around the corner." His smile chased away any vestiges of unease. "Glad I could be of service."

He took my hand. "Sorry about not returning your calls. We're working on a huge case. Can't discuss details, but my sergeant has me up to my ear lobes in paper work."

"I'd like to add my thanks, Ray." Teresa walked to the connecting door and turned. "And now I'm going to bed, Maricella. See you tomorrow."

Ray raised his hand in a casual wave. "I need to leave, too. It's been a long day."

"Wait, can we meet sometime tomorrow to discuss my parents' case? And I have more information about Hector."

He grabbed the door handle. "Sure. In fact, I've read the file notes already. How about breakfast?"

We agreed on a time and place.

I double-locked the door after he'd gone and rested against it. What a day. Had it only been twenty-four hours since I'd ventured out to Hector's garage? I needed to unwind. While I ran the bath water, Tom called.

With so much to tell him, I turned off the water and sat on the bed. Having discovered a tiny seed of faith in my anger-hardened soul, I vowed to give Tom all the details. No more lies. I told him everything—even the recent episode with my open room door.

The retelling of my experience at the cemetery nearly destroyed me. I curled up on the bed and poured out my inadequate words. Reliving the grief and loss brought fresh stabs of pain to my heart.

Tom's words, even though they came from New York, were salve to my wounds. "My darling, please know I'm with you in spirit. That must have been so difficult for you."

How I longed for his presence. What I fool I'd been in not including him.

I hesitated in completing the narration. How do you tell the man who's shared twenty-four years of your life that you've only *attended* church with him all this time? That you've never studied the Bible or prayed from the heart before? That you have no relationship with the Lord?

But Tom didn't sound too surprised. Thrilled at my change of heart, yes, but not surprised. Had he known all along? Of course, he had. His strong faith had sustained us both. How could so sincere a man not have known?

It's a good thing our cell phone plan allowed us free family minutes. We talked for over an hour, ending our evening with a shared prayer. The first of our married life.

"I can't wait for Saturday. I want to see this new woman. I can hear it in your voice, and I want to see it."

"I don't look any different."

"You will, sweetheart. God's light makes people change."

"I love you, Tom McDonough. I'm anxious to see you, too. Better go now."

"Love you. God be with you."

I smiled. Yes, I wanted God with me. Needed God with me.

By the time Teresa joined us, Ray and I had devoured a plate of breakfast tacos and downed a carafe of coffee.

"Sorry, folks. Just couldn't manage seven o'clock. Why so early anyway?"

Ray swallowed a bite of tortilla then wiped his mouth on a paper napkin. "My fault. I have to be at the station in an hour."

Teresa ordered orange juice and a potato and egg taco.

"Is that all?" I asked.

"I must have eaten too much last night. Just not hungry this morning. But, Maricella, what have you learned from Ray?"

"I haven't given him a chance to speak. Been telling him about my encounter with Cigar Breath in Bandera and my suspicions he was in Eva's room yesterday."

"She also told me more about Eva's recollections of Hector and her accident." Ray centered his fork on the empty plate and pushed it away. "We've been on the lookout for him, but he hasn't returned home, at least not when we've checked. I have an officer stop by two or three times a day."

"Is there a warrant for his arrest?" Teresa smiled at the waitress who placed her order and a fresh carafe of coffee on the table. "*Gracias.*"

"Um, no. My sergeant said there wasn't enough evidence for a search warrant or arrest warrant yet." Ray scratched his head then smoothed the hair back in place. "But don't lose hope. You've got my full attention and I won't let you down."

"Thanks. This really means a great deal to me, to Eva." I drained my coffee cup and stared into the emptiness. "In fact, I told Tom, my husband, about you coming to our rescue last night and he wants to meet you."

Ray's signature smile and dimples vanished for an instant, but they returned immediately. Had it been my imagination? Why would the notion of meeting Tom disrupt Ray's equilibrium?

"That'll be great, and how about your sons? Will they be coming, too?" Ray's seamless recovery almost slipped by undetected.

With my forearms resting by my plate on the table, I shrugged and tilted my head to the side. "Well, nothing's been planned yet. But I'm taking Eva home with us tomorrow to recuperate, and when we bring her back, I would like José and Mike to come, too. What do you think, Teresa?"

"That will be a good opportunity for them to see where their mother grew up."

Ray's expression darkened again, but this time the joviality remained at bay. "You're taking Eva tomorrow?"

"Yes. Dr. Contreras has agreed to discharge her. Later today, I'll collect her clothes and other personal items from her home." I clapped Ray on the shoulder, but he had no responding repartee. "So, tell your officers we'll be in the house sometime, and not to arrest us for trespassing."

I stared at him. This was a totally new Ray. Serious, focused, no hint of camaraderie. Teresa took a sip of juice and raised her eyebrows when I looked at her.

"What's up, Officer Reyes?" Teresa's question brought him back.

"Oh, nothing, nothing." The dimples returned. "Just been thinking about you two going to Eva's, I mean Hector's house alone. Don't think that's wise. What if Hector comes back while you're there?"

"Uh-oh. I didn't think of that. But I need to pick up her clothes."

Ray leaned back in his chair and folded his arms. The muscles bulged under the dark fabric of his shirt. "If you can wait until late afternoon, I'll be able to meet you there."

I looked at Teresa and nodded. "We can wait."

"Okay, let's say," he pulled a small notebook from his shirt pocket and flipped through several pages, "five o'clock."

"Five it is. And thanks again for watching out for us." I shuddered as fingers of remembered fear from my night excursion to Hector's garage pinched my neck.

Teresa stood, effectively wiping the image from my mind. "Maricella, there're a few things I need to buy. Would you mind if I take the car?"

"Not at all." I pulled the keys from my purse and handed them to her. "I'll return to the hotel when we're done here."

"Thanks. I'll be back by ten, in time to visit Eva." She meandered through the tables on the patio and left the restaurant.

The waitress removed our plates. When she placed the bill down, I snatched it away before Ray could touch it. "My treat, please."

He laughed and closed the little notebook. "If you insist. But before I give you details about your parents' case, I have a question. Whatever happened to you and Eva after the... incident?"

I shared Eva's story and included my hasty departure to San Antonio.

"No wonder I hadn't seen either of you again until recently." He glanced at his watch then at me. "I don't have much time. Are you ready?"

Warmth from the morning sun shining through the patio's latticed cover and consumed coffee dissipated. Icy tentacles aimed for my heart and shudders traveled down my body like slow moving serpents. But resolving to include God in all aspects of my life, I shook them off and sent a silent prayer heavenward.

I laced my fingers in my lap to control their involuntary spasms. "Yes, tell me."

He flipped close to the back of the notebook and stared at the pages for a moment. "First of all, it's still open, although it's been in the cold case file for many years. No one was ever arrested for the murders. There were a total of seven deaths."

I cleared my throat and hoped my voice would cooperate. "Were they all shot?" Although I'd read the brief newspaper report for June 1977, I wanted to hear the words from Ray. I wanted the information confirmed officially.

"No. Five died from gunshot wounds, two from smoke inhalation."

I closed my eyes and forced words out of my mouth. "Of the seven, I know about Eva's parents and my... my parents. Who else died?"

Ray checked his notes again. "Your parents, Eva's parents, and Paul Matthews were shot. Gilbert and Esther Treviño died of smoke inhalation."

I groaned. Smoke inhalation. So it was true. They died because of me. Because I started the fire. I thought I had prepared myself mentally for this information, but I was mistaken. Nothing could have prepared me for the stark reality of my guilt.

Ray's voice floated over me like a cocoon. It wasn't until his warm hand touched my arm that I acknowledged his presence.

He peered at me and frowned. "Maricella, we don't have to do this right now. I can see it's rough on you."

Rough on me. He didn't know the half of it. His words were like daggers piercing my soul. They confirmed my guilt, my role in the tragedy that night.

Unable to keep my hands still a moment longer, I picked up the carafe, but it almost slipped from my shaky grasp.

Ray removed it and poured coffee into my mug. "I don't have much more information. Do you want me to continue?"

I toyed with the sugar and sweetener packets in a red chili-shaped container. "Before you do, I remember Paul as one of our *quinceañera* court, but who were the Treviños? The names ring a bell, but I can't place them."

"Um," Ray turned a page in his note pad, "they were Eva's godparents."

"Oh, yes. Now I remember." I opened a packet of sweetener and stirred it into my coffee. Why, I don't know because I couldn't have held the mug to my lips without dousing myself in the hot liquid. Instead, I wrapped my icy hands around the mug.

More note pad pages examined. "There were several leads on a suspect, but descriptions of him varied too much for a positive I.D."

Haphazard images darted through my brain. Ray's explanation roused old memories. Had I heard shots from two different locations? I removed my warmed hands and traced the pattern on the tiled table top.

"Were they... were our parents and Paul all shot with the same gun?"

Ray referred to his notes. "Yes. Only one gun."

Chewing on my bottom lip, I sighed. "Good."

"Why? Did you think there was more than one gun?"

I hesitated. Should I tell a law enforcement officer, even one I considered a friend, what I had witnessed that night, what part I'd played in the catastrophe? In my nervousness, my fingers strayed to the sugar container again. It toppled over, spilling pink, white and yellow packets across the table.

Refilling the red bowl gave me an excuse to avoid looking at Ray when I said, "I saw the man. The one who might have shot all those people."

A sudden movement from Ray forced my attention to him. He leaned so far across the table I could see the gold flecks in his dark eyes.

"You what?" No smile now. No dimples. Only brute strength.

"Mr. Cuellar, my dad, and another man were arguing in the storeroom. I saw the third man with a gun, and then Mr. Cuellar pulled a gun."

Ray scowled as he searched my face. "What can you remember about the man?"

Ever since finding the heart necklace, I'd relived that night so many times, but details of the third man remained vague.

"He was shorter than my father, had long, dark hair, but he wore a baseball cap low over his forehead. I don't remember much about his face."

Squinting to concentrate on a smidgen of memory, I pictured something in the mystery man's shirt pocket, but the image faded.

"What?"

"Nothing. I thought—but, no. I can't recall any more about him." Then I remembered my conversation with Eva. "But I think he was a loan shark."

This time Ray's expression darkened so much I blinked. With hints of anger in his eyes he glared at me for a brief second, but his professional visage emerged again.

"How do you know? Where are you getting your information?"

Not sure how to interpret Ray's change in demeanor, I held onto my reply.

Maybe because of my uncertainty, he reached over and covered my hand with his. "I'm just looking out for you, remember. Visiting garages late at night, wanting to go back to Hector's house alone, and now talking about loan sharks. You're going to get in over your head if you're not careful." His smile charmed my cautiousness away.

Removing my hand from the table, I related how Eva had found the money and note from her father. After hearing the details, Ray agreed with our assumption.

"Do you think you would recognize the loan shark if you saw him again? If I let you look at mug shots down at the station?"

The man's shaggy dark hair under a blue baseball cap flickered in my mind, but I shook my head. "I don't think so. Too much time has passed, and like I said earlier, I didn't get a good look at his face. I was too busy gawking at the guns."

Ray closed his note pad and placed it in his pocket. "That's all I have about the murders. Sorry I couldn't be more helpful, but knowing now the perpetrator may have been a loan shark, I'll see how my sergeant wants us to proceed with the information."

"Thank you for sharing what you did. I suppose we may never know."

"True. But I do have something else for you. I found out a lawyer, a Mr. Vicente Ortiz, handled your parent's affairs when they died. He still has an office on Adams Street. Here's the address." He placed a square piece of paper on the table.

My heart plummeted to my feet. The naiveté with which I'd handled my parents' passing revealed itself again. But now I could fill in some of the blanks—and there were many blanks.

I nodded at Ray and took the paper. "Thank you. I'd like to meet him."

Ray picked up his hat from the chair next to him. "I really must be going now, Maricella." He scooted back and stood. "See you at five." He pulled my chair out and placed a hand on my shoulder. "Promise me you won't go to Hector's house before five."

Remembering my stint in the garage, I nodded. "Promise."

The dimples, the eye catching smile, the self assured posture wiped away any niggling doubts I had about sharing all this information with him.

We walked through the restaurant and Ray nodded to acquaintances at various tables. Once on the sidewalk, he turned and looked deep into my eyes. "Remember what you promised."

"Don't worry. I won't go near the house before five." I raised my hand in a little wave and turned toward the hotel.

"Want a ride?"

"No, thanks. The one block walk won't kill me. See you later."

The shaded sidewalk hadn't yet absorbed the morning heat. A balmy breeze played with the strands of hair that had escaped from my ponytail. I brushed them away and glanced around. So much had changed in the years I'd been gone, and yet the familiarity comforted my soul.

When I'd set out on this trip, I don't think I realized exactly how it would affect me. I'd come for knowledge, for information, and while finding answers to many questions, I'd also discovered other personal details. I'd had to face the realities of my parents' deaths, and how I had allowed this hole in my past to imprison my life.

The built-up anger had turned my heart to stone. Although I loved Tom and the boys, I realized now I'd always kept a part of my heart, a part of my love, locked away, in case this family was taken from me, too. But experiences of the past few days had made me appreciate all I have, all I have to give, and I wanted to get home and share this revelation with my family.

But the most dramatic truth to strike me had been that God had never left my side. I'm the one who had drifted, who had built the wall, who had blocked Him out of my life. I discovered that not only was God close by, I could talk to Him with ease.

Saying a prayer of thanksgiving, my step jaunty, my spirit alive, I entered the hotel. Eager to visit Eva, I opened my door, hoping Teresa had returned from shopping.

Before I could call out to her, my phone rang.

"*Holá*, Maricella." It was Eva.

"I was just thinking about you. We're almost ready to leave."

"That's why I'm calling. Don't come right now. Dr. Contreras has several university students here and I'm their guinea pig. He says I'll be occupied with them for several hours."

"Okay. This will work out fine. Ray gave me the name of a man I can talk to about my parents."

"Then how about coming after lunch? And I've made a list of things I'll need from my house," said Eva.

"Sure. After lunch. Well, work hard and show those students what a star you are."

Teresa, standing by the open connecting door, had heard my conversation. I slipped the phone into my pocket and plopped onto the bed. She asked about the information Ray had shared and I gave her the details, hiding the pain another retelling ignited.

When she saw the lawyer's name, she said, "Why don't we take advantage of the free time we have and go visit him?"

"Good idea."

I found Vicente Ortiz's office number in the phone book—Ray had only given me his name—and called. The secretary explained he worked part-time now and had a light case load at present. When I told her why I wanted to meet him, she put me on hold and came back a minute later to say we could come at ten o'clock.

With an hour to fill, Teresa and I drove around Eagle Pass, exploring haunts from my childhood and other places of interest. Mindful of Ray's admonition, we avoided the neighborhood where I used to live.

The houses on Ceylon Avenue were just as majestic and the view of the Rio Grande River from downtown just as peaceful as I remembered. Naturally, many things had changed, but overall, Eagle Pass still had a charm and warmth I'd not often found in larger cities.

Driving back into town on Main Street, I stopped at a traffic light and glanced at people strolling along the sidewalk. I saw a man turn the corner and head down a side street. Short, stocky, smoking a cigar. A baseball cap covered what I knew would be a bald head.

I flicked on my blinker and pointed. "Look at that man, Teresa. I'm certain it's Cigar Breath. I'm going to follow him."

"Maricella, don't do anything crazy."

"I won't. Just want to see where he goes."

The light changed and I turned left, keeping the man in sight. He strode with his head down, hands in jeans pockets, like he had a destination in mind. At the corner, he slowed and entered a building.

I found a parking space and pulled in yards from the door.

Teresa placed her hand on my arm as I turned off the ignition. "I don't think you should do this."

I reached for my purse and pulled out Ray's card. "I have to follow him, Teresa. Here's Ray's number. If I don't come out in a few minutes, call him."

Before she could protest, I opened the car and ran to the building. At the door, I hesitated. Not just any building. It was a bar. I'd never been in a bar before and sincerely doubted my sanity when I grabbed the door handle.

CHAPTER SIXTEEN

Vicente Ortiz's wide smile welcomed us to his office. A large, portly man with silver hair, beard and mustache, he epitomized the Santa Claus grandfather figure. Three-piece gray suit, crisp white shirt and navy blue tie completed the picture.

After leading us to a plush maroon sofa, he removed a folder from his desk and sank into a leather chair opposite us. When he spoke, his voice, as silver as his hair, flowed over us like a calm river. I could imagine hearing him in a courtroom and being mesmerized by the silken tones. What jury wouldn't believe his every word?

"When my secretary told me why you'd called, I unearthed this file on your parents, Mrs. McDonough."

"Please, call me Maricella."

"Very well, Maricella. I usually keep my files. In fact, I think I have documentation on every case I've ever worked. My wife, God rest her soul, never could understand why I needed so many file cabinets." Mr. Ortiz smiled at us then opened the folder. "Before you arrived, I read the details again, to familiarize myself with the case." He crossed one leg over the other and balanced the file on his lap. "Did you know, Maricella, your father and I were friends for many years?"

"No." I scrunched my brows together. "I don't remember much about life before the fire. I tried so hard to forget, to keep the past buried, but now being back in Eagle Pass—this is the first time I've been back—I find sights and sounds are triggering other memories."

"Well, let me share the good, positive things first," said the lawyer.

I relaxed against the sofa cushions. Teresa patted my hand and smiled.

"José's father, that is your grandfather, and my father came... um... across together in the early '30s. You understand?"

"Yes." I looked at Teresa and she nodded.

"They lived near each other, and after they married and had children, well that's how José and I met. We were friends all the way through school."

"If you knew my father and grandfather so well, can you tell me about any other family, uncles, aunts, cousins?"

Mr. Ortiz rubbed his short beard. "I recall your grandfather, Manuel, talking once about his wife. Experiences had hardened him—"

"I know. He scared me. When he'd visit, I'd hide behind my mother's skirts and leave the house as soon as I'd greeted him."

"Manuel sent his wife, your grandmother, away. Some scandal people refused to discuss in front of us kids." Frown lines furrowed Mr. Ortiz's brow. "I never did find out the details. José was the only child and Manuel never remarried. He died when you were about ten."

"I remember. But what about my mother's family? Other than the aunt I lived with in San Antonio, did she have anyone else?"

A page slipped out of the file and Mr. Ortiz bent to retrieve it. "I didn't know your mother well. After high school, I lost touch with José. I attended college and law school in San Antonio, then joined a law firm in Houston. I returned to Eagle Pass in the early '70s, and sorry to say, didn't try to reconnect with José. That is, until he contacted me to review the purchase agreement for the restaurant."

The lawyer shuffled the file pages and the corners of his mouth turned down. "Most of what I do know about your mother I discovered after her death. Do you want me to discuss that now?"

Although his change in demeanor sent a warning flag to my heart, I nodded. "Please. It doesn't matter how... what, I want to hear it all."

He lowered his gaze, staring at the folder. "When your parents were killed, as you know the authorities contacted Gloria Galvan in San Antonio as next of kin. She later called me to say you'd arrived safely. Your father had given me an envelope to be opened in the event of his death."

The break in conversation generated an electric silence in the office.

I stared at Mr. Ortiz. "And what did you find in it?"

"It won't be easy to read." He looked at Teresa, then at me.

"Do you want me to leave?" asked Teresa.

"No, please stay. You're family and already know all my warts. Might as well hear about my... my mother's."

"Maria's generosity overshadowed her hidden pain." Mr. Ortiz held up his hand to abort my question. "Wait until I'm done, *mija*. It will be easier after you've heard the whole story." His brows bushed together. "You know about her miscarriages?"

My purse lay in my lap. I twisted the strap and nodded.

"Maria had two before you were born and two after. She wanted desperately to give José a son, but you were her only child to survive. She became extremely depressed and blamed herself. José didn't comprehend the seriousness of the situation until you were about three years old and Maria tried to steal a baby."

I clutched my throat and shot forward on the seat. "Mama tried to do what?"

The lawyer pulled out a large brown envelope and handed it to me. "Here is the information your father gave me for safekeeping. Go on. Open it."

With quivering fingers, I took the envelope. Inside, I found a single sheet of yellowed paper covered with my father's handwriting and official looking signatures. I pulled it out.

Teresa leaned closer. "What does it say?"

Angling the paper to focus light on the faded ink, I read my father's words. "I, José Eduardo Farias, do solemnly swear to pay Blanca Esther Aguilar one hundred dollars a month until the sum of ten thousand dollars is paid. In return, she will not report the attempted kidnapping of her infant son by Maria Maricella Farias. Signed by my father and Blanca, November fourth, nineteen sixty-five."

Stunned silence.

Mami, what terrible pain and guilt you bore. I'd never known. But why would any of this have been shared with me at the time? All I remember is *Mami* being happy at times, sad at times. Of course, depression. And *Papi*, always solicitous of her health, keeping a watchful eye on her. Now I know why.

"Maricella." Teresa touched my arm. "Are you okay?"

I placed the letter back in the envelope, and not trusting my voice to cooperate, just nodded.

"Do you want to keep the letter?" asked Mr. Ortiz.

Looking down at the brown envelope, then up at him, the outline of his face blurred as tears filled my eyes. How would keeping the letter ease the pinching in my chest or the closing up of my throat? How would this reminder of my mother's crime convince me I had been family enough for her?

"No. Take it." The whispered words tore at my heart. I handed the envelope back to the lawyer and slumped against the sofa cushions.

"I know this has all come as a shock, but I have more to tell you. When your father hired me to review paperwork for the restaurant, we renewed our friendship to a degree. When he gave me this envelope, he asked that you never see it, unless I deemed the circumstances warranted it."

A knock at the door interrupted our session. I used the secretary's entrance as an opportunity to wipe my eyes and blow my nose. Mr. Ortiz signed two documents and the young lady left the office.

"Sorry about that. We needed to catch the morning mail. Where was I? Oh, yes. Now that you've read the letter, do you have any questions?"

Still stunned by his revelation, I could only think of one. "Whatever happened to Blanca and her son?" I hoped he wouldn't turn out to be someone I'd remember from school.

"They moved away, about 1974. I did a bit of investigating after I'd opened the envelope. I was also curious."

After completing the mental computation, I nodded. "That would have been enough time for Papa to have kept his end of the deal."

"Right. I guess they both kept their word." Mr. Ortiz placed the envelope in the folder and closed it.

He related how he'd supervised the selling of my parents' property, which didn't amount to much, and helped settle the insurance claim to repay their debts.

"Just enough funds remained to cover burial costs, and I did manage to send a little money to your aunt in San Antonio."

Her lined face and twinkling brown eyes replaced the image of my father's letter. "I didn't know that. She never said. In fact, she never discussed anything about my parents or the fire with me."

"Mrs. Galvan and I communicated all we needed to by mail and by phone. I believe she couldn't walk."

"She could, but with difficulty. I guess that's why she didn't come for the funeral. I wouldn't have either. I just wanted to block it all out of my mind."

Mr. Ortiz consulted his watch, then smiled at me. "I have another appointment in about thirty minutes. Can I do anything else for you?"

I took in a deep breath, then shook my head. "No, thank you, sir. This has been painful, but necessary. I appreciate you taking the time. But wait, there is something. Can you give me the names of other people who may remember my folks? I'd like to... to talk with them."

He thought for a moment, then consulted the Rolodex on his desk. He thumbed through it and rattled off seven names which I jotted down.

"They might not all still live in Eagle Pass. I've had these cards for a long, long time."

"Thanks. I'll check the phone book."

Teresa and I stood and headed to the door, followed by the lawyer.

He extended his hand. "Sorry we met under these circumstances. You know, José invited me to your *quinceañera*, but I had a previous engagement. It's too bad the murderer was never caught."

"Right." My hand sank into the warmth of his. "Thanks again." When I knew more about the *loan shark* can of worms, I'd share it with him. At this point, I just wanted to retreat.

We walked to the car. Not in any frame of mind to drive, I handed the keys to Teresa.

Once in the car, she switched on the ignition. "Where to now?"

"I need a drink."

"What?"

"You know—coffee."

Teresa eased into the traffic and chuckled. "For a minute there, Maricella, I had visions of taking you back to the bar where you thought you saw Cigar Breath."

As it turned out, the man I'd followed had a scar running from his right eye down his cheek, and a barbed wire design tattoo encircling his neck. Cigar Breath had neither. I shuddered, recalling the stale tobacco and alcohol odors that had assaulted my senses when I'd opened the bar door.

"No, no. Let's try the coffee shop close to the hotel. *The Jumpin' Java Bean*. Sounds very caffeinated."

While we sipped cappuccinos, wisdom beyond her years graced Teresa's actions and words. She helped me process the information Mr. Ortiz had provided. Coffee and conversation are good companions to shared emotions.

When we returned to the car parked along the curb, she leaned against the fender. "I hate to sound like a wimp, but I'm really bushed. I'm going to my room for a while."

Shielding my eyes from the sun, I squinted up at her. "You *are* a little pale."

"I'm sure it's nothing. I don't have a fever. Just tired. And don't worry about me for lunch. Give me a call when you're ready to visit Eva."

Teresa walked across the street to the hotel and I scanned the list of names Mr. Ortiz had given me. While in the coffee shop, I'd used the phone book to collect their numbers and addresses. I'd located four of the seven.

Outside the shop, a wooden bench in dappled shade looked very inviting. I sat and called the first number. No answer. Then the second. Mrs. Garcia had an out of state trip scheduled and couldn't meet me. Disappointment and the heat drained my energy. I contemplated taking a nap, too, but the knowledge we'd be leaving Eagle Pass the next day strengthened my resolve.

Third number. Mrs. Lopez answered. Yes, she remembered my parents, and she'd love to see me.

Following the directions she provided, I turned into her driveway ten minutes later. We were several blocks from the old neighborhood. As I stepped out of the car, I searched in my purse for my recorder. Not there. Must have left it in the hotel room. Teresa was right. I needed to strap it to my wrist.

Mr. and Mrs. Lopez welcomed me into their modest home. The elderly couple, both tall and lean, had weathered faces and callused hands, a silent testimony to a hard life.

She offered iced tea, which I accepted, and directed me to an armchair in the corner of the living room. They sat together on the sofa and proceeded to describe their decades of friendship with my parents. They'd lived on the same street in the early years, and their youngest son and I had been an item.

"I'm sorry, but I don't remember."

"It didn't last long. A neighbor's grandson came to visit and you switched your affection to him." Mrs. Lopez chuckled. "Nearly broke our Raul's heart, didn't it Rueben?"

Mr. Lopez grinned and nodded. "He refused to go to your house for weeks."

As they talked, I glanced around the room, my eyes taking in the family portraits, the worn carpet, the knickknack covered shelves. When I spotted a patch-work quilt lying folded over a trunk in the corner, fluttering knots tickled my stomach. Those patterns, those colors. I'd seen them before.

Mrs. Lopez, noticing my interest, focused on the quilt. "Do you recognize it?"

"I'm not sure, but something is familiar."

Mr. Lopez pushed up from the sofa, reached over and pulled the quilt off the trunk. "Here, look for yourself." He handed it to me, then sat again.

I fingered the faded, delicate fabric and opened the quilt to reveal more squares. A piece of pink and white gingham. Red roses on a blue background. Yellow polka dots. Why did those fabrics jog my memory?

Mrs. Lopez's wrinkled cheeks encased her smile. "You do recognize it, don't you?"

"I think I do. That piece, and that one and," I turned the quilt over, "that one. My dresses."

"That's right *mija*. Your mother made me this quilt because I used to babysit for you. All the time when you were little, and also when..." Her voice trailed.

"When what? I don't know what you're talking about."

"It's okay if you don't remember. It was a long time ago. And we lived in a different house then."

"But wait, I do remember something. You had two older sons, and they used to tease Raul and me all the time."

She patted her husband's knee and sent him a little smile. "*Sí*. Rueben and Roberto."

The wall clock ticked away the years, and memories flooded around me. Mr. and Mrs. Lopez held hands, looking at me as if I were their long-lost child.

"Would you like to have it?" she asked.

Hugging the quilt to me I buried my face in it. "Yes, please."

"It's yours then *mija*. Your mother would want you to have it."

The softness of the fabric eased a nagging thought vying for attention. But what about the baby she'd wanted? Maybe Mrs. Lopez would—

"Mrs. Lopez, I need to ask you a question. Did my mother... love me?"

"How could you ask that? Of course, she did." Mrs. Lopez struggled up from the sofa and came to my chair, stroking the hair back from my eyes. "She loved you more than anything."

She pulled over a stool and sat next to me. "Do you know about the miscarriages?"

"Yes. My father told me before my *quinceañera*."

"Each one crushed her spirit, but after you were born she cherished you all the more. You were her precious child, her *chiquita querida*."

"But what about—" I couldn't complete the question without revealing the information my father had given the lawyer in confidence.

"The baby? Yes, we knew. It was a particularly dark time for your mother. She lost control for a time." Mrs. Lopez turned and glanced at her husband and he nodded. She looked back at me, her eyes soft with concern. "Your father told us because it was right afterward the accident occurred."

"What accident?"

Mr. Lopez leaned forward, elbows on his knees. "Maricella, who told you about the baby?"

"Vicente Ortiz, my parents' lawyer."

"I see. Well he also knew about the accident and I'm surprised he didn't tell you. But, I—we—think you should know. Tell her, Anita."

Mrs. Lopez placed an arm around my shoulders. "You have already heard enough today to darken your spirit forever, but be strong. Draw on the strength of your parents' love for you and for each other."

I snuggled into the quilt, prepared to hear heart-twisting news.

"Your mother was the oldest of four children. Her parents came to Texas just before her second birthday, and many years later, three siblings were born. They settled in Del Rio, but Maria came to Eagle Pass when she married. After the incident with the baby, her parents insisted on taking you and her with them on a vacation to Sabinas in Mexico, not too far from here. They had friends who offered them a cabin along the river."

Mr. Lopez stood, pulled up another chair beside me and took my hand.

He resumed the story. "Your mother refused to go. Before the family reached Sabinas, their car skidded off the rain-slick road and they were all killed."

"All? So if we'd gone with them—"

Mr. Lopez squeezed my fingers and nodded. "Right. You would doubtless have died, too."

"Wow." I couldn't think of anything else to say.

With Mr. and Mrs. Lopez on either side of me, my mother's quilt clutched to my chest, I rocked back and forth, until the elderly woman's voice penetrated the fog.

"Maria loved you, *mija*. The accident brought home to her how she'd almost lost it all. Not only had she lost her parents, her brother and two sisters, but she could have lost you, too. And, of course, she could have died. She realized she needed help to deal with her depression, and I kept you for two months while she received treatment. But never doubt she loved you."

I glanced from one to the other, their sympathy washing over me. "When I used to ask Mama about her family, she never said anything. Papa would just tell me they had passed away. Afterward, Mama would be quiet and sad." I stroked the quilt. "I guess it was too difficult for her to discuss the details."

We talked and reminisced, and when Mrs. Lopez offered to share their lunch of leftover *chiles rellenos*, I agreed.

Clock chimes reminded me of the time. I needed to visit Eva. I promised to bring my family by the next time we came to Eagle Pass, and hugged the Lopezes before leaving their home.

With my mother's fragile quilt in my lap as I drove, I sensed her love flowing from each pain-filled hand sewn patch to my slowly mending heart.

CHAPTER SEVENTEEN

Teresa fingered the quilt. "It's beautiful, Maricella. Something from your past to cherish."

"I know. And I *will* cherish it. The more I examine it, the more pieces I recognize."

I folded the quilt and snuggled into it. Comforting scents wafted around me. I couldn't quite identify all of them. Maybe cinnamon, with a hint of coriander, and wood polish. The oak trunk it had covered had been polished to a high gloss. And certainly love. The aromas would always remind me of the Lopez family and my mother.

Placing the quilt into a plastic bag in my suitcase, I smoothed it flat and closed the case. I gazed into the mirror right above the luggage rack.

Would Tom notice any difference? Searching my reflection, naturally, I couldn't find any physical alterations, but I knew I'd changed. The innermost part of me had been cleansed and scoured. My computer savvy sons always talked about defragmentation. Well, I felt like my hard drive had been defragged.

I closed my eyes and folded my hands over my heart. Although I'd received horrendous information about my parents today, instead of trying to shoulder the burden alone— as I would have in the past—I placed it at Jesus' feet. Pastor Ward, at the Bandera Community Church, often preached about Jesus' willingness to bear our burdens. I took him at his word.

On my return to the hotel, I'd prayed in the car. I prayed for understanding, for patience and for peace. The past was the past and couldn't be changed. How I reacted to events from the past was completely in my control, and with the Lord's guidance, I could be strong.

♦♦♦

We entered Eva's room just as she returned from therapy. A healthy glow infused her skin and a smile graced her beautiful face.

"*Mis amigas*," she said. "So good to see you. Come. Come, sit."

We greeted her and pulled up chairs to flank her wheelchair at the window.

Eva described the session she'd had with Dr. Contreras and the students. Her legs had been prodded and poked, and moved this way and that. The staff all cheered when she'd responded to tickles across her right foot and ankle. The left foot still showed no sign of movement. After the students left, the therapist had reviewed an array of additional exercises Eva would have to do. Eva had a folder filled with printed instructions and illustrations depicting each exercise. We'd have our work cut out for us once home in Hanson Ridge.

In the middle of my sharing the information given by the lawyer and Mr. and Mrs. Lopez, Dr. Contreras entered the room.

"*Buenos tardes, señoras*. Did Eva tell you about her workout?"

I stood and shook his hand. "Yes, she did. You're a slave driver, sir."

"But soon *you'll* be the slave driver, right?" He adjusted his tie while giving us all a cheery grin.

"I've been reviewing her folder. I can borrow the equipment we need from my clinic." I sat again and patted Eva's knee. "You'll have no time to rest."

She feigned distress, but laughed. "I'll do whatever you say, *mi amiga*."

Dr. Contreras looked at me and asked, "Do you know what time you'll come tomorrow?"

"Whenever you say. We're going to Eva's house today to collect her clothes, and we'll be packed, ready to travel when we arrive here."

"Come about nine. There will be paperwork to sign and final instructions to review. Eva, you'll be able to get out of the hospital gown and into your own clothes. Which reminds me, Maricella, but you may already know this. It will be easier for Eva to wear skirts or dresses. No long pants until she gains more muscle control in her legs."

I nodded and smiled at Eva. "Even though your legs aren't cooperating right now, they're still shapely. We'll show off your dainty feet in a fancy pair of *chanclas*, and I'll paint your toenails. But first we'll have to destroy those ugly gray socks."

"Please do." Eva bent over and tugged at them. "Can't wait to wear my own clothes."

"I need to leave you ladies now. See you in the morning. *Adios*." Dr. Contreras closed the door as he left.

Eva wheeled herself to the bedside table. "Here is a list of items I'll need from my house, and," she opened the drawer and reached inside, "here are my keys."

Reading through the list, I noticed Eva had indicated where most items would be located. Included on the list were some of Angel's things, too. A wave of sadness darkened my heart. If my boys were gone, what physical items of theirs would I want to salvage? I couldn't even conceive of making such a list.

Eva watched as I read. When I glanced at her, a comprehending quiver of a smile creased her mouth. I folded the paper and placed it with the keys in my purse.

Teresa slouched down in her chair and placed her feet up on the sill. She wore another sundress and tucked the skirt around her legs. "For some reason, this is comfortable. Hope you don't mind."

"My sill is your sill," said Eva. "Maybe one day I can say *mi casa es tu casa*." She sighed, then looked up. "Speaking of my house, when will you go? You must make sure Hector isn't there."

Teresa crossed her ankles and smoothed out a crease in her blue skirt. "Ray has it under control. He told Maricella he'd meet us there about five."

"Good. I wouldn't want you to run into Hector. He can't be trusted. But enough of him. Maricella, can I look at the names the lawyer gave you? I may know someone on the list."

After visiting with Mr. and Mrs. Lopez, I'd forgotten there were other names on the list. I scrounged around in my purse, pushing aside the recorder I'd remembered to bring, and pulled out the crumpled paper.

Eva smoothed it out and scanned the names. "Juan and Perla Hernandez moved away last year, and I don't know these people," she pointed, "but Albert Holguin is still in Eagle Pass. Remember, Maricella, he and his wife Martha attended our q*uinceañera*. He was our math teacher in junior high."

I thought for a moment. "And he always had candy in his shirt pocket and offered it to kids all the time."

"That's Albert. He still does it. I've seen him around town a few times since being back in Eagle Pass, but I didn't realize he may have known our parents. I thought he came to our celebration because he was our favorite teacher." Eva handed the paper back to me.

Meeting the Lopezes had added another dimension to my past. Perhaps Mr. Holguin could add more. I pulled my cell phone from my purse and consulted the list.

"Do you mind if I call him? Maybe he can come over."

Eva looked around the room and gave me an amused stare. "Sure. It's not like I'm going anywhere. It will be good to visit with him again. Give him a call."

Mr. Holguin, although long retired, remembered Eva and me, and agreed to come by the rehab center later in the afternoon. I'd explained to him I wanted to pick his brain about my parents, and he said I was welcome to whatever brain he had left. His sense of humor had not diminished with age.

While waiting for him, the three of us talked about a variety of topics, none of which taxed our emotions too heavily.

The man who entered Eva's room stood about six foot, with thinning gray hair, slicked back, and an infectious grin spread from ear to ear. I remembered the smile. He always made math more interesting because he enjoyed it so much. His leathery cheeks, permanently creased by laugh lines and age accentuated the perfect set of dentures. A neatly pressed blue shirt and navy slacks, brown cowboy boots and large buckled belt completed his attire.

"Maricella?" He glanced at each of us.

I stood and extended my hand. "Mr. Holguin. Good to see you again."

His gaze flowed to Teresa and Eva. "*Tres señoras.* I was expecting two, but I see three beautiful women. This is my lucky day." His smile encompassed us all.

"Mr. Holguin—"

"Please, Maricella, I'm not your teacher anymore. Call me Al. This is a big occasion for me. Don't often get calls from ladies these days."

I introduced him to Teresa, and he recognized Eva. Teresa brought another chair in from the hall and we visited for a few minutes, explaining the reason for Eva's stay at the facility and her need for a wheelchair.

When the conversation veered to the past, I asked if I could record his recollections of my parents.

He pointed to the recorder. "On that little gadget? I can't keep up with technology. I do good to use e-mail. But yes, record away."

I stated his name into the device, then held it out to him.

After taking it, he cleared his throat and grinned at us. "Got to have my best Hollywood pipes. Okay, I met your father, Maricella, at the telephone company. I worked there part-time while attending college, and he was my supervisor."

"What year was that?" I asked.

The grin disappeared as he thought back. "Must have been mid '60s. Yes, because I graduated in 1966."

"My dad worked there a long time. I never knew."

Eva settled back in her wheelchair and sighed. "I wonder why he decided to leave and open the restaurant with my father."

Sad memories surfaced as we sat in silence.

"I don't know, but *hermosas señoras*, let's focus on good things, okay?"

Albert changed the mood by telling funny stories about his time at the phone company and his early teaching experiences.

"And your parents, Eva. I first met your father when he helped with renovations on my house, and your mother volunteered at the school.

"We became good friends." Albert's eyes dimmed and lost their sparkle. "Things did not stay that way."

Eva leaned forward and frowned. "Tell me, please, Mr. Holguin. I must know."

"Are you sure? It may not be pleasant."

"It doesn't matter. If it's the gambling, I know about his problem."

"Yes, it is *mija*." Albert smoothed back his hair and sighed. "First, Juan borrowed money from me. Which he paid back after six months, but when he wanted to borrow more, I said no. By then I'd heard about his gambling and... other involvements, and—"

"What other involvements?" Eva asked.

Albert sat up straighter, placing gnarled hands on his knees. "He started borrowing from questionable people."

I looked at Eva and Teresa. "We sort of know about one of them."

Concern furrows mixed with the old man's wrinkles. "How so?"

Starting with events the night of our *quinceañera*, I explained to Albert what we knew about the loan shark and the shooting that night.

"But no one was ever arrested, right?" Albert asked.

"Right. I've talked with Ray Reyes. Remember him? He was also in our class."

Albert raised his eyes as if he examined a picture on the ceiling. "I think so. Good looking. Class clown?"

"That's him. He's now a police officer, and because of the new information I gave him about the third man, he told us the investigation may be reopened."

"Glad to hear that." Albert stroked his chin for a moment. "It was a bad night. Martha and I, we had seats close to the door, so we got out quickly." He stood and stepped to the window, then turned. "But I don't have to remind you ladies about that night."

I could tell Albert loathed continuing this line of conversation. His confused expression alarmed me. Had his mind been clouded by memories of his late wife?

Joining him at the window, I placed my arm through his. "Albert, would you like something to drink? Teresa is adept at using the vending machines."

He turned to Teresa and smiled. "Yes. Root beer, if they have it, or a Coke, please."

I pulled a handful of dollar bills from my purse and gave them to Teresa. She returned a few minutes later with four sodas, and we talked about more pleasant things as we enjoyed our drinks.

Albert stood and threw his empty can in the trash. "It's about time for me to go. I have my weekly dominoes game tonight. Can't be late."

Teresa chuckled. "Uh-oh, Albert. They recycle here." She retrieved the can and placed it on the window sill with hers.

"Oops, sorry. Too bad they can't recycle all this extra skin I have. Looked in the mirror this morning and nearly fell over. There's enough skin here" he pulled at his cheeks, "to cover another face."

We joined in his laughter.

"But, seriously, I have to go." He approached Eva and stooped to hug her. "It's been good to see you after all these years. Who did you marry again?"

With a catch in her voice, Eva replied, "Miguel Valdez. I met him in Mexico, but after he passed away, I married Hector Alonzo."

Albert frowned. "Alonzo. Alonzo. That name rings a bell." He rubbed his forehead. "No. Don't think he was a student of mine, but..."

I caught the beginnings of a question in his eyes, but he shook his head and hugged Teresa and me. When he reached the door, he stopped and turned. Teresa and Eva were engrossed in watching a bird out the window and didn't notice. I did, however.

Hurrying toward him, I guided him out the door and down the hall a few steps. "What is it, Albert? You've remembered something haven't you?"

"Yes. Yes. Alonzo. Now I know why the name is familiar. But before I make any false statements, how old is this Hector Eva married?"

"Not sure. I just know he's quite a bit older than us. Why?"

Albert stuck his hands into his pants pockets and frowned. "Have you seen him? Do you know what he looks like?"

I shook my head.

"Too bad. Because the Hector Alonzo I've heard about is a loan shark."

CHAPTER EIGHTEEN

Ray stood in the driveway as we drove up. He opened my door and offered me a hand. "Do you have the house key?"

I gave him Eva's key ring and waited while he climbed the porch steps and unlocked the door. He stepped in and after a few minutes returned to the doorway and motioned for Teresa and me to join him.

"There's no one here. Come on in."

Once inside the hot, stuffy room, I gazed around, and although the furnishings were different, the layout of the house transported me back to childhood. The happy, carefree hours, days, I'd spent in this house with Eva and her parents. Closing my eyes, I could hear our parents chatting in the kitchen. I could smell the tortillas and cinnamon drenched *buñelos*, Mrs. Cuellar's specialty.

In the deep caverns of my mind, I heard Ray turn on the window air conditioner unit and call my name, but I didn't want to leave the pleasant, innocent memories.

Ray cleared his throat. "Maricella?"

At his repeated calling of my name, I opened my eyes on the present.

"Sorry. Must have been daydreaming."

I handed Eva's list to Teresa. "Can you get started please? I need to ask Ray something."

Teresa took the list and headed back toward the bedrooms.

Ray stood with his hands on his hips. "What is it?" Pressed blue jeans and crisp white shirt with sleeves rolled up exposing toned forearms added to his allure.

"I need to tell you something."

I shared the information Mr. Holguin had given me and expected surprise or disbelief from Ray, but I was mistaken.

He shook his head as he moved to the mantel and leaned against it. "No, not possible. Remember I told you Hector's been a person of interest to the EPPD, but not for loaning money."

His expressionless face puzzled me.

"But Albert was so sure." I gazed around the living room and spotted a photograph of Eva. "I know. What does Hector look like? Is there a photo of him here? If I find one I could call Albert and show him. See if he recognizes him."

The only photographs I could see were of Eva and Angel. Strange. Why didn't Eva have any pictures of Hector?

I hadn't told her about Albert's accusation. She'd been in such a good mood when we were ready to leave her room I hadn't wanted to destroy it. But now Ray had provided conflicting information. Whom to believe? Ray or Albert? I should have told Eva.

"Maricella, I can see this is really bothering you. Why don't you give me Mr. Holguin's number and I'll discuss it with him."

I plopped down on the burnt orange sofa and sighed in frustration. "Maybe I'm making too much of all this. First, Eva thinks Hector tried to kill her, and now Albert says he is a loan shark." I found the list of names in my purse and Ray copied down Albert Holguin's phone number. "I don't know what to believe. But wait, Ray, since you're here, can we check in the garage and I'll show you his green truck?"

"You don't give up, do you? Okay, let's go."

"Teresa, we're going to look in the garage. Want to come?"

She brought items she'd gathered and placed them on the sofa. "Sure."

Ray led the way to the kitchen, unlocked the back door, and we crossed the porch. As we traversed the backyard, I noticed the hole where obviously the money had been buried. Money. It had caused so much pain. What would happen to the $75,000 Angel had in the bag when I found her body?

The garage doors were locked. Ray riffled through Eva's keys and opened the padlock. "Just for the record, I'm opening these doors for a friend and not as a police officer."

He swung the doors wide.

Empty.

No old green pickup. Nothing but three boxes, scattered tools, a lawn mower and my flashlight.

"He moved it. It was here. I saw it, right here. And there's my flashlight."

Teresa touched my arm. "I believe you, Maricella."

Ray tramped in and grabbed the flashlight. "Here, Chella. I believe you, too. Hector must have been afraid the vehicle would be found and moved it."

With her hands on her hips, Teresa scanned the dingy space. "But you had the house under surveillance, didn't you?"

Ray motioned for us to leave, and relocked the doors. "He obviously moved it undetected. So much for the truck. Sorry, Maricella. I'll see what the word is on the street, so don't give up yet. If Hector caused Eva's wreck, I'm sure we'll find some evidence soon."

We traipsed back to the house. A gust of wind stirred up loose dirt from the garden and I squinted against the flying grit.

Teresa gathered her loose hair into a ponytail and looked up. "Dark clouds are moving in. We may get rain."

"Sure wouldn't hurt." I looped my arm through hers until we climbed the back steps and entered the house.

She had already collected most of the items on Eva's list. I squeezed the flashlight into my purse, and then hurried to the bedroom in search of a suitcase we could take to the hospital. I'd remembered the closet in the main bedroom had storage above, concealed by a curtain. Sure enough Eva had the area covered by fabric matching her drapes.

I glanced around the room. Clothes strewn on the floor, unmade bed, dirty dishes on the bedside table—not what I would have expected of my friend's housekeeping skills. But it had been a lifetime since we'd had intimate knowledge of each other's day-to-day habits. Maybe she'd changed. Maybe Hector made her change. Or maybe Hector had created this mess since Eva's accident.

She wouldn't have to deal with him any longer.

Pushing a pile of clothes off the dresser stool, I scooted it over to the closet. I held onto the door handle, stood on the stool, and pulled the curtain aside. Several cases stacked on top of each other rested against the side wall. I reached for the middle one, but a twinge knifed through my abdomen. Dr. Fordyce's admonition rang in my ears and I called for Teresa's assistance. She yanked out the suitcase like it was made of Styrofoam and set it down on the floor.

"Thanks, Teresa. I'll take it to the living room."

"Okay. There's a trinket box Eva wants, but I couldn't find it the first time I looked." She opened and closed the dresser drawers. "Oh, there it is."

Objects rattled in the case as I carried it to the living room. I set it down on the sofa, but as I reached for the zipper, Teresa walked to the front door.

She peered through the small slanted window. "There's a pickup truck pulling into the driveway."

"Is it old and green?" I ran to join her and looked outside. "Now *that's* a fancy ride."

Teresa clicked her tongue. "You and Mike and Joey and your cars."

"You have no idea what it was like when the boys were kids. They'd devour automobile magazines, and would compete to see who could identify the most cars as we drove anywhere together. I had no choice. I learned about cars, too, and still compete with Joey sometimes."

Teresa placed her arm on my shoulder. "Poor Maricella. But I wonder who the visitor is. Ray may know. Where is he?"

"He didn't come back in when he closed the garage. Wait." I tapped on the glass. "Look, there he is."

Ray jogged from the direction of the garage and stopped at the truck to talk to the driver through the open window.

Teresa and I watched, but couldn't hear the conversation. "I'm going out there."

Teresa grabbed my arm.

"Maricella, be careful. You don't—"

"I'll be fine. If it was Hector, wouldn't Ray be arresting him right now?" I opened the door.

"There're still a few things I need to locate for Eva." Teresa held the door open. "I'll stay inside, but please be careful."

Ray heard me clomping down the porch steps and turned, his expressive eyes hidden behind dark glasses. He stood by the window, shielding the truck's occupant from my view.

The usual warmth was absent from his voice. "What you need, Chella?"

"I'm nosy, and checking to see if Hector—"

"Hector—" The driver spoke, but Ray interrupted by turning and clapping him on the shoulder.

"Maricella, I'd like you to meet my oldest, Ray Junior. We call him Raymond." He moved aside as I inched closer.

"Pleased to meet you, Raymond." I shook his hand through the window and surveyed the black pickup and whistled. "Some ride you have here. It's the new Ford F-150, isn't it?" I stepped back and admired the body molding, running boards and cab roof lights.

The young man beamed. "Yeah. It's a Lariat. You sure know your trucks."

"My son was a good teacher."

Again Ray interrupted. "Are you and Teresa finished in the house? Ready to leave yet?"

Still ogling the truck, I shook my head. "We're almost done." Studying Ray's face, I became more and more curious. Agitation seeped out of his pores. Maybe his son embarrassed him or annoyed him. But I decided our business at the house superseded my concern for Ray's relationship with his son.

Back-stepping up the sidewalk, I waved to Raymond. "I'd better go in and help Teresa. Again, nice to meet—" I stopped mid-step. "Is that a UT cap?" I watched the young man place a hat on his head.

Raymond adjusted the orange bill. "Yeah."

Returning to the truck I ignored the scowl on Ray's face and focused on his son. "Do you go to the University of Texas? Which campus?"

Raymond stroked the leather steering wheel cover. "In San Antonio."

"At UTSA? No kidding. My youngest son, the auto enthusiast, will be a junior there in the fall. Maybe you met him last year? José McDonough?"

The young man pushed the cap back off his forehead and the smile, a juvenile replica of his father's, slid from his face.

"Um, maybe I've heard of him. Did he live on campus?"

"Yes. In the university apartments."

Raymond nodded and shot a look at his father. "I did, too."

"Will you be back in the fall? I can ask Joey to call you. Maybe you could come out to the house for a meal."

Before Raymond could answer, Ray's bulky body wedged me away from the window.

I took a step backward and frowned at him. "What's wrong?"

His scowl gave way to a false grin. "Sorry to interrupt, Chella, but my son won't be back at UTSA next year, and he needs to leave. Now."

I glanced at man and boy. A tense undercurrent bounced between them, splashing me with leftover vibes. Had my questions aggravated the situation?

Signs of the beginnings of a family feud were in the air. I smiled briefly, waved to Raymond, then turned and climbed the steps.

Heated voices from the driveway slowed my pace.

"You need to go now."

"But Dad, I—"

Inquisitiveness took over. I opened the door, but remained on the threshold. While eavesdropping I noticed the lawn needed watering. I glanced at the sky. Blue predominated, so there'd be no rain today. Maybe Eva had been the gardener and the lawn suffered without her care.

Ray stood by the pickup, pointing down the driveway. "Raymond, I won't tell you again. Leave now."

Raymond turned the ignition and gunned the engine. Whatever he said to his father disappeared in the noise. Teresa came to the door and I told her about Ray's son. She shrugged and returned to her task in the living room.

I held the door open, the cool air refreshing on my legs, and stepped inside, only to be brought back out by the motor's sudden silence. I pulled the door closed.

"Dad, I just want to pick up—"

Ray leaned into the cab, his words inaudible from the porch, but the body language and hand gestures I witnessed assured me his son received a lecture.

The engine revved again. Ray stepped back onto the grass, hands on hips, back military straight.

A feeble last attempt. "Please, Dad?"

Ray pointed to the street. "*Suficiente, mi hijo. Váyase.* Go now."

The black pickup snailed down the driveway, but once on the road, Raymond floored the accelerator, leaving trails of burning rubber. He must really be annoyed with his father.

Still standing by the door, I waited for Ray to join me.

"Sorry you had to witness that, Chella."

"What did he want? He sure was persistent."

"Kids. You must know what they're like. Don't take no for an answer."

Determined to find out more, I stood with my hand on the door knob and raised my eyebrows at Ray. "I remember."

After Ray removed his sunglasses, he produced his most charming of smiles. "Raymond wanted to get his gym bag from my car. I told him it was at home." He reached for the door knob, covering my hand with his. "He didn't believe me. Thought I had it in my trunk."

I slackened my grasp, pulled my hand away and searched the street. "Where's your car?"

He pointed two houses over. "I parked on the other side, down there."

A silver convertible glinted in the sunlight.

"Another fancy car. It's a Mercedes, isn't it?" I avoided asking the obvious question. How could a cop afford such a vehicle?

"Yeah. A Mercedes CLK 320. And," he held up his hands, "before you ask, an uncle, a rich uncle, gave Raymond and me the money."

"Must be nice." My attention focused back on Ray. The jovial, confident persona returned. His chocolate eyes sparkled, the dimples danced on his cheeks.

Opening the door to remove myself from his too masculine presence, I chatted to cover my embarrassment. "So, Mr. Reyes, you have children. Where's the wife?"

Ray tucked his sunglasses in his shirt pocket and picked up the stack of mail on the coffee table. "Raymond's mother, my first wife, died a few years back. Cancer. And Jean, my second ex, lives in Houston."

He returned the mail to the table and wiped a hand across his forehead. "She has custody. My job... you know. Not conducive to a stable home environment."

"I understand." Compassion for his pain touched my heart. "How old are your other kids?"

A tentative smile popped out. "Raymond is nineteen, and there's Carlos, twelve, Paul, ten and my *chiquita*, Yolanda is seven."

The air conditioner's hum filled the space between us.

"You must miss them."

He nodded and turned to the window. "Very much. Only see them twice a year."

I took one step, two steps toward him and stopped. No, I couldn't, shouldn't try to offer comfort. His affect on me sent warning signals like strobe lights to my brain.

Teresa's voice from the kitchen forced us both to turn. "Hey, you guys. You've got to come see what I've found."

"What, Teresa?" I headed to the kitchen with Ray on my heels.

She stood by the open refrigerator. "Look in here. There's a box of leftovers from a restaurant—can't be more than a day old. Half a tomato, still smells fresh, and the expiration date on this milk carton is a week away. Hector's been here. Recently."

"Let me see." Ray examined the items Teresa mentioned and several others. "You're right. This food is a sure sign someone has been living here."

I punched his arm. "So much for your surveillance personnel."

He straightened and closed the refrigerator. "*Está bien.* It's okay. I'm in agreement with you." He perched on the kitchen table, arms folded across his chest. "All I can say is Hector must know the house is being watched and he sneaks in at night. Doesn't turn on any lights. Is very careful. I'll have to tell my guys to be more vigilant."

Dirty dishes in the sink, crumbs on the counter and an overflowing trash can, were further proof of Eva's absence. I pointed to the mess. "That trash is starting to smell."

"I'll take care of it." Ray opened a drawer and pulled out a large black trash bag.

I stepped out of his way. "We'd better complete our job, or rather, I'd better help Teresa, since she's done all the work. Have you found everything?"

"Yes. I'm ready to pack the suitcase."

I took Teresa's arm and we walked back to the living room. "Sorry I didn't help much."

She smiled and patted my hand. "No problem. Open the case and let's get busy."

After unzipping the top, I flipped it open and found several picture frames inside, partially wrapped in tissue paper. I pulled back the fragile covering and picked up the top frame. The exposed photograph sent arctic blood through my body and I clutched at my heart. No sound escaped from my closed throat.

Teresa reached for my teetering body. "What's the matter?"

I pointed to the man standing next to Eva in their wedding photograph. "I can't believe it. It's... Cigar Breath. Hector is the man who accosted me in the Bandera grocery store. Hector is Cigar Breath."

CHAPTER NINETEEN

Visions of angels clouded my brain as I fell backward onto the sofa. Glass from the photograph lay shattered at my feet.

Hector in Bandera. Hector on my property. Hector, the money, Angel.

Teresa leaned over me. "Maricella. Maricella. Don't faint on me. Take a breath." She pushed the suitcase aside and sat next to me.

I opened my eyes and focused on her. "I'm not going to pass out, Teresa. I just need to sort out the craziness dashing around my brain."

The back door slammed and Ray's footsteps clomped on the old wooden floor. I called for him to join us.

"What's up? You ready to go?" He stopped at the door when he saw Teresa and me on the sofa with glass scattered all over the floor.

"Not yet. I have to show you something." I picked up the wedding picture and stabbed my finger at Hector's face. "This man killed Angel. I'm sure of it."

Ray rubbed his hands on his blue jeans and took the picture from me. "Hector? Killed Angel? Where'd you get such a wild idea?" He sank into the brown armchair opposite the sofa.

"Remember I told you about a man who accosted me in Bandera a few days after I'd found Angel's body and I nicknamed him Cigar Breath. Well, he is Hector. They're the same person."

Ray scratched his head, confusion furrowing his brow. "Hector in Bandera? I don't believe it."

"Ray—"

"Oh, not that I don't believe you, Chella, but why would Hector be in Bandera?"

"This is my theory. Hector harassed Eva about the money's location. After Eva's accident he must have assumed Angel took the money with her when she left town."

"And he followed her to Bandera," said Teresa.

"Right, because he more than likely read the same article Eva had and knew I lived close to Bandera."

Ray leaned forward in the chair, elbows on knees, the worry lines deepening on his forehead. "Let me get this straight. You say Hector bumped into you a few days after you'd found the body."

"Yes. He told me he'd read about the death in our county newspaper, *The Bandera Bulletin*. I think he would have asked me more questions—questions about the money—if he hadn't seen cops enter the store."

I stood up, stepping over the splintered glass and broken frame, and walked to the window. "It may not be the proof you need as a law enforcement officer, Ray, but I'm sure Hector killed Angel. He was in the area. He knew about the money. He followed me."

As I turned, I scanned the room filled with Eva's knickknacks, her personality stamped in every corner, and folded my arms to keep my heart from breaking.

"I know he did it."

Teresa joined me at the window. "You'll have to tell Eva."

I nodded, but words stuck in my throat.

She raised her eyebrows at Ray. "Shouldn't someone also tell the officials in Bandera?"

"Leave that to the EPPD. We'll liaise with the Bandera Sheriff's Department." Ray threw the photograph on the coffee table. "I'll have to give my sergeant all this information. He may want to interview you, Maricella."

That would be good. The more people who knew about Hector, the better. I looked up at Teresa.

She pulled me into a half hug and squeezed my shoulder. "Maybe in the morning, before we go to the rehab center?"

"Um, no. Wait till I talk with him. You may have to delay your departure. In fact," Ray consulted his watch, "I'll call him after we leave here."

Stomping back to the sofa, I took two more framed pictures of Hector and Eva out of the case and dumped them on the coffee table. "Then let's get busy." I started packing Eva's things.

Teresa helped fold and pack while Ray picked up the glass shards. With everything in the case, I looked around one last time.

I gathered up the mail Ray had strewn on the coffee table and glanced at the names. Few were addressed just to Mrs. Alonzo. I took those items and placed them in the suitcase.

When Ray returned with a hand-held vacuum to pick up the smaller glass fragments, I asked, "What should we do about the mail? Maybe stop at the post office tomorrow?"

"That would be a good idea. Eva can ask to have her mail held for a month or two. How long do you think she'll be with you?"

Teresa closed the case and carried it to the door.

I picked up my purse and brushed lint off my Capris. "Don't know for sure. It all depends on her rate of recovery."

The noise of the vacuum prevented further conversation. When the last slivers had been removed, Ray unplugged the machine and wrapped the cord around the contraption.

A melodious tune coming from behind a sofa cushion caught our attention.

"That's my phone." Teresa dashed to the sofa, unearthed her purse and pulled out her phone. She read the caller I.D. and said, "It's Mike. I'll take it outside."

Her eyes twinkled and her smile stretched a mile as she put the phone to her ear, closing the front door behind her.

Ray and I stared at each other.

"So, Maricella Farias, you'll be leaving tomorrow."

I clutched my purse and nodded.

"I'll call the sergeant after we leave here, but I have a favor to ask." He dropped the hand vac onto the chair, turned off the window air conditioner unit and stepped toward me.

I backed away until the coffee table stopped my motion. "What's that, Officer Reyes?"

Ray smiled, teeth flashing between dimpled cheeks. "Not officer. Just Ray. Have dinner with me tonight? Just the two of us. I'm sure Teresa won't mind."

He stopped an arm's length away. I couldn't deny his physical attractiveness, but I knew there would be no intimate dinner.

After a deep breath, I twisted my wedding ring round and round. "I can't, Ray. It's not a good idea."

His intense gaze scoured my soul and his soft words floated to my ears. "Are you sure, Chella?"

"I'm sure." Side-stepping around the table, I walked to the door. "Thank you for all your help and support, Ray. It's been a pleasure meeting you again."

He took his sunglasses from his pocket. "Believe me, Chella, the pleasure has been mine." Clearing his throat, he strode over, picked up the case and opened the door. "I had hoped for a different ending to this reunion, but I'll respect your decision."

I placed my hand on his arm and smiled. "Thank you."

Ray covered my hand with his.

Hot August air rushed into the house. My cheeks burned as he flashed a smile and lowered his head.

Teresa came up the porch steps and stopped abruptly. "Mike said—oh, am I interrupting?"

I pulled my hand away, and stepped onto the porch. "No, Teresa. We can leave now." I blinked up at Ray. "Officer Reyes is going to call his sergeant, and he knows he has my profound appreciation."

"Mine, too. Let me take the case." Teresa held out her hand.

"No, no. I'll see you to your car." Ray closed and locked the door, handing Eva's keys to me as we left the porch.

With the suitcase stowed in the trunk, Ray leaned in the driver's window. "I have your cell number. I'll let you know what the sergeant says. Maybe I'll see you tomorrow. If not, have a safe trip and I'm looking forward to meeting Tom. He's a lucky guy."

I started the car. "*Adios. Muchas gracias.*"

Teresa waved, and I reversed out onto the street. Checking the rearview mirror, I saw Ray raise his hand, then drop it and lower his head.

Halfway down the block, Teresa turned to me. "Maricella, do you have something to tell me?"

I stared straight ahead, not wanting to give Teresa a chance to read my emotions. "Ray asked me to dinner tonight." I turned the corner. "I said no."

"I see. I thought he may be smitten."

"Smitten? No." I shrugged off the vague feeling she may be right. "Oh, Teresa, you goose. He's a flirt, a ladies' man. Not used to being turned down. But not smitten."

"If you say so." She looked at the street name as we turned another corner. "Hey, where are you going? This isn't the way to the hotel."

"Thought I'd pay one last visit to my old house. Do you mind?"

"Of course, not."

Driving by as slowly as I could, sadness replaced the gut-wrenching pain I'd experienced before. I stopped the car and closed my eyes. A wordless prayer welled up and coated my heart in peace. My parents were gone, but the foundation they'd provided had molded and shaped me into the person I'd become. Would they be proud? Would they approve of the foundation I'd provided my children?

When I opened my eyes, the sun peeked out from the low clouds, shedding golden rays on the peeling yellow paint. The rays were like smiles from my parents tickling my heart.

Teresa tapped my arm. "Okay?"

A goliath sigh escaped and I took one last look at the house. "Fine. Let's go. And what did Mike have to say?"

"He's home. Arrived earlier this afternoon. I can't wait to see him. He has a report to prepare in the morning, but should be off tomorrow afternoon and Friday."

"And I'll have you home tomorrow as soon as I can."

I could see the excitement beaming from her eyes. Teresa had been a tower of strength to me, an example of faith, and a true friend.

"Words are not enough to convey my gratitude to you, Teresa. I know I couldn't have survived this ordeal without your support."

Teresa gave me a little nod of acknowledgment, then stared out the side window. We drove the rest of the way in silence.

I stopped in the hotel parking lot, but hesitated to turn off the engine. A nagging little voice kept whispering in my ear.

"Teresa, do you mind? I want to take Eva's case to her now."

"Um, I'm hot and tired and want to shower. Why don't you go by yourself? I'll order room service and see you tomorrow."

With Teresa safely in the hotel's side entrance, I headed toward the rehab center, hoping I'd be allowed in at this late hour.

When I explained the reason for my visit, the night duty nurse agreed. "You can only stay fifteen minutes. And please be quiet in the halls."

I nodded and hurried to Eva's room.

Her joy at seeing her clothes reassured me I'd made the right decision. She rummaged through the selection and chose items she'd wear when discharged. Tan T-shirt, floral skirt, and black *chanclas*, sandals with thin gold braid on the straps.

Basking in her pleasure, I decided not to tell her about Hector's visit to Bandera and its tragic consequences. We would discuss many things after we'd left Eagle Pass.

She folded the clothes and placed them next to her on the bed. "I didn't tell you where the cases were kept. How did you find one?"

I placed the case on the floor and sat on the edge of the bed. "I remembered the storage space above the closet. My parents had the same thing."

"Oh, yes. We tried to hide up there once."

I chuckled at the memory. "And did we ever get in trouble for using the closet shelves as steps!"

Eva clasped my right hand in both of hers. "We had so much fun. You were the best friend I ever had."

I added my left hand to the mix and smiled. "And we'll always be best friends. Right?"

She closed her eyes and rested against the pillows, turning her head away. Thick emotion-laden air surrounded us. I couldn't trust my vocal chords to speak without crackling. I cleared my throat and glanced around the room, focusing on the suitcase.

Suitcases, stacked behind the curtain. One containing all photographs of Hector. Who had hidden them?

I peeked at Eva. Her eyes were closed, but her grasp on my hand indicated she wasn't asleep.

"Eva, I have a question."

She turned and stared at me. "What is it, *mi amiga?*"

I squeezed her hand and told her what I'd found in the case.

Tears pooled in her eyes and spilled down her cheeks, like summer rain drops. She bit her bottom lip and pulled her hand away to wipe the moisture from her face.

"Angel. She must have taken down all Hector's photos and hidden them. She must have done it after my accident, before she left town."

I handed her a tissue and also took one. We sat in silence and mopped at our tears, remembering times of love and times of sadness.

The night nurse's knock and unpleasant scowl interrupted our grief and hastened my departure.

I slipped off the bed and hugged Eva. "*Hasta mañana, mi querida amiga.*"

"*Sí,* my friend. See you tomorrow."

"God bless. *Adios.*"

I stood at the door. An irresistible urge to see Eva again struck me. I turned. She smiled from the bed and waved.

I hurried to my car. The almost empty parking area took on a menacing air. Whatever speed limit existed in the lot was broken as I raced to the street. But once surrounded by other vehicles my palpitating heart settled down.

The idea of ordering a meal in a restaurant did not appeal to me. I stopped at a Chinese fast-food outlet and, several minutes later, headed for the hotel with a container of steamed rice and General Joe's chicken.

Sparse evening traffic and savory aromas lulled my senses. The green light beckoned me on. I drove through the intersection and noticed vehicle headlights in my rearview mirror.

Closer. Closer.

I signaled and changed lanes. The lights followed. I wanted to speed up, but the next traffic light flashed to amber, then red.

I stopped.

The vehicle stopped so close behind me he nudged my car.

Main Street. Other vehicles, people. I was not alone, but hot waves of panic surged into my bloodstream, and a colony of ants marched up my neck and cavorted on my scalp.

Three more blocks to the hotel. When the light changed, I raced forward, hoping to get ahead of the car in the next lane. But the vehicle behind seemed glued to my bumper.

A nudge forward.

My head jerked from the force. What should I do? The steering wheel required both hands. I couldn't even reach my cell phone, since the nudge had sent my purse to the floor by the passenger door.

One more block. I slowed, tensing for another jolt, but none came. When I turned into the hotel entrance, the vehicle kept going. I stopped, heart racing, sweat inching from my hairline down my neck.

No. I refused to succumb to intimidation. I climbed out of the car and peered down the street in time to see an old green pickup truck screech to a stop at the next traffic light.

Fearing it could have been Hector, and he could return, I jumped back in the car and parked close to the side entrance. Key card ready, I ran to the door. Once inside, I slumped against the wall, legs like jelly, fear a bitter taste in my mouth.

Did I really see Hector's green truck? Or had my conviction of his guilt conjured up his vehicle? There must be other green trucks in Eagle Pass. Right?

I stood in the hall and rubbed my damp palms on my pant legs. After shallow gulps of air refilled my lungs and normal breathing patterns returned, I staggered to my room. My stomach growled. I giggled and wailed, on odd mix of nerves and relief. My food was still in the car.

Should I brave the trip? I checked around the parking lot before dashing to my car.

The risk was worth it. Some of the best General Joe's chicken I'd ever had. Almost tasty enough to erase the truck from my mind.

No light peeked from under the connecting door, so I figured Teresa may already be asleep. I prepared for bed and, just as I snuggled under the clean, cool sheets, Tom called.

We talked till my cell phone battery faded. I left out the green truck incident, but his amused reaction to Ray's dinner invitation took me by surprise.

"Sweetheart, I trust you. I know you love me and would never betray me—no matter how much attention another man pays you."

Tom, my Tom. I would never betray him. I'd deceived him about my past, but he was right. I would never do anything to jeopardize our love. "Good night, sweetheart. God bless."

"*Dios te bendiga*, my love."

CHAPTER TWENTY

Teresa leaned against the frame of the connecting door, dressed in a pale pink sundress. "Are you ready to check out?"

"Um, no. I'm packed, but I want to wait until after we pick up Eva."

"Okay. You're the driver." Teresa placed her suitcase in my room. "Can I ask why? You mentioned before that when we picked up Eva we would be ready to travel."

I pulled the drapes open and looked out the window. "I don't have a logical reason, except I know something about rehab facilities. They are notorious for agreeing a patient will be discharged, only to find a reason to change their minds." I stepped to the bed, straightening a pillow. "And I hope we hear from Ray or his sergeant soon. About Hector in Bandera and his possible involvement in Angel's death."

"I see. But we have to check out by noon."

"I know, but I still want to wait." I grabbed my purse and moved to the door. "Let's go to breakfast, so we can be at the rehab center by nine."

The hotel's continental breakfast provided enough variety to satisfy us both. As usual, Teresa ate very little. Maybe she just wasn't a morning eater. My boys, on the other hand, always ate a huge breakfast—when they lived at home.

While we ate, I recounted the near rear-ending from the previous night.

"Maricella, it's a good thing we're going home today. I can't trust you to stay out of trouble when I'm not around."

"You sound like a true parent." I stirred sweetener into my coffee. "You'll make a good mother one day."

Teresa blushed and picked up a slice of cantaloupe. "Hope so. But seriously, are you going to tell Ray about the incident?"

After taking a sip of the strong brew, I thought for a moment. "Don't think so. I hadn't planned on contacting him again, unless his sergeant wants to talk to me." I set my cup down. "And the more I think about the truck, the more I'm not certain it was Hector's. Different shade of green maybe. I just want to get Eva away from here and go home."

"Me, too."

We arrived at the rehab center just before nine. Visiting hours hadn't begun yet, but we entered unheeded. What a difference a few days made. Three days ago, when I'd first traversed these halls, knots fought for space in my stomach, and my heart beat inside my chest like it wanted to escape.

Now, I practically skipped along in anticipation. No one manned the nurses' station when we passed by, allowing us to proceed straight to Eva's room.

Empty. Bed stripped, wheelchair missing, balloon bouquet gone.

"They've worked fast to remove her things. Wonder where she is?" I stepped into the hall and looked around.

Teresa plopped onto a chair. "You go find her. I'll stay here in case she comes back while you're gone."

Agitated voices coming from the nurses' station drew me. As I walked, the familiar knots formed tentative tangles in my gut.

I rounded the corner and saw Dr. Contreras and Nurse Williams, who'd worked with Eva, bending over a chart on the desk.

Dr. Contreras glanced up at my approach. "Oh, Mrs. McDonough. We've been trying to reach you." His strained words gave the knots permission to grow.

"But my phone hasn't rung." I opened my purse. "Oh, no. I must have left it recharging in the hotel room."

We'd never given them Teresa's cell number. Mine was the only contact information they had.

"Why? Has Eva had a set back?"

Dr. Contreras handed a folder to another nurse who entered the area. "You could say that." He stepped away from the desk and placed his hand in the small of my back. "Come. Let's go to her room. Is your daughter-in-law with you?"

I nodded, my throat welded shut with apprehension.

"Good."

He steered me down the hall.

Our footsteps on the beige tiled floor echoed against the beige walls. Beige. What a strange word. What a bland color. Beige. Beige. Beige.

Teresa sat up when we entered. She took one look at me and bolted out of the chair. "What's wrong?"

I shrugged, sitting on the bed, the first surface I found to relieve the weight off my rubbery legs.

Teresa sat next to me and asked, "Dr. Contreras, where's Eva?"

He settled in the chair Teresa had vacated and clasped his hands.

"I have bad news." His ashen face sent the blood curdling through my body. "Eva died last night."

Whoosh. Whoosh. Whoosh. My head exploded. My heart burst. The tree outside the window swayed back and forth in the breeze. How could it be so calm outside? The room tipped sideways and I collapsed onto the bed.

Gentle pats on my cheek, my name called by various voices. The fog lifted, my eyes fluttered open.

Dr. Contreras and Teresa stared at me. I rubbed my eyes. Was this for real? Was I lying on a bed with an anxious doctor and my daughter-in-law bending over me?

Blinking away the film that clouded my consciousness, I tried to sit up.

"Stay still, Maricella," said the doctor, picking up my wrist to take my pulse. "You've had a shock. Lie here a few more minutes."

Teresa took my other hand, tears filling her eyes.

"So it's true? I didn't dream it. Eva's dead?" I knew the words came from my mouth, but they sounded like they'd been uttered by someone outside my head.

Wiping her hand across her cheeks, Teresa nodded.

Thoughts, ideas, words climbed over each other like hyperactive kids in my brain. I couldn't be still any longer.

I sat up and grabbed the bed rail as the room spun. "Oooh."

"Maricella—"

"It's okay. Let me up." I sat on the edge of the bed with Teresa ready to offer support at the side.

"Now, Dr. Contreras, what happened to my friend?"

He sat again and leaned forward, elbows on knees. "It appears she had a heart attack during the night. She didn't ring for help and at last bed check, eleven-thirty, she was sleeping peacefully."

My mind couldn't focus on anything but the basics. "Heart attack? Did she have heart problems?"

"Only elevated blood pressure occasionally. But an autopsy will be performed. It's routine in situations like this."

Minutes ticked by. I knew there were scores of questions to ask, but my Swiss cheese brain slowed to a crawl.

Teresa whispered, "Where's the... where is she?"

"In a special room. Waiting for the medical examiner." Dr. Contreras stood. "Would you like to see her?"

"No. No. I want to remember her the way she was the last time I saw her. Last night." I grabbed my purse and hugged it to my chest. "She smiled and waved. She was so happy to be leaving here."

Dr. Contreras stepped over to the bed and touched my shoulder. "There's nothing more for you to do here today. We will have to make arrangements for her things to be picked up, but that can wait." He looked at Teresa. "Take Maricella back to the hotel for now. See that she gets some rest."

He left us in Eva's room.

The rubber in my legs had turned to stone. I couldn't move. Teresa stood and pulled me up. With heavy feet, I plodded after her as we left the room and turned down the hall.

Although each step revived sensation in my limbs, I held onto Teresa's arm. As we passed the nurses' station, I stopped. An idea vied for attention in my scrambled brain.

"I wonder?" I approached the desk and Nurse Williams. "At night, are the front doors locked?"

She looked from Teresa to me and shook her head. "No, ma'am. The side and rear entrances are locked, but not the front."

"So someone could come in undetected?"

"I suppose. We do have a security guard and the night duty staff, but if a person wanted to sneak in, I guess it's possible."

"Maricella, what are you doing?" Teresa asked. "You're supposed to be going back to the hotel to rest."

"I know. I'm ready now." I turned to the nurse and thanked her, then still clutching Teresa's arm, staggered to the parking lot.

"Wait here, and I'll get the car."

"Nonsense. I'm fine. But you can drive." I handed her the keys.

Once in the car, she turned to me. "Okay, Maricella, I know you well enough by now. What's up?"

"I don't think Eva died of a heart attack.

"Of course, you wouldn't. She was your friend. She was healthy and in good spirits the last time you saw her."

I leaned back in the seat and stared at the morning traffic. "No, it's not that. Hector caused her accident. What if the wreck had been an unsuccessful attempt on her life? What if he tried again?"

"You're not serious?"

"I am. You heard the nurse. Someone could sneak in at night. What if Hector came in and... and... killed her?"

Teresa turned into the hotel parking lot. "An autopsy would reveal how she died, right?"

"Depends on how he did it, but it would certainly confirm or refute a heart attack."

The engine off, we sat in the rapidly warming car.

Teresa handed the keys back to me. "What now?"

"I'm going to lie down. Hammers are driving nails into every cell in my brain, and I need to call Tom. And Ray."

We walked down the hall to our rooms. Teresa came into mine and picked up her suitcase.

"Guess we won't be checking out today after all. I'll call the front desk and ask for these rooms for one more night." She stood in the doorway to her room.

I placed my case on the luggage rack and winced. "Ouch. That's a good idea." I grabbed my abdomen.

"Hey, Maricella. What's wrong?"

"Just my incision. Haven't been bothered by it much, but it seems to react to stress."

"Stress." She hiked her shoulders and rolled her eyes. "What stress? I'm going to leave this door open. Now, make sure you lie down."

"Yes, ma'am. I will."

Teresa acknowledged my statement with a weak smile and disappeared into her room. Forcing my intellect to override my emotions, I unplugged my phone—the phone I should have had with me—and called Tom. I had to leave him a message, which allowed me to keep the tears at bay.

Next, I called Ray. He arrived at the hotel within ten minutes. Teresa joined us and together we gave Ray all the details.

When I told him my fears about Hector, his brow furrowed. "That's a serious accusation."

I crossed to the window and paced in front of it. "I know. But what if it's true? We all saw evidence yesterday at their house that he's still in town."

Ray tossed his hat onto the bed. "I agree he may still be in Eagle Pass, but why would he kill Eva now?"

With a shrug I leaned against the sill. "Because—I don't know. Because he found out she's leaving. Because he's a sore loser. Because—"

"Maricella, I think you're clutching at straws." Ray approached me and took my hand. "Come, sit down. You're not thinking rationally."

"Do you want me to get you a soda, or something?" Teresa asked.

"No, thanks." I sat on the edge of the bed. "I know you're both trying to distract me, but there have been too many coincidences for me not to think Hector is involved. I just know he is."

Memories of his strange questions in the Bandera grocery store, of his cigar—

I jumped up, sending Ray staggering backward.

"Ray, you doubt I saw Hector in Bandera, don't you?" I gave him no time to respond. "I have proof. I have a cigar end he dropped. I'm sure a lab somewhere could get his DNA from it."

Teresa pulled me down next to her on the bed and held my hand. "Hey, Chella." She'd never used my nickname before. "Calm down."

Traffic noise from the street pierced through my head, sending whatever coherent thoughts I had left into outer space.

Ray bent over me, hand on my slumped shoulders. "I don't think I can help the situation any more by staying here. I'm going back to the station, and then I'll go to the rehab center. See what I can discover."

Teresa slipped her arm around my shoulders. "Did you tell your sergeant about Hector being in Bandera at the time of Angel's death?"

How did she know I needed an answer to that question?

"I... he... yes, I spoke with him this morning. And he'll increase surveillance at Hector's home. After he hears about Eva's death, he may issue a BOLO."

I frowned up at Ray. "A what?"

"Be On the Lookout. A bulletin for—"

"We get the point," Teresa said.

Ray picked up his hat and stepped away from the bed. "I'll keep you informed, and sorry about all this, Maricella." He raised his hand in a semi-wave. "Good-bye."

After he closed the door, my mind shut down completely. Teresa's arm around my shoulders kept me from floating off the bed, but I lost all touch with reality. The red and gray patterns on the carpet swirled around my feet, clutching at my ankles. I raised my legs to escape their tentacles, and pulling away from Teresa, curled up in a fetal ball on the pillows.

"Oh, God, why? Why?" Whispered words wrenched the plea from my tortured soul.

Teresa knelt by the bed, stroking my forehead, shoulders, and arms with feather lightness. She prayed. Her words calmed my agony, allowing the oblivion of sleep to take over.

CHAPTER TWENTY-ONE

Teresa sat in the armchair by my bed. "I could go by myself."

"Thanks, but I want to go. I have to do this for my friend." I picked up my purse and handed Teresa the keys. She took them and nodded. She knew the drill by now.

The administrator of the rehab center, Flora Gonzalez, had called late afternoon to tell me Eva's personal items were ready for collection. Since Eva had signed a consent form, the center could legally allow me to take her things.

As we drove down Main Street, the events of the day kept replaying over and over like tired summer TV reruns.

Tom had called on his break. Hearing his familiar, concerned voice finally broke the dam of tears. At one point, Teresa had to take my phone and explain the details to Tom when my wailing rendered my words incoherent.

He had offered to cut short his session in New York and fly home early, but even if he did, he'd still have to drive down to Eagle Pass. We hoped to be home before he'd even left New York.

"Sweetheart, I can't begin to know what you're going through, but please keep in mind, I love you, and I'm praying for you." He waited for me to control my sniffles. "And don't let this tragedy come between you and God."

I wasn't sure how I felt about God at this point. I know when I'd woken up the sour taste of denial had coated my throat. But Teresa's expression convinced me it hadn't been a dream. My friend was dead. I couldn't pray, had no desire to pray. What could I ask for? That Eva wouldn't be dead? That I wouldn't have a canyon where my heart used to be?

Like a mechanical robot, I'd washed my face, reapplied makeup and took out my notebook. Making lists had always helped me keep organized. I needed a list now to force me to take care of business, when all my body wanted was escape.

I knew I couldn't handle the nitty-gritty details alone, so I called Vicente Ortiz and solicited his services for Eva's estate. He already knew about Angel's suspicious death, and I trusted him to do all in his legal power for Eva.

Teresa had ordered room service for lunch. I know I ate something, because I remember chewing and swallowing, but I couldn't have told anyone what I'd eaten if a cash reward had been offered.

She was resting in her room when Ray called.

"Good news, Maricella. Hector has been arrested."

Overjoyed, I jumped up and down, but sat when my incision objected to the motion. "Fantastic, Ray. That's the best news. What will happen to him now?"

"He'll be questioned and if charged he'll be held over for trial. I don't want to bore you with the specifics. Just thought you'd want to know."

"Thanks. Appreciate the call so much. Have you notified Carlos Quintanilla yet?"

"Who?"

I frowned at his response. "You remember, the Chief Deputy in Bandera. He'll need to know about Hector."

"Not yet, but I'll make the call right away."

"Thank you for all your help since I've been in Eagle Pass. I really appreciate you giving me details about my parents. And now, with Eva..."

His voice softened. "You're welcome. Wish I could have done more, especially about your folks. But we'll see what happens with the new information we have. Um, when will you be going home?"

I stared at my packed suitcase and said, "We're waiting to hear from the rehab center so we can collect Eva's things. And now, since Hector's out of the picture, we'll take everything back to her house."

After I'd explained Vicente Ortiz's involvement, I said good-bye, put away my phone and knocked on Teresa's door.

She called for me to enter, her cell phone still in her hand. "Just been on the phone with your son. He wanted to know if he should drive down. But I told him no. If he did, it would mean you driving home by yourself."

"That's right, although it would be comforting to have him here. Thanks for thinking of me. And now I have news for you." I told her about Hector's arrest.

"Is he being held for causing Eva's accident and for Angel's murder?"

"Ray didn't elaborate. But Hector's off the streets and can't hurt anyone else." I fingered the heart necklace and added, "He's hurt too many people already."

Teresa raised her face to the ceiling. "Father God, bless our endeavors today and our trip home tomorrow, and send someone Hector's way, so he'll soften his heart and accept you."

This time I had no words to add.

◆◆◆

My recollections of the day's events came to a halt when Teresa stopped in the rehab parking lot.

"Here we are. Are you ready?"

After taking a deep breath, I nodded and climbed out of the car. I squared my shoulders, raised my chin and walked into the facility.

Flora Gonzalez met us outside her office. "We're sorry for your loss, Mrs. McDonough. I know this is a shock for you. It was for us, too. Everything is right here. Come in." She pointed to items on the floor. "There's this bag and the suitcase you brought yesterday."

Holding emotions in check, I said, "We were just informed that her... husband has been arrested for causing her accident. We're taking her things back to her house." I waited a moment for my heart to catch up with my head. "Mr. Vicente Ortiz, a lawyer, is handling her affairs. You may hear from him."

Mrs. Gonzalez released a thin smile, accompanied by a business-first frown. "Thank you for the information. Please sign here," she pushed a form across her desk, "and then you can take Eva's belongings."

I squiggled my name.

Teresa carried the case, while I took the plastic bag. When the items were stowed in the trunk, I covered my face with my hands and stood by the yawning opening. No tears flowed—I'd drained the reservoir earlier—but grief gnawed at my insides.

I lowered my hands and turned to Teresa. "When we get to the house, I don't want to go in."

"That's okay. I'll take care of the bags."

"But first—I don't think Eva would mind—I want one of her photographs. And the necklace."

Teresa unzipped the suitcase. "Which picture do you want?"

"The one of Eva and Angel. You know—the one of them together, at Angel's *quinceañera*."

Moving clothes aside, Teresa pulled out the oak framed picture and handed it to me. She then rummaged through the plastic bag and found the half heart necklace. I placed the necklace in my purse and clutching the precious picture, climbed into the car.

Teresa drove in silence to the old neighborhood and parked in the driveway of Eva's house.

How did a house know? It looked sad. Windows on either side of the front door had shades pulled halfway down like shuttered eyes. The drying grass and weed-filled flower beds echoed my dying soul. I closed my eyes, wishing tears to fall, but the heat building up in the car seared my cheeks instead.

The car door closing signaled Teresa's return. Cool conditioned air blowing in my face forced my eyes open.

"It's done." Teresa backed into the street. "What should we do with Eva's keys?"

I took them from her and studied each one, as if the answer to their fate would be revealed upon intense scrutiny.

"Maricella?"

"Let's give them to Mr. Ortiz." I riffled through images in my memory. "I know. We can take them to his office. Even if it's closed, I noticed a mail slot in the door we could use."

While Teresa drove, I tore a sheet from my notebook and fashioned an envelope around the keys. On the outside, I wrote a message to Mr. Ortiz. When we reached his office I pushed the makeshift container through the mail slot.

Expecting to return to the hotel, a stop at a restaurant caught me by surprise.

"You're always concerned about how little I eat. Well, now it's my turn. Chella, you've eaten next to nothing all day. We're going to sit down and order a decent meal, and," placing the car keys in her purse, "we're not leaving here until I'm satisfied you've eaten enough to keep from collapsing on me."

She laced her arm through mine and we entered the Italian restaurant.

Soaking in the tub later that evening, I appreciated Teresa's concern. The good meal had done much to quiet the gnawing knots in my gut. Now if only I could find something as readily available to satisfy the hunger in my soul.

As if reading my mind, Tom called as I crawled into bed. The sound of his voice brought immediate soothing aid to my wounds.

After a brief recounting of events since his last call, he asked me to locate the hotel Bible, a pen and paper. I rummaged through the bedside table drawer and located the items.

"I'm ready, Tom, *mi amor*. What now?"

"Sweetheart, in all our years together, I've never said this to you, but I'll say it now. I want you to sit down and listen to me. Okay?"

"Okay. I'm sitting in bed. Is that good enough?"

"Perfect." He cleared his throat. "If I could sit next to you, I'd put my arms around you and still say this. I know you've been through a trying few days, especially today, but I want you to write down some Scriptures and read them whenever you begin to have doubts."

I didn't know if I could read them, but at least I could do as Tom asked and note the references. "I'm ready."

"The first one is Romans 12:12. The apostle Paul tells us to be joyful in hope, patient in affliction and faithful in prayer. The second is in II Timothy 1:7. We're reminded that God didn't give us a spirit of timidity, but a spirit of power, of love and self discipline. And then in James 1:13 we're told that God doesn't tempt us."

"Okay, Tom. I've got those down. I'll... I'll try to study them later."

He sighed. "Sweetheart, there's one more thing I want to stress. You don't know how it pleased my soul when you told me you'd realized you needed to do something to mend the breach between you and God. I may be speaking in circles, but—"

"I know, Tom. When I acknowledged I'd never had a personal relationship with Jesus."

"Right. And now I don't want you to allow this... this tragedy to build that wall again."

Similar thoughts had been circulating in my mind all evening, but I lacked the spiritual depth to flesh them out like Tom did. My silence seemed to concern him.

"Maricella?"

"I'm still here."

"I know you, sweetheart. I know you'll try to analyze today's events and try to make some sense out of them, but it can't be done. Philosophers and authors have tried for centuries to provide answers to the big question of why bad things happen to good people."

Why, indeed? Why had Angel been taken so early? Why has Eva left us just when I'd found her? "And what is the answer?"

"I don't have one. All I can offer is this: remember when my dad was killed?"

I leaned back against the pillows and doodled on the note pad in my lap. "Of course, I do."

"I endured the same struggle then."

"What?" The pen went flying as I reacted to his words. "Oh, Tom. I didn't know... didn't realize."

Tom's voice wavered. "I didn't tell you. Couldn't let you know of my doubt. You saw strength in me I didn't always have. I couldn't let you know I was weak."

He was right. It never crossed my mind that *he* needed spiritual guidance. "So what did you do? How did you handle it?"

"Daniel Ward's wisdom pulled me through."

I knew Tom and the pastor of our Community Church often spent time together. Now I know more than football scores and community affairs had been discussed.

"I'm sorry I wasn't the one who helped you then. I'm not sure I could have—"

"Don't be sorry. That's in the past. From now on, we'll lean on each other, with Jesus' guidance."

"But, Tom, how do you reconcile the way your father died? In that he was helping someone else when it happened?"

He had been killed on the interstate when he'd stopped to help a young woman change a flat tire.

"I can't. Mother and I have often discussed the incident. And all we can say is the little boy in that car has a mother today because my Daddy was changing the tire instead of that young lady."

I closed the Bible and set it next to me. "It doesn't seem fair."

"You're right. It's not. It's not fair Eva died just when you'd found her again. It's not fair your parents were taken from you at age fifteen. It's not fair—"

"Tom, I know life's not fair."

"Sweetie pie, all I'm trying to say is, we mortals can rationalize till we run out of paper and ink, but we'll never understand the mind of God. Not until we meet Him face to face, that is. But until then, we live each day, believing in Him, following His commands, getting a little closer to eternity."

Digesting his words, I nibbled on a fingernail. "Thanks, *mi amor*. This is just what I needed."

"A verbal reprimand?"

"No. An anchor to hold on to. A light in the darkness of death."

"I wish I was there to comfort you. To reassure you. But I want to leave you with two more Scriptures. They're both from the Old Testament, but they'll speak to you."

"Hold on. I have to get the pen." I stretched across the bed and grabbed it. "Okay, go ahead."

"The first is Psalm 95:8. The writer says don't harden your heart. Sweetie, now that you've opened your heart to Jesus, don't let doubt and pain interfere. And finally, in Psalm 41:10,

God says not to fear, because He is with you; don't be dismayed for He is your God; He will strengthen and help you; He will hold you in His right hand."

I wrote down the verses Tom quoted. We said our good-byes and I clutched the Bible to my chest. God would hold me in His right hand. He promised. Closing my eyes, I tried to form a prayer asking for the presence of His hand. The words never emerged from my lips but the void in my soul filled drop by drop. The night sounds drifted away like clouds in a breeze. My breathing slowed to normal, my heart relaxed its beat.

"Thank you, God. Thank you for my Tom."

The beep, beep signal from my depleted cell phone battery roused me from near sleep. We'd talked so long today the phone needed recharging again. I plugged it in and placed my voice recorder and purse by the outlet so I wouldn't forget my phone again. Teresa and I would be leaving in the morning. I'd done all I could for Eva, and with Hector in jail, I could leave Eagle Pass confident the murderer had been caught.

Images of Angel, Eva, and Hector punctuated my dreams. I awoke with the unpleasant sensation of something in my dream clamoring to be remembered. But the more I tried to recall the specifics, the more the dream evaporated.

CHAPTER TWENTY-TWO

I placed my suitcase on the floor and glanced around the room one last time.

"I knew it."

There sat my charger, phone, and recorder. In my grief-induced fog, I'd picked up my purse, but had forgotten the other items.

Not wanting to bother with unzipping the suitcase, I placed the charger in my purse, and cell phone and recorder in the spacious pockets of my teal Capri pants.

Teresa had called to say she wouldn't be at breakfast, and we agreed to meet at the car in thirty minutes. She said she'd pick up something to eat on the way out of town. I carried my case out the back entrance, and stowed it in the trunk, then returned for my last hotel meal. Coffee, scrambled eggs and bacon satisfied my hunger.

With the windows down, I sat in the car scanning the morning newspaper. Teresa appeared after a few minutes.

Her pale face and the downward turn of her mouth had me out of the car in a second. "Let me take your case, *mija*. What's up? Didn't you sleep well?"

She squinted against the slanted sunrays and said, "No. Slept fine. It's just an upset stomach, I think."

"Are you ready to travel? Do you need Pepto-Bismol or something?"

Teresa set her case in the trunk and chuckled. "Not as serious as that. I'm ready." She patted her pocket then checked in her purse. "No, I'm not. Pulled one of your tricks, Chella. I left my cell phone still charging in my room."

"Let me go."

"No. I'll go. And I think I left my robe behind the door of the bathroom. Be right back."

Since we were going to checkout after loading up, Teresa still had her key card. She took it out of her purse and ran inside.

The morning breeze kept the car bearable as I finished reading the paper. I glanced at my watch and realized Teresa had been gone almost twenty minutes. I turned on the ignition to close the windows, and took my key card out of my billfold. I hid my purse under the seat and locked the car.

A family congregating by the side entrance blocked my way. The father motioned for his children to move, and I scooted by them. Both our room doors were closed. I opened my door and looked around. The open communicating door drew me like a magnet. Peering into Teresa's room, I saw her blue robe on the unmade bed, her phone still plugged in, but no Teresa.

"Teresa, where are you? Are you okay?"

No answer.

I stepped in and turned to check the bathroom. A shaft of light through the partially open door gave me a glimmer of hope.

I called again, this time a little louder. "Teresa."

Nothing.

With one hand on the bathroom door, I held my breath and listened, but the clamor of my heart drowned out the unspoken cry on my lips.

I pushed the door and it moved a fraction then stopped. Resistance kept it stationary. I poked my head around the door and discovered why it wouldn't open any farther.

Teresa lay sprawled on the floor, her bent legs wedged between the door and the wall.

"Teresa, what happened?"

I squeezed into the bathroom and knelt beside her. A weak pulse answered my probing fingers. At first, I thought she may have fallen or collapsed, but when I saw the blood at the base of her skull, I knew the wound could not be from a fall in such a confined space.

Fumbling for a towel to place under her head, I heard a door squeak as though being opened.

"Hello. Is anyone there? Please call 911. My daughter-in-law's been hurt."

Silence.

I hurried into the room intent on calling the front desk, but before I reached the phone next to the bed, two strong arms grabbed me. One pinned my arms to my body. One clapped a calloused hand over my mouth.

Struggling brought a vice grip around my waist. Warm garlicky breath next to my ear sent shivers down my neck. What did he want?

A hoarse whisper gurgled from my assailant. "If you promise not to scream, I'll remove my hand."

The voice. Did I recognize it?

I nodded as best I could.

The hand slipped from my mouth allowing me a half turn. Who was he?

"Don't. Don't look at me."

I kept my eyes forward, searching the bucolic landscape reproduction above the bed for help. The man reached into his pocket, but the arm around me kept its wrestler hold.

My senses heightened. I tried to capture every detail that would help identify this miscreant. Olive skin. Spanish accent. Body odor, but not the needing a bath kind of odor. Alcohol, maybe. Tobacco, yes. Stale tobacco.

"Oh, no!"

"*Silencio.*" He spat the word in my ear. "I have a gun and I'll use it. Now, be quiet!"

For emphasis, he prodded my back. The vice grip relaxed. I took a deep breath, peeking out of the corner of my eye. What could I use as a weapon?

I saw a shadow rise above me. Then a dull thud and sharp pain forced my eyes closed as I collapsed to the floor.

Pain. Cramped muscles. Blackness. Whiffs of oil, gasoline, garbage.

Silence.

I had long since determined my situation. Tied up in the trunk of a car.

When I had regained consciousness, the car had been jerking through traffic, judging by honking horns and engine noises. Then the pace increased and the absence of other vehicle sounds indicated we were leaving the downtown area. Air gushed in through a sliver of light above me. After anxious miles, the car abruptly stopped. The driver got out, but returned seconds later, and the car moved forward. Dust seeped into the trunk. We were on a dirt road, a rough country road. My body jostled back and forth in the tight space.

My first order of business had been to free my hands and remove the vile smelling gag from around my mouth. During my college days, I had been the envy of roommates for my ability to perform the most complicated yoga positions. I now used my limberness to my advantage. I ignored twinges from the incision in my abdomen and twisted and wriggled my body through the loop my tied hands formed. I swiveled my shoulders until the knotted rope was in front.

I pulled the gag down, spat out fragments of who knows what, and took a deep breath, almost choking on the stuffy, fume-filled air. Teeth at work, I loosened the knot and wiggled my hand free.

I patted the cramped area, searching for something, anything to use as a weapon.

Nothing.

The only objects sharing my space were a pile of rags, and by the odor, a slew of half empty fast food containers.

The bumpy ride ended. I waited, muscles tensed, ready to pounce on my abductor.

A slammed car door sent shock waves reverberating through the metal frame to my teeth. Footsteps crunching on gravel, like final steps before a firing squad.

I swallowed. The movement made my throat ache as if I'd had rocks in my mouth. Sweat drenched my clothes, covered my face and stung the wound on the back of my head. Ears on alert for approaching sounds. Eyes scanning the black interior. Shallow breaths, heart pounding.

But he didn't come.

Muscles relaxed. I touched the painful swelling at the base of my skull and winced. I pulled my hand away and rubbed my fingers together. Wet with sweat not blood. That was a good sign. My head throbbed, probably from inhaling carbon monoxide. The Scrünchie holding my hair in place had slipped to the end of my damp ponytail. I pulled it off and snapped it around my wrist. No way could I twist it back on lying on my side in the confined space.

Now what? Should I try to escape? Should I wait?

I couldn't see my watch so I had no way of knowing the time. I had no way of knowing how long I'd been unconscious either.

Why wait? I hoped the vehicle was new enough to have an emergency latch. Several years ago when we'd purchased a car for Mike, the salesman had made a point of demonstrating the trunk's emergency latch. He said all new cars were required by law to have them. I know my Chevy Impala had one.

I fumbled along the edge of the trunk and located the latch. I pulled one way. Nothing.

I tried the other direction and with a quiet click, the trunk popped open.

Bright light and fresh, sweet smelling air tumbled in. I squinted against the light and the rush of unpolluted air filled my lungs.

I waited.

Swaying branches sprinkled dappled shade on the ground outside, but no human movement caught my eye.

Deep breath. I pushed the top up and swung my legs over the rim, relishing the breeze that cooled the damp clothing stuck to my skin. I climbed out of the cavity, flexing stiff joints. I held onto the car and searched the area.

Squatty trees, scrubby grass, rocks. No buildings. No people.

The rope used to tie my hands dangled over the trunk rim. I bundled it into a pocket and squealed when my fingers caught the edge of my cell phone.

If my abductor looked this way I wanted to give the illusion nothing had changed. I pulled the trunk down and pushed it until I heard the click indicating it had latched closed. My attempts at stealth almost failed when I saw familiar dark brown metal surrounding my hands. I yanked them away from the offending car part and covered my mouth to stifle a scream.

A dark brown trunk.

I stumbled around the car. The dark brown right, rear fender confirmed my horror.

Cigar Breath's car—Hector's car. The one I'd seen in the Bandera grocery store parking lot and at the rehab facility.

But who had placed me in the trunk of Hector's car and driven me out here? Icicles trampled down my spine, sending a shudder through my body.

Hector had been arrested. Surely, he hadn't been released already, but the final impression before I blacked out now made sense. Words spoken in my ear indicated a short man; Spanish accent; tobacco odor on his breath.

Hector. It had to be him.

My vulnerable position by the car forced action. I crouched down as low as I could and skulked along to a line of stubby trees.

I listened for my abductor, but only heard wind rustling the leaves and occasional chirping birds. Where was he?

The need for help overcame my fear of his appearing. My cell phone had a San Antonio number. When I dialed 911 I wasn't sure what would happen.

I punched in the numbers but *No Service* blinked on the screen.

Spying a foot path through the dense undergrowth, I followed it, and when I came to a clearing, dialed 911 again.

This time I reached the operator. First, I asked her to have someone sent to the hotel to check on Teresa, and after recounting my abduction, tried to describe my location.

There were no visible land marks. The dispatcher advised me to stay on the line and to keep following the track. I must have trekked in circles, because after ten minutes the sight of a tan Chevy Cavalier sent the blood from my brain to my feet.

I staggered and grabbed a tree limb for support. "Oh, no," I whispered to the dispatcher. "I'm back where I started. I can see his car—"

A strong arm encircled my waist while a stubby hand grabbed my phone. I clutched at the arm which came perilously close to my incision and gouged at his skin.

Adrenaline-fueled muscles tensed for action. I kicked back, heel catching shin, but the grip around my body intensified when he used both arms to lift me off my feet.

Kicking and screaming were my only weapons. "Let go. Put me down. You're hurting me."

A grunt response. He carried me to a rough wooden picnic table, weatherworn and lop-sided, shaded by a robust mesquite tree. Released with a shove, I braced my fall against the table. Sharp splinters pierced my palms.

"Ouch, you brute!"

I turned and scowled.

Hector.

I knew it.

He wore a sweat-stained brown shirt half tucked into dirty blue jeans. A faded red bandana snaked around his throat.

He placed his hands in his pockets and smirked. "*Sientese.*"

The effective demand worked. I sat down on the bench and examined my palms.

"I have splinters."

"Too bad. I have a gun."

His emphatic tone commanded my attention. Standing by the table, he glared at me. "How'd you get out of the trunk?"

"How'd you get out of jail?"

"What?" He leaned forward. "Don't confuse me. How'd you get out of the trunk?"

"There's an emergency latch."

"Oh. I didn't know that." He eyed me up and down. "But I tied your hands."

I shrugged, unsure how much information to give him. Regretting now I'd told him about the latch in case he put me back in the trunk. "The knot came... came undone."

I pulled a large splinter out and turned my wrist over. Ten forty-five. Time crawls when you're not having fun. Hector sat opposite me, elbows on the table, sleeves rolled up to expose thick, hair-covered arms.

No wonder I couldn't break loose.

I rubbed my abdomen and realized those arms could have done serious damage to my incision if he'd grabbed me any lower.

"What now?"

I shook my head. My vulnerability needed to stay my secret. "Nothing. Other than you. Why have you brought me here? And why did you hurt Teresa? And," I picked at another splinter, "what happened to your arrest?"

"Arrest? Oh, that's a long story. I'll tell you later."

Hector leaned to the side and reached into his back pocket. Expecting a weapon, I blinked when he produced a small, half-empty bottle of alcohol.

Opening it, he grinned. "Want a swig?"

"No. I want answers." I pulled the yellow Scrünchie off my wrist and wound it around a hastily fashioned ponytail.

"All in good time. I'm thirsty. Too bad you don't want any of this. I don't have a refrigerator for sodas or *agua*."

He swallowed once, pulled the bottle away and wiped his mouth with the back of his hand. "Aah, good tequila."

He twisted the top back on, moved the bottle a few inches and scowled at me. "So, you want answers. First of all, if you're talking about the young woman in the hotel, don't worry about her. I didn't hit her very hard, but when she fell maybe she hit her head on the floor or something."

I pushed up. "You cruel—"

"Sit down!" Hector's shout hushed the birds. "Do you want me to tie you up again?"

I plopped down, restraints the last thing I wanted, and waited for answers.

But he swallowed more tequila, lit a cigar and blew the smoke in my direction. I averted my face, thankful a slight breeze kept the nauseating odor from my nose.

"You want to know why I brought you here?"

I nodded.

"First, I have a question for you. Do you recognize me?" He sat up straight, chin out, shoulders back, then offered his profile.

The bizarre act almost made me laugh. "Of course, I do. You accosted me in the Bandera grocery store, and you're Eva's husband. And," I pointed to his cigar, "you dropped one of those on my property, so I can prove you were there."

A deep-throated chortle erupted from his lips. "Oh, yes, my cigar. Heard about that. But it won't do you any good out here. Alone with me."

The implications of his words tried to enter my brain, but I denied them access. My nerves may be tingling, sweat may be dripping down my neck, but I would not let Hector discover the extent of my anxiety.

"What do you mean?" I causally asked, as if the answer hadn't already suffocated me in the trunk.

"Never mind. I still want to know if you recognize me. Think younger." He pulled a grimy base ball cap from his other back pocket and placed it on his head. "How about now? Think of a cap like this covering some hair. I haven't always been bald."

Again he posed.

I shook my head. "I told you already."

"Oh, *Chiquita*. You must think back, many years, to—"

Nuggets of fear nibbled at my heart. "How far back?" My brain retreated to my past.

"Why don't you try ten years, make it twenty. Or even better, make it your *quinceañera* party."

His beady, dark eyes squinted against the cigar smoke. Menace emanated from his face.

"At my *quinceañera*? You were there?" My words echoed in my head.

"You saw me, *Chiquita*."

Fear paralyzed my vocal chords.

Hector removed the cigar from his mouth and tapped the ash on the table between us. I observed the pile build, then disintegrate when hit by the breeze. He had been at my party. Although I'd had reason over the past two weeks to revisit every aspect of that night, I couldn't place Hector in the scene.

I had to ask, but dreaded the answer. "Where were you?"

"In the storeroom."

I clenched my fists, ignoring the splinters' sharp stabs. Shadows danced on the table top. Cigar smoke spiraled this way, then that. My vision blurred. I blinked.

Stammered words finally spilled out. "You were there with my... my father and... and Mr. Cuellar?"

Hector raised the tequila bottle and allowed the filtered sunlight to sparkle through the amber fluid.

"What a sight." He took a swig. "Yes, I was there." He pushed the bottle aside.

Memories of the night darted back and forth in my brain, leaving bruises I'm sure would never heal. "You liked cigars back then, too. Didn't you?" Vestiges of one poking out of the third man's pocket assaulted my fifteen-year-old eyes again.

He nodded. "I just wanted my money. But then Cuellar pulled a gun. So what was I to do? I had to—"

"You shot all those people? You killed my parents?"

Hector puffed on the cigar. "*Sí.*"

CHAPTER TWENTY-THREE

Hector's alcohol consumption began to take effect. Not that I'd had much experience with heavy drinkers, but his words slurred, his eyes were slow to focus, and his rubbery spine slouched his upper body on the table.

Determined to avoid the same fate as Angel, Eva and my parents, I bided my time. I encouraged him to drink and kept alert eyes on the surroundings. Soon he'd be too drunk to detain me.

While Hector was still somewhat coherent, I decided to discover the exact extent of his involvement in the deaths of Angel and Eva. Since he'd already confessed to the shootings the night of my *quinceañera*, I began with the money.

"So, were you the loan shark Mr. Cuellar borrowed from?"

"Loan shark? No, no." He drained the tequila bottle. "I consider myself *un banquero*."

Smirking, I repeated, "Banker. But you loaned him the money?"

"Sure, and he never paid me back. That's why—" He picked up the empty bottle. "Hey, who drank all this? Did you?" He shoved the bottle in my face.

I backed away, the fumes enough to churn my stomach.

"Got to get more. Come." He stood and gestured for me to follow.

Hoping this may be my escape opportunity, I didn't move. But he still had sufficient acumen to distrust me. He strode around the table and yanked me up by one arm. Although well on his way to inebriation, his strength alarmed me.

No escape yet.

Trudging through the undergrowth, shoulder almost dislocated, I stepped over clumps of grass and broken branches, trying to keep up with him. I could see his gun peeking out from the waistband at his back.

He slowed when we neared a dilapidated metal shack. The rusty structure had no door and leaned so far to the left I expected it to fall any second.

He released my arm and stooped to enter the opening, saying over his shoulder, "Don't try anything. If you run, I will shoot you."

Vitriol dripped from his words. Combined with the brute force with which he'd brought me here, and the reminder his gun was conveniently close, his words convinced me I needed to wait. I remained where he deposited me.

But when I placed my hands in my Capri pants pockets and found my mini voice recorder, I had a blinding light-bulb moment. I could record Hector's confession. With eyes glued to the shack opening, I turned on the recorder and pulled my hands out of my pockets.

Although I believed Hector's warning not to run away, nothing could prevent me looking around for clues to our location. Thick brush surrounded the shack. Mesquite trees were the only vegetation I recognized. Keeping an ear open for Hector, I took a few steps forward to a large rock, and once I balanced on top, it added height to my view.

Above the immediate tree line, I caught a glimpse of taller trees, maybe ash. Standing on tiptoe, I could see a shingled roof covering a building large enough to be more than a shack. It had to be a dwelling of some kind. No one in his right mind installs shingles on a barn.

Could it be inhabited? I doubted it. Hector would not have risked bringing me to a place where there were other people. But it offered the first light of hope since I'd woken up in the trunk.

Objects crashing on the ground near the rock distracted me and I lost my balance. Jumping off the rock I identified the projectiles. Hector had tossed out one empty bottle after another. I moved closer to the shack and stopped dead in my tracks when an insect-like hum floated up from my pocket. I turned my back on the shack and slid my hand over the recorder, gently shaking it. The humming stopped.

Hector's hollering behind me rooted my feet to the spot.

"Found one. Thought I'd die of thirst before—" He prodded my back. "Hey, what you doing?"

I turned a one-eighty, hands held open before me and took a step backward. "Nothing."

Eyeing me up and down, he broke the bottle's seal, careful not to spill a drop. I inched my hands down. He noticed nothing amiss, but ambled over until his hand brushed my arm.

Alcohol, tobacco, body odor, assaulted my senses. I didn't flinch. My stomach muscles somersaulted over each other, but I retuned his glare.

When my breakfast felt like it wanted to make a return visit, he backed away and motioned for me to follow.

I swallowed the bitter taste and coughed, but conscious of the hidden recorder, I kept as close to him as I could. "So, is this your home away from home?"

"My what?"

"You know, when you can't go to the house in town, you come here."

He stepped over a large log and surprised me by offering his hand in assistance. The log almost came to my knees. I grabbed his hand and stepped on, then over the fallen tree.

"I come here to conduct... business. But what do you mean when I can't go to my house?"

"Because of the surveillance, the arrest warrant."

"Arrest warrant. That's nothing. I don't worry about stuff like that. I have... friends."

"What friends?"

He turned his head a bit, eyed me for a second, then chuckled like a fast-food clown. "Wouldn't you like to know, but I'm not telling."

This was leading nowhere. I needed to change my line of questioning, but I didn't want him to know I'd seen the building behind his shack. "What is this place anyway?"

"This is my land. I have a hunting cabin here, and rent it out during the season. So don't get your hopes up. We're the only ones here now."

Hunting cabin. That's what I'd seen.

By now, I knew we had followed a different return route. We emerged by his car, and I noticed a vehicle track in the distance. Information to add to my store for possible use in an escape plan.

We approached the table, now shaded completely by the tree. He gestured and I sat in my place. Hector opened the bottle of tequila and took a drink, standing with one foot resting on the bench opposite me.

I needed to keep him talking. "I want to know more about the night you shot all those people. Why did you kill so many?"

He wiped his mouth on his sleeve. "Things got out of hand. I didn't know Juan had a gun. And then the fire." He sat and faced me. "I heard someone else shooting, so maybe I didn't kill them all."

"But—" Should I reveal what I knew by telling him about Ray? I decided not to. "The police report indicated all bullets came from the same gun."

"That doesn't make sense." He pulled the stained baseball cap off and threw it across the table. "I know someone else, besides Juan, had a gun." He shrugged. "Oh, well. Why all the questions? You're not going to live long enough to do anything with this information."

I laced my fingers together and winced at a splinter prick. With my elbows on the table, I willed a nervous quiver away. "In that case, why don't you just humor me? What harm can that do?"

Another swig. Another smirk. "A dying man's, oh, sorry, woman's last wish. Ask away."

"Tell me about Angel. Did you kill her?" I don't know how I managed such mundane speech. My outer shell might appear intact, but my heart had already broken into a trillion pieces.

"I'm really not such a bad person. I didn't mean to kill her either. But she wouldn't give me the bag of money."

"How did you know Angel had the money?"

Hector admitted he'd harassed Eva after he'd found her father's note. He'd caused her car accident, never anticipating she'd be seriously injured.

"I only meant to scare Eva. But she goes and turns into a crip—"

"Don't you dare talk about my friend like that." I stood and leaned forward, but changed my mind when his cold eyes bored into mine.

"*Sientese.*"

I sat, chest heaving with anger and fear.

"Now, do you want to hear my story or not?"

"Sorry. Yes. Go on." I couldn't believe I'd apologized to this thug.

He'd visited Eva soon after she'd been transferred to the rehab center. She'd been sleeping when he snuck into her room and read my article in the journal she'd left open on the bed.

Hector pointed a stubby finger at me and chuckled. "Eva had often spoken about you, so when I saw your name and address, I wrote them down. I knew they'd be useful."

A day later, when Angel didn't come home from work, he'd become suspicious. She'd left a bus schedule in her room and when he'd described her as his dearly beloved daughter, the ticket clerk revealed her destination.

"I tracked her easily after that. She was tall and beautiful. But you saw her, right?"

Not wanting to hinder his confession, I ignored his bait. I swallowed the lump in my throat, choking as it scraped my insides.

His self-satisfied smirk almost blinded me. I closed my eyes, his words gouging new holes in my soul.

Angel had left the San Antonio-bound bus in Uvalde. There she'd purchased a ticket on a small private van that would take her as far as Bandera.

Hector confirmed everything Chief Deputy Quintanilla had already told me.

"That's where I found her. She'd stopped at a convenience store to ask for directions to Hanson Ridge. And we both know she made it there."

He raised his eyebrows, but I gave no hint of a response.

"We argued. I tried to pry one of the gym bags away from her." Again he looked at me. "The money was in the gray bag, wasn't it?"

I blacked out the painful memory his words conjured up, but had to respond when he nudged me with his foot. "Huh?"

"The money. Where is it now?"

I picked at a splinter. "The Bandera Sheriff has it."

"Wish I'd known that sooner. Might have saved me... Never mind. Angel wouldn't give me the bag. I pulled my knife to scare her, but she fought like *un gato de monté*, hissing and clawing, and she fell against my knife."

Anger erased a chunk of my fear and I lashed out at him. "She fell against your knife? Two times? Three times? You're insane if you expect anyone to believe you."

"Okay, so I stabbed her. But I didn't think she'd die. I tried to follow her, but a truckload of teenagers came to get gas and she disappeared in the crowd."

The callous nonchalance with which he related the murder astounded me. I inhaled and folded my arms to keep from striking Hector.

"Angel bled to death." The words stammered out between breaths.

"I know. I read the newspaper account."

My anger bubbled and I couldn't stop. "Why did you accost me in the grocery store?"

Hector rolled his head from side to side. "Accost is such a strong word. I just wanted to find out if you'd found the money."

"Did you come on my property?"

He grabbed the tequila bottle and twisted off the cap. After a swallow, he left the remnants around his mouth while he closed the bottle. Eyes glued to mine, his snake tongue whipped out and ran over his lips.

I blinked and turned away, wanting more confession on record, but despising myself for keeping in such close proximity to this animal.

"Not only did I check out the crime scene where Angel's body was found, but I walked all around your house. Cute dog. Brutus, right?"

The dog's name was inscribed on his collar tag. Hector must have picked him up to read it.

I stared at the dead leaves and rocks at my feet. Jittery muscles quivered in my legs. I shifted on the bench, partly to ease my body, but also to quell the desire to run.

A few more swigs. Surely he'd pass out soon.

Loud booms coming from the west had Hector on his feet. I stopped breathing as hope surged through me. Could this be my rescue?

We listened. Hector ran on unsteady legs. At the car he stopped and strained to see down the track. I stood.

Silence. Even the birds cooperated.

Hector shuffled back and shrugged. "Don't know what that was, but now I'm thirsty again." The amber liquid was fast disappearing.

How much more could I record before he became incoherent? I thought of a different tack. "Did you follow me to Eagle Pass?"

Hector's chest heaved in and out from his recent exertion. "Not exactly. When I got home and there were no cops at my door, I knew I'd made it. I didn't know you were here until I saw you in the rehab center's parking lot."

"So that *was* your car." Glancing over at the vehicle in question, I asked, "If you're *un competente banquero*, why do you drive such a beat up old car?"

Hector also looked at the car then hiked a shoulder. "I like to keep a low profile. Spend my money on other things. You were in my house. Did you see the nice furniture I bought Eva?"

"Don't talk about Eva." The recorder shifted in my pocket when I straightened my leg under the table. "No, do talk about her. I mean, tell me, did you kill her, too?"

Hector's malevolent grin dropped the temperature twenty degrees.

I shivered.

CHAPTER TWENTY-FOUR

Hector rubbed his temples. "Oh, *Chiquita*, you're asking too many questions. My head hurts." He tipped the bottle back.

I frowned as he swigged. "That's not because of the questions. It's the alcohol."

Hector guffawed, spraying the table with tequila. "No, no. This," he patted the bottle, "is my friend."

Anxious to record his involvement in Eva's death before alcohol further impaired his speech, I ignored the droplets of liquid close to my arms.

"Hector, please. Just a few more questions. Then I promise I'll be quiet." Oops. I shouldn't have used those words.

"Maricella, when you're right, you're right. Okay, what now?"

"You were going to tell me about Eva."

Hector had extinguished the cigar, but he chewed on the stump, twirling it from one side of his mouth to the other.

"We had some happy months." He took the cigar stub out and inspected it as if deep in thought.

"Did you know she was Juan Cuellar's daughter when you married her?"

Placing his hand over his heart he feigned pain. "I'm crushed you think so poorly of me. No. I didn't know until she told me the house I'd rented had been her childhood home. And then the whole pathetic story came out."

"Pathetic?"

"Yes. I'd forgotten the incident. After all, it had been nearly thirty years. Time to let go, I told her. I tried to be nice about it and agreed we could move when the lease was up. My offer didn't help. She became too inquisitive and stuck her nose in my affairs. But that's not what you want to hear, is it?"

He slouched on the table, arms supporting his chin. "When I heard Eva would be going home with you, I had to see her one last time."

A troubling idea niggled my stress-numbed brain. "How did you know I was taking her?"

Hector raised his red-rimmed eyes to my face. "Never mind how I knew."

His answer bothered me, but I had more important questions to pursue. "Why did you want to see her again? To say good-bye?"

My sarcasm flew right over his head.

"No. To find out for sure you didn't have the money." He fiddled with the baseball cap on the table. "I'd discovered it wasn't in your room."

"I knew it." I poked his forearm, then pulled back when his muscles tensed. "You broke into our hotel rooms. How dare you?"

Sitting up a little straighter, he waggled a finger at me. "No, no. You have it wrong again, *Chiquita*. I didn't break in. I have friends. I told you."

Another incident slammed into my memory. "Did you try to run me off the road a couple of nights ago?"

"On Main Street?"

"Yes."

He nodded, then grabbed his head as if to steady it. "So that was you. Thought I'd bumped into someone. If I'd known it was you, I would have tried a bit harder."

There were so many nasty comments on the tip of my tongue, but I held back and ignored the lop-sided smirk on his unshaven face.

Determined to keep him focused on Eva, I tapped the table. "So you visited Eva to see if I'd given the money back to her?"

"No. Yes. To see if you'd told her where it was." His brow furrowed in confusion. "Or if she'd told you where it was. That's all." Hector placed the cap on his shiny bald head and tweaked the bill. "But she wouldn't talk to me."

With my heart in my throat, I asked, "What did you do when she wouldn't talk?"

Hector stared at a point behind me, eyes unfocused, but intent on avoiding my gaze. "I told you, *Chiquita*, I'm not a bad man. I didn't mean to hurt her, but I needed the money."

It all came back to the money. "Didn't it occur to you, if Angel had it when she died, the sheriff would have taken it as evidence?"

After rubbing his eyes, he toyed with the half empty bottle. "Now you're getting too technical or legal or whatever it is." He put the bottle to his mouth and smacked his lips after a large swallow. "I just know my wife lied to me, and I don't like being lied to."

Hector stood and leaned over the table, his potent breath choking me. I backed away, glaring at him, but wary of his heightened emotion.

"You women are all alike. Liars—" He stretched out to prod my chest, but I swung my legs over the bench and moved out of his reach.

"Come back here. I didn't say you could get up." Hector, hampered by the bench, squeezed his stocky body away from the table and staggered after me.

I knew I could outrun him at this point, but he still had the gun. "I'm not going anywhere, Hector."

"That's right, *Chiquita*. But I can see it's going to be harder to kill you."

Still backing away from his swaying body, I said, "Harder than what?" I knew the answer, but wanted to record the words from his mouth.

"Eva, of course. She didn't put up much of a fight. I just held the pillow over her face, and... and it was over in a few minutes." Hector downed the last of the tequila and threw the bottle in my direction.

I dodged to the side, my anger and revulsion giving me strength. "You are a cruel, heartless excuse for a man, Hector Alonzo. I've heard enough. If you're going to kill me, you'd better do it now, because I'm leaving."

Turning, I stomped to the car, praying he'd left the keys in the ignition.

"Wait, *Chiquita*. Wait. I—"

Thump.

My scalp tingled, sending anxious waves down my neck.

I glanced over my shoulder. Hector had tripped over a rock at the base of the tree.

Reaching a shaky hand out to me he pleaded, "Don't go. I'm not finished." His arm fell to the earth and a puff of dust burst out around it. "He's going to be so mad at me."

Hector rolled over onto his back and chuckled.

I rushed to the car, ignoring his situation.

No keys in the ignition. No keys behind the sun visor.

I looked back at Hector. Flaying arms and a throaty laugh signaled his semi-consciousness. I scanned the area. I had no idea where I was, but Hector's mention of someone being mad at him and the possibility he'd appear, forced me to quickly consider my options.

Hector's mirth ceased. His arms lay folded across his chest. I approached on tiptoe, at least as tiptoed as I could in sandals on gravel, and saw the tip of my cell phone protruding from his shirt pocket. Closed eyes and heaving chest. Asleep maybe? I watched and waited. He lay motionless.

Stepping closer, I pried my phone out of his pocket. Hector's fingers twitched, sending panic spasms down my legs.

I froze.

He slept. I stared at him. A threat awake; vulnerable in sleep. But my enemy all the same.

Where had he placed the car keys? His back pockets had contained the first bottle of tequila and the baseball cap. Could the keys be there too? His front shirt pocket appeared flat, now that my cell phone had been removed. The only other place would be the front pockets of his jeans.

Keeping alert to any movement, I eased around to his side and bent down to determine which pocket housed the keys. Neither betrayed its contents.

I knew I couldn't reach into the tight pockets without waking Hector. I stood and decided to escape on foot.

The track I'd seen earlier led off to the right. I dashed down it and dialed 911 again. This time I gave the dispatcher more details of my location and told her about the hunting cabin I'd seen. She advised me to stay on the track. I jogged down an incline, keeping the friendly voice apprised of my situation.

At a fork in the track, I hesitated, because each seemed equally overgrown. Just as I described my predicament, the phone lost service again.

I placed it in my pocket, and turned off the recorder. If ever I got out of here, I'd have Hector's confession to two recent murders and several from the night of my *quinceañera*.

Standing at the divide, I closed my eyes. My parched throat, dry lips and rumbling stomach became more and more insistent as my fear dissipated.

I whispered a prayer of sorts. *Please, God, help me.* Can that be considered a prayer? Since hearing of Eva's death, I'd had ambivalent feelings about God. Just when I'd arrived at a point in my life where I acknowledged God's guidance, my world had revolted, and the chasm between us grew wider by the hour. I knew God hadn't moved. But I wasn't sure my fledgling faith could carry me through the abyss. Even Tom's words of encouragement were dissolving like wisps of fog in a storm.

Off to the right, the gurgling of water trickling over rocks emerged from the silence. I headed in the direction, stepping over bushes and stumps, and came to a small stream.

The water appeared clear. At this point, I dared not contemplate its source. I knelt down and scooped the cool liquid to my mouth. *Oh, what sweetness.*

After I'd quenched my thirst, I splashed my face and neck, and wiped the scratches on my legs and arms. The cool water washed away the last trace of my headache. Heading back to the path, I resumed my trek down the right fork.

My cell phone still had no service, but I kept dialing. The afternoon sun beat down through the scraggly trees. My refreshing drink at the stream seemed like a dream. Sweat drenched my shirt and trickled down my brow.

I drew my hand across my face, trying to keep the droplets from stinging my eyes.

A noise.

I stopped.

Yes. Maybe a vehicle.

I scurried into the bushes and hid behind a clump of tall grass. Could the 911 dispatcher have located me from my cell phone call? Or was this the person Hector expected?

The vehicle came closer. Engine noises. Tires on gravel. And lights. Lights?

I peered over the grass and saw flashing lights.

Red and blue.

The police.

I abandoned my hiding place and returned to the track, keeping a wary eye on the surroundings. A police car rounded the curve.

The driver stopped and opened the door. A familiar face emerged.

"Ray! Am I ever glad to see you!" I dashed to his side.

He held his arms open. "Maricella."

His hug brought instant relief, but I pushed away and asked, "Are you here because of my 911 call?"

Ray nodded and placed a hand on my back, ushering me to the passenger side. "Yes. Come, get in."

"But what about Hector?"

He opened my door and waited for me to buckle my seat belt. "Hector?"

"Yes. He brought me here, abducted me and said he was going to kill me." I gestured with my chin. "I left him up there. He's been drinking."

Ray climbed into the car and turned off the flashing lights. "How did you manage to get away from him?"

"I waited until he... collapsed. He's so drunk, he couldn't detain me any longer."

Ray slid the gear into drive and we headed up the trail. "Since I'm here, I'll arrest him for assault and the abduction. By the way, Teresa is okay."

"She is? That's wonderful news." I was so happy to hear about Teresa that Ray's first statement flew under my radar.

His matter-of-fact words sounded so professional. "I heard about your first 911 call and talked with the officer who checked out the hotel. Teresa told him she couldn't identify the man who attacked her."

A shudder rattled down my spine at the memory. "I didn't see who it was either in the hotel. But, of course, now I know it's Hector."

We maneuvered up the rough track, the police car jostling us from side to side. A subtle change in Ray's demeanor confounded me. Tight, thin lips replaced his usual quick smile; relaxed confidence changed to a tense vise grip on the steering wheel.

If only I could see his eyes. They'd help me gauge his emotional state, but they were shielded behind mirrored sunglasses.

"Ray, I have a question. Whatever happened to Hector?"
He flicked a quick glance my way. "What do you mean?"
"His arrest. You told me yesterday he'd been arrested."
He negotiated a sharp turn. "Oh, that. I think the arresting officer forgot to read him his rights. Something like that. He had to be released."

"I see." But I didn't understand. I knew all the legalities had to be followed, but Hector seemed to have more than his fair share of good fortune.

Ray slowed to avoid a large rock. "How much farther, do you know?"

I surveyed the surroundings, recognizing a clump of cactus. "Not far now."

"Where did you last see Hector?"

"He'd tripped over a rock and lay on his back under a tree. There's an old picnic bench where we sat, and a run-down shack not far away, close to the hunting cabin."

"Oh, I think—"

My cell phone rang, jolting my mind away from Ray's words.

"I have service again. Great." I pulled the phone from my pocket and opened it. "Hello."

"This is the 911 dispatcher. Mrs. McDonough?"

"Yes."

"Are you all right? Have you found any landmarks yet? We're still trying to locate you based on the cell tower use. Unfortunately, we haven't been able to verify any land owned by a Hector Alonzo."

Although her calm voice reassured me, I frowned at her last bit of information, but filed it away. "I'm fine, thank you. I'm in a police car with—"

"Let me talk to them." Ray took my phone without waiting for my okay. "This is Officer Reyes, badge number 27985. I have Mrs. McDonough safe in my car. I'm on my way to arrest her abductor."

He listened a moment, then said, "Right. We're out on Highway 1021, about five miles passed El Indio." He listened again. "Thanks." He closed my phone and glanced at me. "They're sending back-up."

I nodded, still wishing I could see his eyes.

"You must be hungry and thirsty. I don't have any food, but I carry bottled water in the trunk. Want some?"

The relief at seeing Ray step from his police car had assuaged my physical discomfort at the time. But now the thought of fresh water sent my salivary glands into high gear.

"That would be great. I don't suppose it's on ice?" I smiled as he stopped the car.

Chuckling, he put the car in park, opened the door and stepped around to the trunk.

Two seconds later he handed me the precious liquid. "Here. Wet, I promise, but tepid is the temperature of the day."

"Thanks." I opened the bottle and, tipping my head, glugged down half the contents.

Ray continued along the track. "What have you and Hector been doing all this time?"

I replaced the bottle cap and slid my hand into my pocket, touching the recorder. Should I tell Ray about the taped confession? I glanced at him; his strong hands on the wheel, guiding the vehicle expertly along the rough surface; his mouth set in a firm line; his eyes still shielded by dark glasses.

A niggling little prickle on my neck sent the kernel of a knot to my stomach. I withdrew my hand and chose to keep the confession to myself for now.

"Hector talked about his exploits. He's led a colorful life."

"I'm sure. Did he tell you anything about Eva?"

Again, I hesitated, not sure why, but when Ray's characteristic smile returned, I gave in. "Yes. He confessed to stabbing Angel and to suffocating Eva." The lump in my throat threatened to suffocate me. "He's a cruel, mean excuse—"

"Now, now, Chella. Don't upset yourself. I'm here and Hector's going to face my justice."

Ray's words, meant to calm and reassure, confused me instead. What did he mean, face his justice?

But I didn't get a chance to challenge him. We rounded a turn and arrived at the clearing.

The picnic bench, the trees.

But no Hector.

"Is this the spot?" Ray asked, surveying the area.

I nodded and pointed to the large mesquite. "He lay under that tree when I left."

Ray turned off the engine. "Let me check it out. Stay here, Maricella." He opened his door and stepped onto the rocky track.

He stalked toward the tree, hand on his holster. My fingers tightened around the water bottle. Sweat popped on my upper lip—from anxiety and build-up of late summer Texas heat.

I opened the door. A breath of a breeze meandered in, bringing no relief to my anxiousness.

Keeping my eyes on Ray, I swung my legs out of the car.

He stopped and slowly drew his gun.

I sat motionless, straining to hear any noise from Hector. The seconds ticked by like slow molasses. Dry, baked air swirled around my head, loosening a strand of hair, fluttering it against my cheek.

Crunching gravel.

Ray dashed to the picnic table and crouched behind it. I slid off the seat, ducked down by the car door and peered through the windshield.

No one appeared.

Ray glanced in my direction and motioned for me to stay put. Knees feeling the effects of squatting for eons, I shifted my legs and sat on the ground. From my new vantage point, I had a clear view under the passenger seat. A scrap of paper. A match book. And a cigar wrapping.

With hand shaking, I reached for the cellophane wrapper. The red circular medallion surrounded by gold filigree acted like a hot plate.

I dropped it on the car floor and covered my mouth with both hands, trying to stifle a scream of dismay.

My life flashed before my eyes. At least, the last two weeks did.

Hector. Ray. The coincidences. The near misses. No search warrant for the garage. Ray's familiarity with Eva's, rather Hector's house. Hector's arrest. Ha! Some arrest.

But why would Ray be helping Hector? Every instinct in my being told me to flee, but my numb soul wouldn't cooperate.

I pushed to my knees again, moving away loose rocks to make the position tolerable. Ray now stood by the table, gun aimed at the brush beyond.

A shape emerged.

Hector.

Forcing air into lungs pinched tight with panic, I watched the characters act out their scene. Hector stumbled forward, new tequila bottle proudly held high. Ray stepped closer, mumbling.

Hector stopped by the tree, leaning against its sturdy trunk. Ray turned to me, gun still aimed at the man. "Maricella, you can come out now."

I know he saw me. What now? If I ran, he still had the gun and could shoot me. And he had the car.

Pulling myself up into a half-squat, I saw the keys in the ignition. Hector had Ray's attention again. I grabbed the keys.

Thank you, Capri pants manufacturers for making such voluminous pockets. Ray's keys mingled with mine.

I brushed the debris from my pock-marked knees and shins. Stepping around the car, I tromped closer and closer to the men.

Ray pocketed his sunglasses. "Come, Chella. Let's hear what Hector has to say for himself."

The sound of my nickname coming from his lips grated in my ears and on my heart. But because I wanted to keep my discovery to myself, I forced a smile.

Hector's slurred words reverberated through the trees. "Too late."

"What do you mean, old man?"

"I told her everything."

Ray lowered the gun, holding it by his holster. "You stupid, drunken fool. If you weren't family, I'd kill you right now."

Hector staggered toward me. I stopped, rumbling heart beats drowning out the whispering leaves. He stood a yard away, swaying like a piñata, fumes emanating from his pores.

"See, *Chiquita*, I told you he'd be mad at me."

CHAPTER TWENTY-FIVE

"Good night, sweetheart. Good night, sweetheart." Tom's last words to me the previous evening echoed over and over in my perforated brain.

The surreal scene in front of me short-circuited any hold I had on reality. Tom's words were the only connection I had to sanity. I wouldn't let them go. Couldn't let them go.

But I wasn't in control of the situation.

Ray grabbed Hector, pushing him to the table. "*Sientese.*"

The intoxicated man swung his legs over the bench, placed the liquor bottle down and slumped on the table.

Roots grew from my sandaled feet and held me in place. Even when Ray turned and used the gun in his hand to motion me forward, I stood with the sun scorching my body, and fear invading every cell like a virus.

"Maricella, I'm not in the mood for games. Come here, now."

I surveyed the scene. Hector, drowsy. Ray, armed, menacing. Ray, the man I had considered a friend.

I had no choice. But if I was going to die, it would be on my terms.

Forcing muscles to obey, I trudged to the table, keeping my eyes on Ray's face.

"Good girl. Sit down." He lowered his gaze and added, "Please."

With Ray standing near Hector, I chose to sit on the opposite bench. Sliding my hand into my pocket, I turned on the recorder and coughed to camouflage the slight click.

Neither man reacted.

I hesitated, then patted my other pocket hunting for my phone. It wasn't there.

What had I done with it?

Oh, yes. Ray. In his police car. He'd talked to the dispatcher and had kept the phone.

Don't react. Don't let him know you're suspicious.

Hector grunted. Ray straddled the bench and laid his gun on the table.

He noticed my interest and chuckled. "Don't even think about it, Chella." He moved the weapon farther away. "Have you ever fired a gun?"

I kept my gaze on his face. "No. Never even held one."

The dimples I'd found so charming just hours ago appeared on his cheeks, but they failed to dampen the threat in his voice.

"Didn't think so. And you won't be starting today." He prodded Hector on the shoulder. "What have you been up to, old man?"

Hector raised his head, bleary, blood-shot eyes trying to focus. He gave up and slumped on the table again.

Ray exaggerated a sigh. "My uncle is a big disappointment to me."

"Your uncle?" Puzzling events from the past week fell into gaping holes of the bizarre picture, finally making sense. Hector and Ray, related.

"Chella, Chella." Ray clucked his tongue and shook his head. "What am I going to do with you?"

Did I want to hear his options or give him ideas? I kept silent.

He rubbed his eyes then swung his leg over the bench and rested his elbows on the table. "Why so quiet? This is not like you. Usually you have plenty to say."

I bit my bottom lip to bridle my tongue. I had questions and accusations by the ton, but needed to rein in my anger.

A hawk soared above the tree line in a slow, majestic arc. Its dark outline accentuated the cobalt sky. Watching the bird for an ephemeral second gave me a chance to corral my jumbled thoughts.

Anger still stoked a fire in my gut, but I couldn't remain quiet any longer.

"Why, Ray? Why all the... the deceit?"

Aware of the hypocritical nature of my question, I swallowed and focused on the table's rough wood.

Spluttering snores erupted from Hector. Ray smirked. "He's such a noisy drunk, isn't he, Chella? Come, let's leave him here, and go—"

"No." I had no idea what Ray had in mind, but I wanted to stay in a somewhat familiar place. "I'm staying here. And I want answers."

Ray's forced chuckle caught me off guard. I'd expected more resistance.

"Okay, we'll stay. Always admired your spunk." He patted my arm. "I know I've said it before. Tom's a lucky man."

I pulled away and placed my jittery hands in my lap. Tom would not be used to distract me. "Ray, answer my questions. Please."

"If it's answers you want, it's answers you'll get. Fire away."

Where to begin? Events from the recent and distant past clamored for attention. My concern for Teresa took precedence.

"In the car, after you picked me up, you assured me Teresa was fine." I looked him square in the eyes. "Is that the truth?"

Without blinking, he returned my stare. "It is. She wasn't unconscious very long, and the bumps on her head weren't serious. I was at the station when her call came through. Didn't speak to her myself, but—"

"What about me, Ray? Am I going to be fine, too?"

Drumming fingers on the table failed to pull my gaze from his face.

"Depends, Chella. Seems *Tio* has been spilling the beans. He may have told you too much."

And I had it on tape. "All I know so far is Hector seems to be responsible for several deaths. If you're involved in any way, he didn't implicate you." I placed my hand over his, stilling the drumming. "Let me go, and I promise I'll—"

"Can't risk it." Ray pulled his hand away and scowled as he shook his head slowly.

The tightening and relaxing of his jaw muscles betrayed his vacillation between determination and doubt.

Could I increase the doubt by calling on our friendship? "So, will I be next?"

"Next?"

"The next to die. If you're not going to let me go, what are you going to do with me?"

He whacked the table and sent the blood in my brain on a brief vacation. I clutched the rough wood to steady myself and kept my eyes on Ray's right hand, perilously close to the gun.

"Why did you have to come to Eagle Pass? Why were you so persistent?" He swung his legs over the bench, but instead of standing, reached around Hector and grabbed the bottle of tequila.

With Ray's back to me, the gun lay unguarded.

Could I grab it in time? And then what? I didn't know how to release the safety, or even know if it was on.

And Ray could overpower me in a second.

My hesitation forestalled any action.

Ray stood and turned. He noticed my focus on the weapon and snickered. "Not again." Placing the gun in his holster, he shook his head. "What were you thinking? Would you have aimed it at me? Pulled the trigger?"

The lump in my throat grated as I swallowed. I studied his hard face and tried to hide the fear I'm sure flooded mine. I couldn't relate to this metamorphosed Ray, one-time friend, now foe.

He opened the tequila bottle and studied the contents as if waiting for a revelation. He sighed and took a swig, smacking his lips in appreciation.

"Mmm. I'd forgotten how good it is."

Another mouthful. He sat opposite me again and closed the bottle. "You should be proud, Chella."

With a shrug, I placed my elbows on the table. "Why?"

"You made me fall off the wagon. Been sober for... let me see... two years. But you came, and interfered, and—"

"No, Ray. Don't blame me for your problems. This is not my fault."

He took another drink. "It is. You came back and stirred all those old feelings."

I knew little about alcoholics and their tolerance for liquor. If he'd been sober for two years, how much tequila would he need to slow his responses? Hector had consumed at least one bottle before he'd passed out. Should I encourage Ray's drinking to facilitate my escape?

I could not.

Placing my hand on the bottle I said, "Ray, stop. You don't have to do this."

He removed my grasp of the bottle, one finger at a time, then held onto my hand, sending a splinter or two deeper into my palm. "You don't understand, *querida*."

"Don't call me sweetheart." I tried to pull my hand away, but his grip remained firm. "And what don't I understand?"

He raised my hand to his mouth and puckered up, but stopped short of kissing it. "If anyone else had come to inquire about Angel and Eva, we wouldn't be in this," he waved his free hand around, "situation. Anyone else would be dead by now. But you, Chella, *you* came."

Ray's dark eyes searched my face. A hint of concern gave me a glimmer of hope.

"What do you mean?"

His grip tightened as his other hand closed over mine. "Hector would have killed someone else, but I told him to leave you alone."

My skin burned where he touched it, but at least he wasn't drinking. "Why? What's so special about me?"

Ray's smile brought the deep dimples to his cheeks. "You really don't know, do you?"

I scoured his expression for a hint, but learned nothing and shook my head.

Still holding my hand, he said, "I suppose there's no harm in telling you everything now. I'll deal with the consequences." He squeezed my fingers. "Later."

A leaf fluttered down from the tree. I sensed Ray's hold relaxing and wiggled my hand free, picking up the leaf and twirling it round and round.

"I'm not going anywhere. Tell me."

He tented his fingers and studied them. "Okay. Might as well start at the beginning. I had the biggest crush on you in junior high."

"No!"

"Yes, but I hesitated—can you believe me hesitating—and by the time I made up my mind in eighth grade, my family moved to Del Rio. Then when we returned the following year, you were going with David and—"

"I was not. David and I were just friends."

He grabbed the tequila bottle and stared at the gold liquid. "That's not the impression I got. Anyway, during the summer I decided to take a chance and got invited to join your *quinceañera* court."

"Wait a minute." I took the bottle away without thinking. "You were invited because Jesse broke his leg two days before the celebration." Through narrowed eyes, I tried to read his body language. "Did you orchestrate that?"

"Sort of. I told Uncle Hector about you and he suggested I... I get invited to your party. So Jesse and I took a little trip out of town, and he... fell." Ray tapped the table. "Okay, so I helped him fall."

"Ray."

"Don't look at me like that, Chella. It's not the worst thing I've done."

An airplane's noisy jet engine miles above us filled the void. Ray focused on his hands, fingers intertwined, and I gazed at his bowed head.

Where would I be right now if I'd acknowledged Ray's interest back then? All I remembered about him flooded into my mind. His good looks and physical attributes had attracted many girls, me included, but there'd also been another characteristic that had deterred me. I doubt if I could have named it at age fourteen, but now I'd label it ruthless arrogance.

No, we would not have been a couple.

And he did not need to hear that. His mood baffled me. Contrite one second, bold the next. But while he was in a reminiscing mode, I wanted more answers.

I shifted on the bench and cleared my throat. "Did you know Hector would be at my celebration that night?"

Ray stretched his legs under the table, his thigh brushing mine. "Yes. I knew he was going to confront Juan Cuellar. I saw you and Eva enter the kitchen, but when she came out alone minutes later, I wanted to go in and find you."

The scene made its way into my mind again. "I didn't see you in there."

"I know." Ray separated his fingers and rubbed his chin. "You ran out before I reached the door, and then the shooting started. I didn't know till a few days ago—when you told me— that you'd seen Hector."

"I didn't recognize him when I saw him again. I wouldn't have been able to identify him."

He bumped my leg under the table. "But you can now."

Our conversation veered off course. I had to redirect his confession to his role that night. "Forget about that for a minute. What did you do when I left the kitchen?"

His words flowed as if he'd rehearsed the story. "When I heard the shots, I knew Hector was in trouble. I deliberately knocked over those candle things you had everywhere."

"*Luminarias.*"

"Whatever, and rushed into the kitchen. I overpowered—"

"Wait. Wait." I leaned farther across the table. "You started the fire?"

Ray shrugged and raised his eyebrows. "I suppose."

Anger tightened the muscles of my jaw. I gawked at him. "You... you started the fire, and all this time I've taken the blame. I've lived under this guilty burden for nearly thirty years."

"Chella, what are you talking about?"

I pushed back, trying to increase the distance between me and Ray without leaving the bench. "Part of the reason I never came back here, or tried to contact anyone from my past, is because I believed I was responsible for all those deaths that night. I'd told Papa I'd seen Mr. Cuellar with the money. I'd knocked over a *luminaria*. But... but the truth is it was you and Hector."

The shackles holding my soul in bondage loosened. The guilt keeping me prisoner dissolved into little pieces.

But Ray's chuckles entering my consciousness reminded me my soul may be free, but my body was still captive.

"*Pobrecita.* You—"

"Don't. Don't pity me, Ray."

He patted my arm. My skin singed at his touch, and I pulled away. I glared at the table while my chest heaved. How much longer could I listen to these painful truths?

I knew Ray had more to tell. His alcohol-loosened tongue and the malevolent glint in his eyes begged for more questions.

So I forced my gaze to his face and kept probing. "You were telling me what happened when you entered the kitchen."

His brow furrowed. "Oh, yes. I told you I heard the shooting and overpowered Mr. Cuellar. I took his gun and followed him into the restaurant."

Unable to face the man who admitted assisting in the murders that night, I stared at the tequila bottle I'd placed on the bench. "Did you... did you shoot anyone?"

"I fired the gun, but don't know if I hit anyone."

"But you told me the ballistics report indicated all bullets had come from the same gun."

Ray pulled his legs back and stood, reaching over the table for the liquor. "Oh, Chella, you shouldn't believe everything you're told." He gulped down several swallows and sat again, grimacing against the liquid's bite.

I searched his face and found no hint of my former friend. "But Ray, I trusted you."

Everything he'd said to me since my meeting him at the police station now became suspect. "So, you didn't read the report of my parents' murder? Didn't pass on the information about Hector's pickup?" Boiling blood roared in my head. "Of course, not. Nothing I told you about Eva's suspicions or Hector's involvement ever made it to your sergeant. Did it? No surveillance. No arrest warrant." I hit the table with my clenched fist. "It's all beginning to make sense now."

I stood and leaned across the table, finger wagging in Ray's face. "You're despicable."

Ray grabbed my finger and forced my hand down, making me sit again, as I grimaced against the sharp stab of splinters finding new flesh.

His chuckle took on an evil note. "Now you're getting the picture, Chella. All this time it's just been me and you. I even told Hector to move his truck before we visited the house to collect Eva's things."

I tried to pull my hand away, the intense pressure of his fingers causing fear to nibble at my gut. "That's why you knew your way around the house so well, and your car, Raymond's car. Did Hector finance them?"

Ray kept a vise grip on my hand and took another drink, almost emptying the bottle. "You could say that. Uncle Hector has been very generous to Raymond and me. In exchange for certain... favors."

I watched Ray's thumb rub circles on the back of my hand. Shivers ran up my arm like an army of ants on patrol.

"You've helped him in his business?"

"Sure. Ran errands and did odd jobs for him all through high school. Then after spending four years in the army, I joined the EPPD. That's when he and I really became a team."

Ray tipped the bottle and drained the last drop of tequila. He slid the empty bottle across the table and rubbed his forehead. "Ooh, shouldn't have drunk it so fast."

"Shouldn't have drunk it at all. Did you mean it when you said you'd been sober for two years?"

A frown scrunched up his forehead and he nodded. "And it's your fault I started drinking again."

"Didn't we just have this conversation? It's not my fault. What did I do?"

Ray raised my hand to his mouth again and kissed it this time. "You came. You saw and heard too much. And now you'll have to die."

CHAPTER TWENTY-SIX

Hector stirred. Ray glanced at him and relaxed his grip on my hand.

I slid it off the table and scooted along the bench. If Ray was going to kill me, he'd have to shoot me. In the back. Because I was going to make a run for it. There were two things in my favor—I had the police car keys and my reflexes weren't dulled by alcohol.

Ray noticed my movement. Quicker than I thought possible, he wrenched his legs from under the table, stood and placed his hands on my shoulders.

"Where do you think you're going?" Vapors from his breath swirled around me.

Ignoring the offensive smell, I raised my head and hoping to appeal to his humanity, said, "I really need to use the restroom. Will you let me, please?" Although not a complete lie, the words still stuck in my throat.

He released me and stepped around the table. His closeness elevated my apprehension, but I smiled, determined to connect with the caring part of him I'd glimpsed so many times during the past four days.

I'm sure my outward calm caught him off guard. He stopped abruptly and scanned my face. "What?" His brow wrinkled as if processing my words hurt his head. "Oh, sure."

Prodding Hector's shoulder, he asked, "*Tio*, is the cabin open?"

Hector sat up, blinking red-rimmed eyes. "Huh?"

"The cabin. Is it open?"

"*Sí*." Hector's chuckle even sounded slurred. "It's hard to lock when the door's broken." With a grin still on his face, he resumed the slumped position.

Ray pulled me up, linked his arm through mine and we tramped down the path. "I haven't been here for a long time. I think the cabin is this way."

We stumbled along the path. Ray kept a firm hold on my arm, thwarting any inclination I had to run.

When we arrived at Hector's shack, Ray hesitated. "Um... I think the cabin is this way." He veered to the left and headed to the dwelling I'd seen earlier.

A few yards into the thick brush brought us to the cabin. The rectangular-shaped building was surrounded by weed-filled beds, an overgrown cobblestone path, and large Rio Grande ash trees. Years of neglect were evident everywhere. The patch of shingles I'd glimpsed with Hector belied the true condition of the roof. Bare patches and gaping holes invited the elements in. We skirted the dirty, gray weathered stone wall and found the entrance on the other side.

Ray pushed on the door, and it squeaked open. I stepped over the crumbling threshold and entered the room. A cursory glance revealed a table, three wooden chairs, bunk beds along the wall, and a crude kitchen sink in a warped counter.

Filtered sunlight streamed through the two windows and holey roof. Dried leaves crunched underfoot as I pushed aside sticky spider webs. As if by reflex, my hand automatically flew to rescue my nose from the unpleasant odors confronting us. Mold, dust, animal waste and who knew what else contributed to the mix. Why would anyone rent this foul, decrepit cabin from Hector?

I stood in the middle of the debris with Ray.

He clucked his tongue. "What a mess? I guess *Tío* hasn't been here for a while."

I turned and grimaced behind me. The room had no other doors. "Where's the bathroom?"

"Over there," Ray pointed to the corner. "Behind that curtain."

"Oh." I took a step toward it and stopped.

"Don't worry. I'll wait outside." Ray returned to the door. "Don't do anything heroic, Chella." He flashed a mirthless smile at me and stepped out.

The dusty green curtain hung on a rod suspended from a ceiling beam. I grabbed it between my thumb and index finger and pushed it aside. The alcove it concealed housed a commode, sink and shower stall, all as revolting as the cabin. Potent ammonia fumes forced me to hold my breath. Broken glass from the high window mingled with leaves and trash on the floor.

Heedless of the mess, I placed my foot closer to the sink, sandal exposed toes curling up in disgust, and turned on the faucet. Brackish water spluttered out. At least, the plumbing still operated. After using the luxurious facilities, I sighed and contemplated my situation.

With Ray right outside the cabin's one door—his muffled off-key humming indicated his closeness—I had to glean whatever help I could from my enclosed cubicle. The window was well out of my reach. Even if I could heave myself up there, the remaining broken glass would have to be removed, and the noise would attract Ray's attention.

Could I sneak out and search the kitchen area for a knife? No. I could never resort to using a knife as a weapon. Knife. Stabbing. Angel. I shuddered as goose flesh crept over my arms.

I rubbed the bumps away and took a step closer to the shower stall. When I stubbed my toes on an object hidden in the leaves, I stifled a groan and stopped dead.

Pushing the trash aside, I found a pile of old plumbing fixtures. Among the stash, I saw two pieces of metal pipe. Pipe. Now that I could use as a weapon.

I grabbed the shortest piece and slid it down my left pant leg. With my hand in my pocket holding it in place, I exited the dilapidated building.

Ray turned, hands on hips. "That was quick. Ready?"

"Sure. Thanks for bringing me." I walked ahead of him, conscious of the rough pipe brushing against my leg with each step.

When we reached Hector's shack, Ray grasped my shoulder. "Wait a minute. I think Hector still keeps his supply of juice in here."

"Ray, do you have to?"

He slid his hand down his throat and sighed. "Yeah, I need it." With head lowered, he turned. "Got to have something to help in case I have to—"

He stuck his head in the opening, but yanked it out again. "Maricella, promise me you won't run away."

Still holding the concealed pipe, I shrugged. "Can't get very far, can I? Don't even know where I am."

Ray snickered, a dimple almost sneaking out. "Good point." He entered the shack, and after thumping, banging and much cussing, came out with a full bottle of tequila.

Against my better judgment, I hoped Ray would suffer the same alcohol-dulled reflexes as Hector had. But as he tramped behind me, smacking his lips after each swallow, I gripped the pipe, a solid reminder of action I may have to take.

When we reached the clearing, Hector no longer slumped on the table. He'd managed to maneuver himself to the tree and lay curled up in the dirt like a baby.

Ray stepped closer behind me, placed his arm around my shoulders and led me to the picnic table. Not wanting to antagonize him, I tolerated his touch, but slipped away as soon as I could. Hector grunted, and with Ray distracted by his uncle for a second, I slid my left leg under the table, adjusted the pipe and sat.

I patted the opposite side of the table. "Come sit, Ray. I have more questions, if you don't mind." The tiny recorder still concealed in my pocket had many hours of memory left.

He shrugged, swung his legs over the bench and faced me. "Okay. What else can I tell you?"

Several leaves had landed on the table in our absence. I gathered them together with my free hand and formed a bouquet. The questions I wanted answered collided in my brain. Where to start?

"Did you... did you know Hector killed Angel?"

Ray played with the tequila bottle, turning it over and over, watching the liquid slosh back and forth.

When he raised his dark eyes to mine, I deciphered a hint of shame or remorse, but before I could capitalize on his brief relapse, he opened the bottle and knocked back several swallows. The next gaze from his eyes shot through me like a cold sword.

"I knew." He closed the bottle, making each twist last an eternity. "Hector told me when he got back home."

"So, all of our conversations were... were just so much hot air?"

"I suppose. But I sure enjoyed our time together." A pensive smile touched his lips. "Especially when you relied on me for—"

"But you took advantage of me."

"I know." He picked up one of the leaves that fell from my bouquet. "Are you disappointed?"

Trying desperately to hold my emotions in check while keeping a wary eye on Ray's chameleon display, I pushed up from the table. The pipe slipped down my leg and caught in the elasticized hem just below my knee.

Ray's focus on the leaf allowed me to grab the pipe before it escaped. Sitting at an awkward angle, I stuck my left leg out straight under the table and eased the pipe back up to where I could again hold it through my pocket. Desperation camouflaged the pinch of the splinters.

He twisted the leaf back and forth. "Well, are you?"

Preoccupation with the pipe had distracted me, but Ray's question, voiced in a hoarse whisper, commanded my response.

"You and Hector have given me so much information today that I think, or rather I know, I'm... numb. Disappointed, incredulous, I don't know what I feel." I threw the leaves down. "But mostly I'm angry that my friend and her daughter had to die."

Ray tore the leaf he held into pieces. "But didn't Hector tell you he had no intention of killing Angel? How was he to know she'd bleed to death?" He blew the leaf pieces off the table. "Stupid girl. She should have gone to a clinic or something. Instead, she—"

How could he be so callous? "Maybe she was too scared. Or maybe she had no idea how serious the stab wounds were."

"She should have realized something was wrong and gone for help. I still say it was her own fault."

It was so hard to keep up my end of this interrogation when all I wanted to do was knock him off the bench. "Don't put the blame on her. Hector's greed—"

"But it was his money."

"Angel didn't know that." My tight words reeked with agitation and anger.

I focused on the branch swaying behind Ray and waited for the ringing in my head to subside. I wanted more information, but I had to maintain a tighter rein on my reactions to his answers. Irritating him at this point would be counter-productive and dangerous.

Returning my gaze to the man in charge of my destiny, I took the tequila bottle he'd discarded and pushed it away. "One more thing I have to know, Ray. Why did Hector abduct me and bring me here?"

He noticed my action and grinned. "Think that will stop me?"

"For now, yes. Answer me, please."

Resting his elbows on the table, his twitching biceps the only outward sign of stress, he fixed his eyes on mine.

"Interesting question, Chella. But I don't know why. We'll have to ask Hector." He stood and eased away from the bench. "I also want to know why he brought you here. It's just complicated everything. He's been acting so weird lately. Wonder what's wrong with him?"

I raised my hand in protest. I wanted to leave Hector asleep. One semi-alert adversary was enough. But I also wanted an answer.

Ray sauntered over to Hector and kicked his feet. "Wake up, old man. Wake up."

Hector stirred, murmuring unintelligible syllables and sat up.

"Hey, Hector. Get up. I want to talk to you."

The drowsy man brushed dirt, twigs and leaves off his shirt sleeves. "No. Not getting up. What's your problem? Can't a man get any sleep around here?" His words slurred together. He bent his knees and hugged them.

Ray glanced at me. I sat on the edge of the bench, tensing against what Hector would say. Dismissing any threat I posed, Ray placed his hands on his hips and faced his uncle.

"Why did you bring Maricella here? Don't you realize what a mess you've created?"

Straining to hear his reply, I left the table and moved closer to the men.

Hector sighed and ran his hand over his pate. "I can't think straight. Need a drink." He raised pleading eyes to his nephew and extended his arm. "*Por favor.*"

"Just get up. Come." Ray grabbed Hector's outstretched hand and pulled him to his feet, steadying him as he teetered forward.

Hector spied the tequila on the far end of the table. "*Muy bien.* That's what I want." He staggered toward his desire.

Ray linked his arm through mine and we followed Hector. Instead of releasing me when we reached the table, he tightened his grip, even placing his other hand over mine, effectively holding me prisoner.

"You have a captive audience, old man." Ray chuckled at his ironic words. His chuckle swelled into a laugh, then a bellow. He let go of me, and doubled over, slapping his legs. "That was funny."

No responding smile creased my face.

"Come on, Chella." Ray straightened and clapped his arm around my shoulders. "You must admit that was funny."

I tolerated his offensive presence and gave him a two second grin. "If you say so. Can we get on with this, please?"

"You're no fun today." He pulled his arm away. "Okay, Hector, what were you thinking? Why did you bring Maricella out here?"

Hector had drained the liquor bottle. He wiped his sleeved arm across his mouth and sighed. "I don't have to answer you."

Ray pushed me aside and dashed to the table. He grabbed Hector by the shirt collar, yanking him off the bench. "Yes, you do, *Tio.*" He spat out the words. "I'm tired of always having to clean up your messes. Don't you know how many times I've intervened to keep you out of jail? The people I've bribed, the favors I've called in?"

Hector's blood-shot eyes bulged out of their sockets, but his dulled senses showed no other response.

I backed away from Ray's wrath, but stopped short when Hector opened his mouth to speak.

"Raymond, *mijo*," he crooned and sat when Ray released him. "Give me a break. I'm getting so tired."

"Just answer this one question and you can sleep. Forever, for all I care." Ray strode over to the tree and grabbed my arm. "Come. You asked for this."

He forced me back to the table. I held onto the pipe and sat opposite Hector with Ray standing behind me, hands on my shoulders. The hairs on the back of my neck prickled, like ants scrambling for cover. I'd managed to conceal my weapon through all my movements, but Ray's proximity concerned me. At any moment, I was sure he'd notice my hand constantly in my pocket.

However, he focused on Hector, and demanded one more time, "Answers now, old man."

The afternoon heat swirled around us. Leaves whispered in the branches above and distant bird calls pierced the silence.

Hector looked up at Ray, then across at me. "You should have stayed in Hanson Ridge. None of this would have happened if you'd stayed home."

I sat statue still.

"You asked too many questions, but," he glanced at his nephew, "because you confided in Ray so often, I knew exactly what you were up to, what your suspicions were. So that made it easy for me."

Ray's fingers tightened their grip on my shoulders.

Hector scratched his bald head and grimaced. "But after my confrontation with Eva, I knew you would be suspicious of me again. You knew too much, and," he stood and shoved a dirty finger in my face, "I don't like it when a woman messes in my business."

I moved a jot to the side to avoid Hector's finger. The scowl on his face and the harsh tone in his voice underscored his words. Women messing in his business. Eva, Angel, and now me. Would I suffer the same consequences they had?

I still made no response, not wanting to give him additional fodder for his anger. But his brief explanation had answered a volume of questions.

Ray removed his hands. "Maricella got into your business, but now you've brought her into mine. You're a fool, Hector."

"You're the fool, Ray. You didn't have to come out here."

"Yes, I did. Do you know she called 911? Would you have preferred another EP police officer to have responded? Or even the Maverick County Sheriff's department?"

Hector plopped back onto the bench and rested his elbows on the table. "Suppose not."

"Do you expect me to take care of her?" Ray placed his hands on my shoulders again and squeezed. He bent down, planting a kiss on the top of my head. "*Chica.*"

I tried to duck, but he held me firm. The gesture of false affection mutated into fire, burning my scalp. Why had I been fooled by his apparent charm? Were there signs I should have seen?

Answers were blocked by Hector's sudden action. He grabbed my hand. "No, *mijo*, let me do it."

Ray's chuckle above me chilled my blood. "We could do it together."

CHAPTER TWENTY-SEVEN

Static and intermittent syllables crackled from Ray's shoulder communicator. "Now what?" He fiddled with the small device.

His adjustments bore fruit. "Dispatcher Eagle Pass to 27985. Officer Reyes, please respond. What's your location?"

Both my captors released me at the same time. Galvanized by the question, Ray backed away and Hector stood up.

Stress, anxiety and hunger had dulled my senses. It took several seconds for me to comprehend I could make my situation known to the Eagle Pass Police Department.

I swung my legs over the bench and, holding onto the pipe, rushed toward Ray.

He covered the communicator and held me at arm's length. "No, you don't." Glaring beyond me, he yelled at Hector. "*Tio,* come and get her."

"Help! Help!"

"It's no good, Chella. I have to press this button to be heard. Your words are wasted."

Hector moved with surprising speed for an intoxicated man. He grabbed my arm and pulled me toward the brush.

With his hand still on the communicator, Ray gestured to his uncle. "Take her away, old man. And don't bring her back."

Stumbling behind Hector, I tried to ignore Ray's words. Their cold savageness destroyed any vestige of hope I had left.

This was it, then. Ray had placed my life in Hector's hands, without a second's pause.

Aching muscles, sweat-drenched clothes, and a friend's betrayal combined to cripple my spirit. My recent reconnection to God seemed eons ago and light years away. Could I call on

Him and ask for help? Was His right hand still ready to hold me?

Before I opened my heart to plead with the heavens, the pipe slipped from my grasp. I yanked my arm free. Hector stopped and turned, but I secured the pipe before his eyes scanned my body.

"What are you doing?"

I lied without flinching. "Nothing."

Hector grunted. "Okay, but walk in front of me."

I followed the rough track, trying to move ahead of Hector, hoping to dash into the dense brush. But he kept right behind me.

The scraggly mesquite branches thickened. I must have strayed off the path, but Hector didn't comment. I pushed aside a low branch which blocked our way and held it until Hector caught it and we moved on. When he let go, it whooshed back in place.

An idea burst into my befuddled brain. Instead of using the pipe on Hector, I'd use the natural weapons all around us.

Another branch blocked the way ahead. I pulled it aside as far as it would bend and as Hector reached the open spot, let it go.

The sapling caught him by surprise, whacking him in the face. He staggered back on alcohol-dulled legs and tripped over a large exposed root. Spurred by his groan as he fell, I rushed to him. I let the pipe slide down my leg then held the weapon high.

I hesitated. Could I hit him?

Even knowing he'd killed Angel and Eva and would end my life without blinking an eye, I couldn't strike him.

The pipe slipped from my hand and landed with a thud next to me. I bowed my head.

A lot of good that did me. Might as well give up and let Hector—

Stray strands of twine poked out of my right pocket. Rope. The rope Hector had used on me in the trunk.

I pulled the prickly coil from my pocket and examined the inert body at my feet. Although Hector's eyes were closed, I needed to be sure he was unconscious or at least stunned. But I had to act quickly.

Stepping closer, I prodded him, certain any second he'd seize my foot. He murmured, but his eyes remained closed. Taking this as a positive sign, for me, at least, I grabbed his hands and bound the rope around them. Undeterred by his infantile struggle, I secured the ends of the rope to the exposed root. I pulled the bandana from his neck, stopping for a breath-stopping second when he grunted. I tied the grimy cloth around his mouth, almost gagging at the action. When he awoke, he wouldn't be able to alert Ray.

Blood rushed from my brain when I stood. I clutched the sapling to prevent myself from joining Hector on the ground. My head ached while I drew in oxygen.

I closed my eyes and voiced a silent prayer. *God, if you're still listening, please help me out of this mess.*

I don't know what I expected, but when I opened my eyes, Hector's hands were still bound, and I was still lost and in danger.

What to do now? Try and locate the police car, or avoid Ray and head through the brush?

I tramped away, but my left leg felt bare. No pipe. I might need it if I encountered Ray.

The pipe lay at Hector's feet. I grabbed it and squinted at the sky through the canopy of fine leaves. The sun appeared on my left. West. And according to the directions Ray gave the 911 dispatcher, we were south of Eagle Pass. But could I trust those directions?

No time for deliberation.

I chose north. No sign of a track, but I didn't care at this point. Any direction away from Hector and Ray was a good direction.

I ignored the twigs scratching my arms, legs and feet. I ignored the hunger growls in my gut and the desert in my throat. But I couldn't ignore the heavy thuds crashing through the brush behind me.

Running was not an option. The intertwining branches in front of me refused to part. I searched for a place to hide. Skinny tree trunks offered no sanctuary.

The noises grew louder. Sweat streamed down my back. My muscles tensed against the closet monster about to pounce.

Ray's hoarse words sent cold waves over me. "Where do you think you're going?"

I raised the pipe and turned, ready to defend myself.

He tore at the branches of a tree separating us and lunged at me. I swung the pipe, but he caught my arm, sending my feeble weapon crashing into a pile of dead leaves. So much for my perseverance in concealing the pipe.

With a fierce grip on my wrist, he gritted his teeth. "Not a smart move, Chella." He turned, forcing me to follow him through the maze of trees. "Where's Hector?" His hard voice carried over his shoulder.

Old standby deceit came to my rescue. "Don't know." Which wasn't exactly a lie. I couldn't direct Ray to the tree where I'd left his uncle.

"How'd you get away from him?"

"You know he consumed several bottles of tequila. He tripped and fell. He's probably... asleep somewhere."

"Trust him to foul up again."

Ray's vicious hold on me and his agitated tone increased my anxiety. The knots, never far away from my gut, tangled again. Ray had expected Hector to do the deed, but now my life was back in his hands.

"Ray," I attempted to keep my voice level, but my dried out vocal chords squeaked. I coughed and tried again. "Ray, you don't have to do this."

He trudged on.

I pleaded. "Ray, you can't do this. You said—"

"Can't, Chella. Can't. Don't tell me what I can and cannot do."

"But you said backup was coming. You told them where we were."

I expected a reaction out of him, but his solid presence right in front of me kept moving forward.

One more time. "Are they coming?"

"No." He stumbled on a rock, but caught himself before he fell. "I lied. I gave them the wrong directions."

Although I'd hoped for a different response, deep down I think I already knew I was on my own.

We trampled through acres of brush. Twigs plucked at my arms and legs. Hope drained out of my body like the final drips of fluid from an I.V. Ray's vise grip on my wrist propelled me onward. I lowered my head in defeat.

A flash of red to my left captured my attention away from Ray's ever-moving legs. Hector's bandana. So that's where I'd left him. Ray hadn't noticed. Hector Alonzo. Hec...

Synapses in my befuddled brain began to fire. I'd told the dispatcher I was on Hector's land, and she reported they hadn't located any such land title yet.

Eternal hope forced words out before I could apply verbal brakes. "Don't be so sure no one's coming."

Instead of slowing, Ray's forward progress increased. "What do you mean?"

"I told the 911 dispatcher I was on Hector's land. I told them I'd seen his hunting cabin. They'll be here soon."

Ray stopped and I careened into his back. He turned and grinned, the hold on my wrist never slackening.

A malevolent chuckle erupted from his barrel chest and spewed over me. "No, Chella. They're not coming. Hector does own this land, but he never puts assets in his name. This place, I believe, is under his step-daughter's name. We are officially on Angel's land."

He turned and pulled my wrist with such force I gasped as tears of anger and hopelessness pooled in my eyes.

I suppressed the sobs. "Ray, where are we going?"

"*Silencio.*"

Crackling twigs, crunching leaves, and occasional bird song accompanied us. I took Ray at his word. Did I really want to know where we were going, or what Ray had in mind?

We skirted Hector's shack, but Ray kept moving. Tramping along the track brought us to the clearing. He pulled me to the bench and reached on his belt for his handcuffs.

The sight of the metal bracelets sent frenzied convulsions through my body. I knew I was in serious trouble. Had known since I'd woken up in the trunk of Hector's car. Each man had a gun, but even the sight of the weapons didn't affect me like seeing the handcuffs did. I don't know what it was about them that brought out the animal in me. I wouldn't let Ray use them on me. I wouldn't give up without a struggle. I wouldn't be restrained again.

Every muscle in my body ached from tension. I tried to pry his fingers loose. They held like glue. I bent down and sank my teeth into his wrist. He let go and pulled his arm away. I staggered back, but kept my balance and turned to run.

Could I out-run Ray? Could I make it to the police car?

I scooted around the bench and sprinted like an Olympian. But the pounding on the earth behind me grew closer and closer.

Muscled arms around my waist pulled me to the ground. A sharp pain shot through my hip. My face was centimeters from the dry, packed earth. With Ray's arms still encircling me and half his body weight pinning me down, I watched the dust particles disperse with each frantic exhalation.

Ray moved his arms and flipped me. He swung one knee over me, imprisoning me to the earth.

With eyes as dark and cold as a midnight winter blizzard, he scanned my face and brushed dirt and leaves off his navy blue shirt.

His voice crackled with ice crystals. "Now you've made me mad, Maricella. You shouldn't have run."

I had never been in a situation like this before. Being forced by Hector to march through the brush was one thing. But when a former friend with rape on his mind attacked me, that was completely different. A monster replaced the Ray I'd known.

He unbuckled his belt and ripped open his shirt, popping one button at a time. "Might as well have some fun before you... leave this world. You should have accepted my dinner invitation, Chella."

I knew pleading with him would be useless. The insane glint in his eyes and the steel cold edge to his words signaled his break from reality.

Arms flaying, fists beating, I screamed and struggled against him. He chuckled. I pawed the ground beside me and closed my right hand over a rock.

As Ray reached his arms back to pull his shirt off, I struck, smacking the side of his head.

The rock flew out of my hand. Waves of nausea undulated in my gut. I puffed out shallow gusts of air.

Stunned, Ray fell sideways. I moved faster than a hunted jackrabbit and scrambled to my knees.

A quick glance at Ray's head revealed an open wound and a series of scratches. Not enough blood to indicate a life threatening wound. Even in his state of intoxication, the blow wouldn't incapacitate him for long.

Ray had dropped the handcuffs in his pursuit. I crawled to them and fumbled with the catch. When they sprang open, I stood and approached the prone body.

Was he faking? Was he still semi-conscious? I couldn't wait around to find out.

He lay on his stomach with his arms by his sides, stuck in the shirt he'd tried to remove. He'd been so taken by surprise he'd been unable to brace his fall.

I snapped the cuff on one wrist and yanked his other arm to secure the second cuff. The bunched up shirt provided a sickening reminder of his intensions. I pulled my hand away and brushed against an object in his pocket. My phone. I snatched it from its hiding place.

Ray groaned. My heart stopped.

He raised his head and blinked. "Chella, what the—"

I stood and backed away, ignoring him.

He lowered his head and sighed. I couldn't bear to hear anymore. I ran to the police car and unearthed the keys from my voluminous pocket.

With fingers shaking like branches in a tornado I started the engine and raced down the track. In the rearview mirror, I glimpsed Ray roll to his side, kneel and hang his head.

CHAPTER TWENTY-EIGHT

Captain Sandoval placed my voice recorder in an evidence bag. I'd remembered it on my frantic escape ride and retrieved it from my pocket. A brief examination revealed it to be intact. I'd assumed it broke when Ray knocked me down, but the pain to my hip had been caused by the two sets of car keys and not the recorder.

"You'll get it back, Mrs. McDonough, when the trial—if we go to trial—is over." Captain Sandoval leaned across the desk. "But for now, we'll put your recording to good use. From what I've heard so far, I think it will help convict Hector Alonzo." He tapped a pencil hard enough on his desk to break the lead. "And I hate to say it, Officer Raymond Reyes, too."

I slumped into the chair. My cuts, scrapes and head wound had been treated, splinters removed, food and beverages supplied in abundance, but I was tired. Bone-numbing tired.

"Can I go now, sir?"

Frank Sandoval, a tall, well-proportioned officer, stood and towered over me. "Yes, you can. But we'll need to see you in the morning to complete your statement and wrap up the loose ends." He helped me out of the chair. "I'll walk with you."

Aching bones and stiff joints accompanied my slow path to the front foyer where my family waited. Teresa rested her head on Mike's shoulder. José paced by the row of windows. Three pairs of eyes examined me as I hobbled in.

José rushed to embrace me. "Mama."

I melted into his arms.

"Take her to the hotel, but be back here by nine in the morning." Sandoval shook hands with my sons. "Your mother is one phenomenal woman."

Mike placed his arm around me, too. "We know, sir. Thank you."

We drove to the hotel in silence. I'd already spent a short time with Teresa and the boys and had nothing else to share at this late hour.

Teresa had been at the police station when I'd driven up in Ray's patrol car. She'd contacted the authorities as soon as she'd regained consciousness. That part of the story Ray had related accurately.

When there'd been no sign of me by ten o'clock, she'd called Mike. He and José had driven down and had been told about my 911 calls, and the subsequent police search. By the time Mike contacted Tom, it was too late for him to reschedule his flight. Even if he'd driven all night, he wouldn't have gotten to Eagle Pass any sooner. Tom had kept in touch with frequent updated phone calls.

We'd been huddled together in Captain Sandoval's office when Hector and Ray had been brought down the hall. I'd hidden behind José as they passed the open door, not wanting to make eye contact. Sadness and relief had washed over me, rendering my muscles to mush.

When we arrived at the hotel close to midnight, José booked a room down the hall and we retired for the night. I had a brief conversation with Tom. He chomped at the bit because he wasn't with me, but he trusted Teresa and the boys to take care of me. Sensing my exhaustion, he reluctantly said good night.

I took the last of my pain pills, and after a quick shower, slipped into bed.

Follow-up at the police station took less than two hours the next morning. We were packed and ready to go home when Captain Sandoval gave the green light.

Teresa and Mike rode together, while José drove my car. By two o'clock, we were in Hanson Ridge. We stopped at the veterinary clinic to get Brutus. Since the dog still needed antibiotics, Joey had boarded him there. I cuddled the exuberant armful and relished his zest for life.

When we arrived home, we had just enough time to unpack, grab a sandwich, and then head to the San Antonio airport to pick up Tom. Teresa and Mike decided not to accompany us and went straight home.

I asked José to drive, partly because it was a relief to have someone to rely on, and because I was a coward and couldn't face Tom alone.

On the phone the previous night, Tom had been anxious with concern, but I'd detected a hint of something else. Something I'd never experienced before. Disappointment still underlined his words, but he was angry.

Along the familiar drive into San Antonio, I contemplated the reunion with my husband. Tom had never expressed anger at me before, but now he had every right to. I'd acted without considering the consequences. I'd put Teresa's and my life in danger. He could add numerous lies and more deception to his list of grievances.

José parked and we walked to the baggage claim area, the best place to await passengers, since security restrictions prevented us from going to the gate.

We'd only been there ten minutes when Tom called to say they'd landed and he was on his way to the baggage area. My throat dried instantly and knots pulled at my stomach. I stood by José and latched onto his arm.

Tom's head, visible above other passengers descending the escalator, sent the knots into disarray and my heart to fluttering. The grin on his face stretched from ear to ear, but his blue eyes held no merriment.

I dashed to him and buried my face in his chest. One arm encircled me and his head rested on mine.

Peace. Sanctuary. Life. But was there forgiveness?

José patted Tom's shoulder. "Hey, Dad."

"Hi, son. Take this, please." Tom handed his briefcase to José. His other arm, now free of its burden, also closed around me.

Why couldn't this be the end of my saga? Why did I have to let go and give him all the gory details of the last week, of the last twenty-odd years of my life?

People scurrying about reminded us of where we were.

Tom removed his arms and grabbed my hand. "Come. Let's collect my luggage and go home."

Teresa called on my cell phone while we waited at the carousel. She offered to order pizza and prepare salad and dessert for all of us. I accepted. This would provide the opportunity for me to confront my whole family and shed my burden of guilt.

I'd known from the time I'd found Angel's body and the necklace that I'd have to tell my family everything. I'd been formulating reasons, excuses and details for several weeks now, but still dreaded the eventual showdown.

◆◆◆

A puckish breeze made the muggy evening bearable on the back porch. Citronella candles lit to ward off mosquitoes; chairs arranged in a semi-circle; appetites satiated; I couldn't procrastinate any longer.

I pulled a chair away from the group and sat. Brutus pawed at my legs and I picked him up. He settled in my lap, exposing his shaved thigh and healing wound. The squirming, warm body provided comfort as I prepared to release my burden. My family filled the other seats. Tom, directly opposite, gave me a reassuring smile, and the quaking waves of trepidation in my gut settled to a mild quiver.

Giving Tom the details of my abduction had been difficult. I'd deliberately told him on the trip home from the airport, with José in the back seat. Tom had been angered by Ray's actions, but his relief at Teresa's and my safety had won out.

But this confrontation proved much harder.

I had to rid my soul of the last layer of deception and lies. The story had to be told, even if it alienated my husband and sons forever.

My saga began with the limited history I knew of my parents, and tumbled through my childhood association with Eva and her parents. I gave details of my *quinceañera*, the fire, the shootings, and my dash to *Tía* Gloria in San Antonio. I included Ray's role in the tragic events.

Facing Tom and discussing my artificial spiritual life added salt to the wounds already bared. I'd told him over the phone several days ago, but witnessing the hurt and disappointment on his face, brought fresh guilt-wrapped chains to my soul.

I took a deep breath and focused on the distant hills, patting Brutus too hard. He yelped and jumped down, curling up at José's feet. Maybe if I kept my eyes on the hills and not on Tom, the restrictions in my throat would ease.

By instinct, my hand sought the necklace I now wore all the time. I'd placed Eva's half-heart on the same chain as mine. The completed heart provided solace when sorrow and regret overwhelmed me.

I held onto the heart and brought my gaze back to my family. The heart gave me confidence. I took off the necklace and handed it to Tom. I recounted the night I'd found Eva's piece and how I'd concluded the young girl had been connected to her.

When all my secrets had been laid bare, I took a tissue Teresa offered and wiped the tears from my face.

"That's all. I'm so ashamed of all the lies." I grabbed another tissue and mopped up more tears. "Please forgive me."

Tom stood and before I could move, knelt down and enveloped me in an embrace. "Of course, darling. Of course."

Mike, José and Teresa added their arms and assurances to the mix. Brutus, unsure of all the commotion, added his yelps.

After a minute or two, Teresa stood. "Mike, José come. Let's clean up the kitchen." Teresa pulled her husband to the door, and José followed.

Still wrapped in Tom's arms, I clung to him like lint on a dark suit. He slackened his hold and peered into my eyes.

Wiping away an errant tear, he said, "Thank you. I know that wasn't easy. But—"

I laced my fingers behind his neck. "But what?"

He pulled my hands apart and stood. "Let's go for a walk."

I took his offered hand and trotted down the stairs with him. He guided me to the fish pond where we sat on the bench. The gurgling water splashing over the small waterfall filled the silence. Tom gave the necklace back to me and placed his arm around my shoulders. Despite the warm night I snuggled next to him.

I couldn't take the suspense any longer. "But what, Tom? What did I miss?"

He removed his arm and turned to face me. I couldn't read his dusk-muted eyes, but the thin line of his lips spoke volumes.

I clutched the necklace. All I'd had from Tom since seeing him at the airport had been support, but this expression sent panic spasms to my heart.

He stood and stepped to the pond, hands in his pockets. "Why didn't you trust me, Maricella? Why did you think you had to lie? Years of lies. Didn't I love you enough?"

My heart's new-found lightness vanished. Familiar knots tangled in my gut. This was no more than I deserved, but I wasn't prepared for the leaded weight of shame holding me captive.

I couldn't move. I stared at Tom's ram-rod back and willed him to turn around.

When he did, his questioning eyes peered right through me. I hung my head, not able to withstand the scrutiny.

No tears. My guilt dried up the well and sent hot waves of blood through my flesh.

Minutes snailed by.

Tom stood motionless.

I sat, head bowed under the load of guilt. I saw his foot move forward a few inches. I held my breath. He came closer. I stood.

We faced each other with the splashing water drowning out my unspoken confession. What could I say? I didn't even know all the reasons why I'd kept part of my past hidden, why I'd lied. Over the years, I'd never believed my deception had hurt anyone.

I was wrong.

The man I loved more than life itself stood before me. The grim line of his mouth, the downward turn of his eyes, the sagging shoulders, all testified to his pain.

I stretched out my hand. "Tom."

He stood still.

What have I done? I'm so close I can smell his aftershave, but I might as well be on the moon.

Lowering my hand, I shrugged. "I don't know, Tom. I don't have any answers."

I sat again, afraid my wobbly legs would betray me. "I thought you... you wouldn't love me if you knew the truth. I thought I had to keep the secrets to... keep you."

My words made no sense to me. How could Tom understand?

I slumped against the bench, hands clenched in my lap, the necklace points stabbing my flesh. Tom's form in front of me held me prisoner. I couldn't leave, although I wanted to run down the hill. Run through the brush and disappear into the approaching night.

A long, slow sigh above me brought me back to reality. I looked up.

Tom held his arms out to me. I stood and clutched his shirt, trying to read the expression in his eyes. But when his arms encased me, I knew I had my answer.

My Tom was back.

He showered my head and neck with kisses. "Oh, Chella, my love. Why would you think that?"

I tried to move, to speak, but he held me tighter.

"No, don't answer. Just know that I've loved you from the moment you sat in front of me in social studies class, and no amount of history from your past will ever change my heart. I love you so much, I would give my life for you. Never doubt my love, darling."

We clung together like newlyweds till Brutus' barking from the back porch forced us to the present.

"But, sweetheart, promise me one thing," Tom whispered in my ear.

"What's that?"

"Never lie to me again."

Choking emotions filled my throat. I squeaked, "I promise."

We strolled arm in arm to the steps, but Tom stopped before we ascended.

"Just one more thing. You've asked us all to forgive you, which we've done, but I think you've forgotten the most important Person."

I placed the necklace in my pocket and reached for the hand rail. "I know. God."

"What do you want to do about it?"

I slid my fingers down his arm and clasped his large, comforting hand. "Tomorrow, at church, I'm going to confess and accept Jesus as my Savior."

Tom squeezed my hand and smiled. We climbed the steps with Brutus bounding along beside us.

CHAPTER TWENTY-NINE

One of the hardest things I've ever done was accepting Jesus as Savior in front of my family and people who'd known me for years. But the love surrounding me at the conclusion of the service added another dimension to my guilt-free spirit.

As we headed to the car, I felt like skipping, but didn't. My heart, however, skipped for me. I'd invited the whole family to attend our community church, and then join us for lunch at our favorite restaurant in Bandera.

We enjoyed the country buffet, which featured platter-sized chicken fried steak, but included other entrees for those of us without a platter-sized appetite. We took two lemon meringue pies home for dessert.

Tom made a pot of decaf, and I gathered small plates and forks.

While waiting for the coffee to brew, I surveyed my family-filled living room from the kitchen. Humidity from the mid-morning thunder storm kept us indoors. Tom separated the newspaper sections. Teresa examined my mother's quilt. Mike and José argued over which NFL teams would win the preseason games.

Joy bubbled up and almost exploded from my heart. I wanted to laugh. I wanted to cry. I wanted to hug each person till they squealed.

Tom headed to his chair, but when his eyes met mine, he tossed the paper down and joined me.

He placed his arm around me and gave my shoulder a gentle squeeze. "Why the Cheshire-cat-grin?"

"Because I'm so happy. And content." I pointed to the kids and cuddled next to Tom. "Can't think of anything else I want, but this."

He planted a kiss on my cheek. "Me neither."

Brutus dashed past us and bounded out the pet door, interrupting our togetherness.

His frantic barking abruptly stopped and changed to a meek yelp.

"Wonder what that's all about?" I disentangled myself from Tom's arms and walked through the kitchen.

Before I reached the back door, it burst open and a man's shape filled the space. In his hand, he held a whining Brutus by the scruff of the neck.

"What in the—?" My question died when I saw the man's face.

Raymond. Ray's son.

"Don't move." Raymond held a gun in his other hand. He peered over my shoulder. "Back up to... to your husband. Careful. I'm watching you both."

Mike, José and Teresa all stood.

Raymond's eyes darted back and forth. "You three, get over here. And... and I won't hesitate to shoot."

Brutus' feeble struggles distracted Raymond. "Here. Take your stupid little mutt before I break his neck."

I grabbed my dog and held him against my fluttering heart, stroking his quivering body, more to soothe my nerves than his.

José and Mike, with Teresa behind him, moved from the living room into the kitchen.

Raymond waved the gun around, pointing at each of us in turn. "That's better, now we're all in the same room."

José took a step forward. "Hey, don't I know you? Aren't you the guy from UT, the one with the fancy truck?"

Tom glanced from Joey to the interloper. "You know this man?"

"So do I. This is Raymond Reyes, Ray's son. From Eagle Pass." I stepped closer to Tom. "Don't do anything rash."

Tom shook his head. "I won't, but I've got some questions for you, young man. Why are you here? What do you want?"

The waving gun held our attention. "I'll tell you exactly why I'm here. Your son, the jerk by your wife, he snitched on me and got me kicked out of UTSA."

"I didn't need to snitch. You were suspected of selling drugs. You—"

"Enough." Raymond spat out the word. "And you," pointing the gun at me, "you got my father arrested. It's your fault he's in jail."

"But he was going to kill me."

"Don't try to blame him. Just," Raymond used the gun to signal me, "get back."

I stepped away from him as Brutus struggled in my grasp. Ignoring Raymond's threats, I placed the dog on the floor. Brutus growled, but cowered behind me.

Tom used the brief distraction to act. He lunged at Raymond, pushing him back to the counter. They struggled, sending the lemon meringue pies to the floor. Yellow and white goop splattered everywhere.

Arms thrashed about. Grunts and groans. Tom out-weighed Raymond, but the younger man's strength kept him in the fray. We watched them swivel and Raymond's gun jammed into Tom's gut.

Mike hovered over the men. "Dad, be careful."

I latched onto the counter to keep from collapsing like a string-less puppet and muttered, "Tom, I can't lose you now."

The fracas lasted less than a minute, but the action played in slow motion in my mind.

My husband could be shot. He could die. How could this be happening? I'd just accepted Christ as my Savior and felt complete for the first time in my life. Could Ray's son destroy my newfound peace?

Blood pulsed in my brain, then drained to my feet. I staggered. José's arms steadied me from behind. What could I do to stop Raymond? Cement filled shoes held me in place. All I could do was watch.

Tom pulled Raymond away from the counter, but slipped on the messy floor, dragging his opponent with him. They landed in a heap on the floor. Tom grabbed Raymond's right wrist, smashing it into the pie debris over and over.

The gun slid across the tiles.

Mike grabbed it. "I've got the gun, Dad."

Without his weapon, Raymond lost his edge. Tom flipped him over and held his wrists behind his back.

Panting and covered in yellow slush, he looked up at his audience. "Check in the garage, Joey, and bring me some rope."

◆◆◆

"Comfy?"

I rested my head on Tom's shoulder. "Uh-huh."

We sat in our side-by-side recliners and watched the evening TV news. Finally able to relax, we wanted nothing more than to get back to normal and move on with our routine lives.

After Chief Deputy Quintanilla had arrested Raymond, we'd cleaned up the pie fiasco. Joey had left with Mike and Teresa, and now we had the house to ourselves.

I cradled the heart pieces on their chain around my neck. Moving forward with my life wouldn't be easy. There were still so many loose ends in Eagle Pass. And there'd always be memories.

Tom shifted in his chair and groaned.

I raised my head and asked, "You okay?"

He rubbed his shoulder and moaned. "Yeah. Just pulled a muscle and bruised a few areas. I need some sympathy."

The awful fight flashed before my eyes. Tom entangled with Raymond. The gun jammed in his gut. But my Tom had prevailed.

The scene vaporized and I turned to Tom, massaging his tight trapezius muscle. "Sympathy, sympathy. There, is that better?"

"Thanks."

I grinned at him, then focused on the weather report.

Brutus roused in his bed with ears perked for sound. He growled and trotted to the kitchen.

Tom muted the TV. "What now?"

The dog's barking brought us out of our chairs. Reminded of his earlier warning, we dashed to the kitchen. Tom opened the door into the garage and stepped out.

"Be careful, *querido*."

Brutus continued barking.

I peered outside and saw Tom standing in the driveway, illuminated by the outdoor lights.

"What is it? Can you see anything?"

With Brutus dangling over one arm, Tom entered the garage and punched the remote to close the door. "It was only a couple of deer."

"Whew. For a moment I thought—"

"I know."

Once back in the living room, Tom placed Brutus in his bed. "Does Ray have any more sons?"

I smiled, and relief bubbled up in giggles. "Yes. But they're grade-school age and live in Houston with their mother."

Tom turned off the TV and stretched. "Good. We don't need any more excitement around here." He took my hand and raised his eyebrows up and down, Marx brothers' style. "That is, unless you consider me exciting."

"Tom!"

"Come, Chella, let's go to bed."

EPILOGUE

We all attended the funeral for Eva and Angel in Eagle Pass. They were buried next to her parents. It had been gut-wrenching to say good-bye to my friend. The one I'd thought dead, but found, only to lose again. And her daughter I'd never met, only seen in a crumpled heap, exposed to the August sun. My family's love and support helped me through. And I'd never been able to say this before—the Lord's calming Spirit sustained me.

After the last of the attendees left, we walked over to my parents' graves. Arm in arm with Tom, flanked by Mike, Teresa and José, I held my head high, willing the tears to evaporate. I'd cried enough for the past, for my mistakes, for my losses.

My sons placed the flowers they'd brought next to the headstone. There were no weeds today. I clutched my bouquet and stared at the simple words etched into the white stone. *Maria and José Farias, beloved parents of Maricella.*

The hot, dry breeze stirred the rose petals, swayed the mottled shade from the mesquite tree, blew a strand of hair across my face. Time stood still. The past and present meshed and made me whole.

I knelt to place my flowers with the others. Peace and completeness filled my being. From a new place I'd found inside my heart, I saw my parents smiling, extending their arms to me, as if giving a blessing.

When I stood, I leaned against Tom and cuddled into his protective arm. I'd finally concluded this chapter of my life. It had been revisited, reviewed and resolved. I could go home now, with a clear conscience and an open heart.

Hector was being held for the double homicide of Eva and Angel, and a variety of other crimes related to his loan shark operation. Once arrested, he'd spewed mountains of details. Revealing more of his unsavory character, he provided evidence against Ray, hoping to reduce his own sentence. He would also be charged with the murders at my *quinceañera*. My recording proved invaluable, and Eva's autopsy revealed she'd been suffocated.

Ray would face his own set of charges, going all the way back to high school. Evidence indicated he'd used his charm to commit petty crimes even then. His admission to starting the fire in my parents' restaurant would also bring charges of murder. Eva's godparents, Gilbert and Esther Treviño, had died of smoke inhalation. Raymond Junior was following in his father's footsteps. Investigations revealed he worked for Hector in a variety of activities.

We'd visited Vicente Ortiz and helped finalize Eva's affairs, and had spent time with Rueben and Anita Lopez. Mrs. Lopez unearthed a photograph of my parents and me, taken when I was six months old. It would find a prominent place in our house, to be a constant reminder to cherish every moment with every family member.

And the McDonough family—we were going home to begin a new chapter. Our first grandbaby was due in March. Teresa had experienced morning sickness the whole week we'd been in Eagle Pass. I hated to remind myself of the danger I'd exposed her to, and yet she'd stood by me, supported me in spite of my foolish actions, and prayed for me.

Now it was my turn. I had so much to be thankful for, how could I find enough time or adequate words to express my soul to the Father? But I was learning. The words came when I needed them.

I scanned the quiet cemetery one last time and sighed.

Tom rubbed my shoulder. "Okay?"

I nodded and gazed at my family. "Are you ready to leave?"

Clasping Tom's hand on one side and José's on the other, I indicated to Teresa and Mike to join us, and we walked to the cars.

I looked up at Tom and smiled. "No more lies. No more secrets."

He squeezed my hand. "*Sí, querida,* my love."

Other Titles from Parson Place Press

For more information regarding discounts, see
www.parsonplacepress.com/store

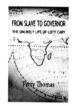

From Slave to Governor: the Unlikely Life of Lott Cary
By Perry Thomas
ISBN 13: 978-0-9786567-9-9

A tribute to God's amazing grace

The Unseen War: Winning the Fight for Life
by David K. Kortje
ISBN 13: 978-0-9786567-7-5

Spiritual warfare may be one of the most significant aspects of the Christian life.

Good News from Indonesia: Heartwarming Stories from the Land of the Tsunami
by Perry Thomas
ISBN 13: 978-0-9786567-6-8

Your vicarious missionary experience begins here

The Robins of St. Lawrence Church
Story and Full-color Illustrations by Amy Dyas
ISBN 13: 978-0-9786567-8-2

Take off on this high-flying adventure

More Titles from Parson Place Press

For more information regarding discounts, see
www.parsonplacepress.com/store

Seasons of the Heart
by Lori Stratton
ISBN 13: 978-0-9786567-2-0

Let your heart be stirred anew

A Time for Everything: the Kevin Zimmerman Story
by Michael L. White
ISBN 13: 978-0-9786567-4-4

God can work miracles in your life

Louisa
by Richard Emmel
ISBN 13: 978-0-9786567-3-7

Based on the life of American poet, Phillis Wheatley

The Resource Book for Louisa: A Guide for Teachers
by Gena McReynolds and Richard Emmel
ISBN 13: 978-0-9786567-5-1

For elementary and middle school teachers

LaVergne, TN USA
17 January 2011
212867LV00001B/79/P